THE LINE BETWEEN LIFE, DEATH & LOVE

THE LINE BETWEEN
LIFE, DEATH & LOVE

Sarah Aila

iUniverse, Inc.
Bloomington

The Line Between Life, Death & Love

iUniverse books may be ordered through booksellers or by contacting:

iUniverse
1663 Liberty Drive
Bloomington, IN 47403
www.iuniverse.com
1-800-Authors (1-800-288-4677)

ISBN: 978-1-4759-5278-0 (sc)
ISBN: 978-1-4759-5363-3 (ebk)

Printed in the United States of America

iUniverse rev. date: 09/28/2012

To my father,
who will forever live on through my work.

PREFACE

You never realize what you've missed out on until it's gone and slapped you in the face about ten times for wasting the preciousness of quality family time. I've written this first novel of mine because thoughts of my father's passing constantly plague me and I needed a way to release all of my emotions without burning someone's ear off. My work is completely based on my own life mixed with fiction from my own imagination.

I'd like to thank my family and best friend for constantly pushing me to complete my first novel and all the encouragement from friends.

CHAPTER 1

"Oomph" *God damnit!*

Jane was on her way to an interview at a fairly large sized law firm. The only thing with her? Her purse, a.k.a her life. Yeah, you know her life? Flying all the way down the sidewalk after tripping over an errant crack in the sidewalk.

That's my life, always tripping over things I never expected to be there. Hi, I'm Jane Rivers. 5'8", white-Hawaiian, hazel eyes, and a muddy dull brown of a mop on my head that's been colored so many times, no hair stylist wants to deal with it so I make do on my own.

Like I said, I'm on my way to an interview when this dumb ass crack decided to move in front of my foot, causing me to fly but catch myself at the last minute. Purse wasn't so lucky though. That went flying. Thank god it's a new satchel; otherwise everything would've spilled out.

Bending down, I picked up my bag and continued on my way up the stairs of the Plaza building my interview was at like nothing happened. Whoever saw, lucky them, hope I made their day good with a laugh. Shaking my head at myself I made it to the elevators without another incident.

Taking a breath I closed my eyes and went over in my head what I knew and why I would get this job.

Ding

Here goes nothing.

About an hour later, I came out feeling victorious. I should be hearing from them in a week, Parker, my interviewer had told me, that she'd also be voting for me in the partner meeting regarding the new peeps.

Bored yet? Well so am I. But this is necessary to let you know what a bad ass multitasker I am. Everyone thinks life is so peachy and easy. Yeah that's easy to say if you've never lost someone close to you . . .

"I can be a freak, I can I can be a freak every day of every week . . ." Stupid phone.

A guy next to me in the elevator looked over at me with interest in his eyes. Rolling my eyes, I answered. "Hey"

"Hey babe, how'd it go?

Sigh my boyfriend of 10 months. We used to be just best friends. I had a crush on him while we were in high school. He never got the hint. I pushed the issue at a rave this past summer. Short story? I saw him, was so excited to see him out of all the people I expected to see, and planted a kiss on him. Oh, one more thing? I was extremely high. Yeah . . . that pretty much factors into why I'm losing interest nowadays plus all his issues coming into play. He's about two years younger than me.

"It went great! She's actually considering pushing for me at the partners meeting."

"Babe, that's great!"

"I know! I'm so excited to hear back from them!"

"So what are you doing now?"

"I'm gonna head home I guess, remember? No money for playing."

"Yeah, true. Well okay, I'm gonna head back to work. Talk to you later?"

"Yeah okay, love you."

"Love you too."

Click.

Let me just say we used to be awesome together but now that I look at it, it was almost like we were still best friends, just added sex into the picture. I feel like there is no partnership and that's what's bringing me down these days. Honestly, I've been thinking about ending it for awhile.

Sigh

Getting into my car I started driving home. Needless to say it was a lonely drive. It's been that way since my birthday to Las Vegas in June. *No.* No I wasn't going to think about it. Thinking I needed some me time, I changed direction to the closest Barnes & Noble's. Parking, I grabbed my faithless bag and strode to the door.

Ah, the smell of new books. Loved. It. Grinning a little, I greeted the worker in the front and made my way to the most interesting section in the entire B&N. Romance. Duh! If I can't have a perfect dream relationship, I'm sure as hell going to read about them and fantasize.

Lightly touching all the covers with my fingertips, I glanced over the titles and covers to see which lucky book was going home with me today. Right now I'm in a paranormal phase of mind so I picked a few authors I recognized and headed to the cashier. Let me just say now, I shortened that for your expense; normally I'd be there for a good hour just enjoying all the could-haves.

I took my place in line and waited patiently for my turn. Glancing around at the knick knacks these poor suckers tried to make us buy while standing in line, a prickling sensation came over me. I rubbed the back of my neck and gave it a good twist to crack the sensation out. Hmm, nope still there. Scrunching my face up, I looked around but didn't notice anything out of the ordinar . . .

Well that's of course unless you notice a dark god the size of a . . . well a . . . okay he just looked god like alright? Staring at you from the Starbucks on the other side of the store. I turned back around swiftly and saw that the line had moved up ahead of me.

Don't turn around. Don't turn around.

I was really good at that. Ignoring things I mean. It was my specialty. As curious as I may be, I knew when to be steadfast.

"Next!"

I placed my books on the counter with my B&N card waiting for the man to ring up everything. Picking up my card and package I swiftly made my way to the door.

Don't you dare fucking look Jane.

Nodding once to myself, I lifted my arm to push the door open. That's when a bigger arm with a lot more muscle than mines beat me to the punch.

"Oop, sorry." I looked up to smile at the gentleman so I could brush this awkward moment off and walk out. No such luck. *Fuck.* Guess who? Yup, God himself would have been please with the specimen before me. Looking up, (His chest was currently in my face) I was facing the same dark god who was standing in the Starbucks earlier.

"No prob."

Oh sweet Jesus he had an accent. Why?? Gulping, I nodded and went ahead of him to find my car before I got caught up in a conversation I wanted no part in. Searching for my keys in my bag I finally made it to my car. Still searching . . . . seriously?? Where were my keys?! Taking my bag off and placing it on my trunk, I frantically started searching through my bag. This was NOT happening. What could have happened to it? There is no way it could have fallen out, it was physically impossible for keys to jump out of bags right? Right?!

"Hey."

"Eeek!" I jumped around and Starbucks God was standing too close for it to be called public space. I tried to back up a step but my car bumped up against my back. Placing my hand over my erratically beating heart, I shot a glare at him. "Are you crazy? What are you trying to do? Give me a heart attack?"

His lips quirked a bit at the side. "Only if you want me to."

"What . . . ? Of course I don't want you to! You scared the life out of me! Do you get off from scaring women or something?" Kay, this guy was whacked. Wanted him to give me a heart attack? Unless . . . ew!

"Ew! You pervert! Get away from me or I'm calling the cops!"

He only stepped closer, making my stomach do a flip flop, of fear surely.

"Well if you call the cops . . ." he pulled his hand out from behind his back dangling a very familiar set of keys, "how will you get your keys back?"

Gasping in outrage, I went to grab for the keys but he pulled them out of reach. "Give me my keys! How'd you even get them? Were you following me the whole time I was in there? Because I know damn well they didn't fall out." I reached again but he only pulled them higher, bringing me closer to him. His chest brushed against mine sending a burning sensation into my stomach. Sucking in some air I stepped back, this was ludicrous! I was not playing keep away with a veritable stranger.

"What is your deal?!" I stomped my foot in frustration. This was so weird! Not to mention frustrating in the extreme.

"Walk with me." He turned around and started to walk away.

"What?! I'm not following you, you're probably a psycho killer!" I can't believe this; he was walking away from me, ignoring me with my keys dangling from his hand.

Crap! I was NOT dealing with this. I reached into my bag for my phone. What? It wasn't in its usual spot. I looked deeper into my bag but it wasn't there. A high pitched whistle brought my attention to the Starbucks God. Okay, you know what I refused to call him that. Psycho was a better match at this point.

At that, I looked up at Psycho and he was unbelievably holding my phone in his other hand. He had that stupid smirk on his face and stuck MY phone in HIS pocket. My jaw had dropped apparently because I had to close it. I can't believe this, how the heck did he get both of those important items? I must've been daydreaming in there because no one was around me at any point in time while I was browsing.

Unable to think of what to do next, I assuredly couldn't ask anyone here for help. He was twice the size of anyone around! My shoulders fell in defeat, well I guess I should just nail my own coffin together, I was probably going to die tonight.

Grabbing my bag, I followed Psycho back into the mall.

CHAPTER 2

I had finally caught up to Psycho around the entrance to B&N. Catching my breath I didn't say anything, just glared at the floor as I followed him through the mall. I tried to figure out where he was taking me but it looked like circles and pointless to me. *Patience, patience.* I was famous for it unless I was hungry, a body part was sore, or if I were irritated/frustrated at something. Considering the latter was a factor at this point, my patience was thin.

"Stop thinking so much."

I snapped my head in his direction. "What?"

"Stop. Thinking. So. Much." He said it as if I was slow or something. *Ass.*

"I'm not thinking a lot. What are you talking about?"

He just looked at me and kept walking.

Patience. Grumpy much? We kept walking for what seemed like another hour until finally he stopped at a fountain secluded on the far end of the mall. It was pretty deserted here I noticed. Oh god this is the part where he rapes me and—"

"Shh!" He glared at me. I glared back. This guy! He had a lot of nerve going around shhing people he stole from and didn't even know.

"YOU SHH! Don't tell me to shh! You STOLE from me and are practically holding me against my will via important life items!" I crossed my arms over my chest and stuck my nose in the air, proud of my rant at him, a for all I knew Psycho killer.

"I'm not a Psycho, 'Azel. I just want to talk."

My eyes widened. Did I say that out loud? I thought back. No, I'm pretty sure I never called him that to his face. Plus he missed the killer part. My eyes widened farther. Or maybe he was a killer and that's why he left that part out! I took a step back for good measure. And did he just notice my eye color? What killer did that? Again he took a step forward. "Stop doing that!"

He looked at me in question. "Don't give me that look, you know what I mean. Stop following me."

He sat down on the border of the fountain. "I believe YOU were following ME."

My jaw dropped. Seriously? "You have MY keys and phone!"

A too finely shaped brow rose in question. "So?"

I sputtered. I couldn't believe this guy! "So? SO?! SO they are MY property and I CAN'T LEAVE THE MALL WITHOUT THEM!" So the patience chant was not working with me on this one and I was now yelling in public with a psy-

"Again, I'm not a psycho." This said with exhaustion.

My face scrunched up in concentration. "Are you reading my mind?"

Now he looked at me like I was the crazy one. I shook my head. "Never mind, okay what do you want to talk about? I really need to get home."

"I can be a freak, I can I can be a freak every day of every week"

His lips twitched as he pulled out my phone. Looking at the screen he looked like he was going to . . . .

Gasping I lunged at him, "NO!"

Simply wrapping one huge arm around me, he banded me to his chest. "Hello?"

I could hear the high pitched tone of my mother's voice as I struggled for freedom. I groaned against his chest in defeat. There would be hell to pay when I got home.

"Yes she's shopping right now, I'm holding onto her stuff. Sure, I'll let her know. Me?" That's when he brought the phone away from his ear and ended the call. He released me from his hold, I was not going to contemplate the butterflies flying around in my stomach right now and the cold air that seemed to seep into me by the second after the release. I shot out my hand for the phone, but he was too quick and pocketed it again.

"What are you thinking answering MY phone!?"

He completely ignored me and sat back down on the border. Not knowing what to do I started pacing in front of him worried about the load of questions I was sure gonna get from my mom as soon as I placed my foot through the door. Groaning inside, I kept pacing trying to calm down and figure out what was happening to me. Why me? I just wanted to do my interview and get a good steady job to live with myself independently. Was that so much to ask? God, why!?

"'AZEL! Sit down before you give me a headache!" His command was like a cracked whip. What else was there to do but listen? Wait, what? I shook my head realizing I had sat down next to him.

I shook my head again in confusion. How'd he do that? I didn't want to sit down, I wanted my stuff and I wanted to get the hell out of here. Oh jeez, what if my boyfriend called, would he answer that call too? Probably, the psy-

Before I knew what happened something pushed me. Hard. I fell backwards and landed in the fountain behind me. I came up sputtering obscenities. "*What the fuck!*"

He was leaning on the border staring down at me with a smirk on his face. That was the last straw. I don't think he expected me to do it, which is the only reason why it worked. I reached up and grabbed both his arms pulling him in right alongside me. It was then I realized too late what I'd done.

"OH MY GOD! OH MY GOD, OHMYGOOOD! GET OUT OF THE WATER, GET OUT, GET OUT, GET OUT!" I screeched at him until I was pushing him out of the fountain and I followed him out soaking wet.

"NO! Oh my god is my phone dead!? Give it to me now!" I ran up to him and began to give him a full pat down to find my phone. Victory gleamed in my mind as I found it in his back pocket. I reached in but he grabbed my wrist and forcefully removed my hand.

"Not so fast." I guess I didn't realize, um, he was pissed.

Not that I cared . . . too much. He held my hand over his head and grabbed my phone himself. Looking at it he pressed the button to power it on. My heart fell and all the air left my chest. It wasn't turning on. "Quick! Open the back and take everything out for it too dry."

"Too late." Ignoring my request he stuck the phone back into his pocket.

In too much disbelief at the fountain, the phone, emotions crashed into me all at once. My shoulders started to convulse and I felt new wetness to my eyes that weren't from the fountain. My shoulders slumped forward to cave in on my body. Why? Why was this happening to me?

"'Azel?" I heard him all right but at the same time I didn't. I ignored him and kept at it. All I had wanted was to grab a couple books and make it home to relax and congratulate myself on a good interview and share the results with my mom. I guess life really didn't want to work out for me in the slightest, I just thought I'd get some kind of break, what with the good news of the interview and . . .

"'Azel?" Strong fingers gripped my chin and turned my face up to his. I really didn't want to do what he commanded my body to do but I lost the fight in me for the moment and just wanted to recoup.

"Why do you call me that?" I just realized he's been calling me hazel (coming out as 'azel because of his accent) this whole time but I never said a word about it. "That's not my name." All I could do was stare into his obsidian eyes. Black as a black hole. Well no, that wasn't quite right, if I stared hard enough there were some silver flecks in there. I almost couldn't differentiate his irises from the rest of his eye. Who had eyes like that? So odd.

"You never told me your name." Well duh, why would I? I snorted in my mind.

"Well Mr. Stranger you've never told me yours either." I pulled my chin from his grasp and out of his hold. He had been holding me this entire time? I guess that made sense since once he let go I almost fell on my ass from mental exhaustion. He started to reach out to steady me but thought better of it pulling back at the last second.

Looking down at myself I'd almost forgotten how soaked I was and now I was starting to feel the cold. "Look . . ." I didn't know what to say but I had to get home and away from this situation. It was growing darker by the minute and Mom would be worried. Now that I had no phone she wouldn't get a txt to warn her about what was keeping me.

I tried again. "Look mister, I don't know what you want to tell me but I need to go. This is insane. You've stolen from me, made me follow you all over this mall, pushed me into the mall fountain, now my phone doesn't work, and I can't leave because of said stolen item. What do you want from me!?" I hadn't noticed but my tone had grown to a level that at least some passersby could hear me.

"Oh and I don't even know who you are OR your name for that matter." My chest was heaving as I waited for an answer to this bazar situation I was in.

"Than." That's all he said and I'm not even sure what that was.

"What?" I scrunched up my face in confusion. "What is a Than?"

He rolled his eyes. "My name is Than."

What kind of name was that? I was going to ask but then I noticed his expectant look. "What? You think I'm going to share my name with you?" I snorted. "Boy you must be kray kray if you think I'm giving you my name."

Another roll of the eyes. "Well then I guess your name is 'Azel until further notice." I know he was trying to egg me on to give him my name but it wasn't going to work.

"Okay, *Than*, what are you making me suffer for." I seriously had doubts about that being his name.

He had a thoughtful expression on his face for a moment. "I'm new to town."

Good start but not so good consequences in my mind. "I'm listening." That's it? That's what all this was about, the fountain, the phone, and the keys? I really needed to understand because that made no sense.

"Look I've lost my way around . . . . and I need help for directions back to the place I rented out."

You've got to be kidding me. "I don't believe you." I said it before I could think about it. What if he was really lost?

He looked confused, and something else flickered in his expression but I must've imagined it. "Why not?"

"You're torturing me for directions? You took my keys, phone, now dead and pushed me into the fountain, and I don't know the why of that one, for directions? There's no way."

He pulled that almost believable confused look again. "It's true; I just didn't want to ask anyone because guys don't do that. Plus you're cute." He shrugged as if this was a normal conversation. Okay . . . the asking directions part was definitely true enough. The cute part . . . doubtful, but still . . .

"Where exactly around here did you come from?"

"I'm on Elm Street, know it?" I almost snickered at his response.

"Really? Elm Street? Does Freddie live next to you?" Now he looked really confused.

"No, I don't know any one of my neighbors, I just finished moving in." This time I did snicker realizing he didn't know the reference to the movie or story behind Elm Street.

"Never mind, okay I'll take you there." I had to get home, and honestly if he was going to kill me he would've done it already.

He seemed surprised. "Really?"

"Yeah, honestly I need to get home and get out of this Wonderland you've pulled me down into." Again with the confused look, but I put my hand out for my keys.

"I'll drive, you direct." My jaw was seriously going to fall off if he kept this up.

"What?! You're not driving my car! I draw the line mister."

"Draw the line wherever you want, I don't trust you to drive me to where I need to be if I hand over the keys."

I gasped in outrage. "What am I going to do, run?! I'll never outrun you." Though it didn't mean I wasn't going to try, hehe.

He seemed to realize my accuracy on this claim and finally handed me the keys. Relief swept me. "See? That wasn't so hard." Just as I turned around and was about to take off on a crazy woman run, he grabbed my free hand. My heart fluttered. What? Wouldn't yours if a handsome, albeit crazy man held your hand? I tried though to tug free, looking at him in question.

"I drive, or you drive and I hold your hand so you don't run. You choose." He stared at me waiting for my answer. I gulped down the nervousness and stood my ground.

"Fine, but if anyone catches wind of this and tells my boyfriend, I'm coming back to your house to damage you permanently." I looked at his package for good measure (NOT checking him out) to make my point clear.

He almost smiled at that, but the hardness never left his eyes. "Whatever you say 'Azel."

One more thing I had to know about this deranged person. "Before I take a stranger into my car, you have to answer one question." He quirked a brow in question. I stared him straight in the face. "Why the F did you push me into the fountain?" At this he merely started pulling me along behind him, grasping my hand loosely as if he knew I wouldn't try anything funny. I thought he wasn't going to answer my question but he glanced back at me and said, "You gave me a headache."

CHAPTER 3

Everything after being pulled along to my car was pretty uneventful. I found the place and let me tell you it was NOT a small rental. I don't know what Than did for a living, but he was doing alright for himself. I had pulled up to his GATE when he looked at me expectantly.

I looked at him *confusingly*. "What?"

He shook his head. "Nothing. Thanks for the ride." He opened the door and stepped out taking the time to take my phone and hand it to me. I dropped it on my seat, useless. He pushed my door closed and started up to the door in the gate, disappearing inside.

I took the moment to compose myself. I felt empty, exhausted and so damned tired. Closing my eyes I decided to rest them a bit before heading home.

—ꟺ—

Thump Thump Thump.

"Hmm?" I became aware, groggily waking up from my nap. What was that?

Thump Thump Thump Thump.

Did I have a headache or something? I don't remember drinking last night or going out. I slowly opened my eyes to blinding light. "Agh!" Jesus! Who opened my windows?? I opened my eyes again, trying to find my bearings. "What the . . . ?"

I was definitely NOT home. Where the hell was I? I looked around taking in the leather interior of my car. Why was I in my car; did I get that wasted last night? But I didn't go out . . .

Thump Thump.

I looked over to the incessant thumping going on to my right and squeaked out a protest. A pissed off looking Than was outside of my window signaling me to roll my window down or get out all together. I dumbly shook my head at him.

He looked heavenward in exasperation, dragging a hand down his face. More forcefully he made the motions again of asking me to roll my window down. I pushed the button for that window. It didn't work. I tried again, checking to see if it was locked. Still not working. I realized the car was off and shock went through me. Shit! Did my car die last night?! I tried the ignition. Nothing but some sputtering and a bunch of clicking. Fuck! I then proceeded, like an idiot to bang my forehead against my wheel. Now that that was out of my system I opened the door and stepped out. Than met me on the other side.

"What are you doing here?" I couldn't help but notice that he seemed to be holding back a smile at my expense.

"Not stalking YOU." I don't know why I said that. Word vomit. I was so angry at myself. I try to rest my eyes and this is what happens. I'm so disgusted with myself right now. My stomach then proceeded to tell me in a very LOUD matter that I haven't eaten since before the interview yesterday. I rubbed my stomach as though that would make it full.

I looked back up at Than and explained myself. "I fell asleep when I attempted to rest my eyes last night." My nose twitched and my eyes were puffy. "I—" *Ah . . . Ah . . . AH CHOO!* Ugh! What was I now, sick? I hung my head in defeat also realizing that I'd fallen asleep in my wet soaking clothes. *Thanks a lot Than.*

"Listen, seeing as you're not going anywhere soon," he glanced at the car making his point, "why don't you come in and eat something, shower, change and maybe call your mom?"

I stared at him in shock. "Really?" I didn't want to impose. What if he wanted me to go inside? Where he proceeded to rape me and cut up my body into tiny little-

"'Azel?" He looked at me as if he interrupted my thoughts on purpose. Do I think too much truly?

"Um . . ." I looked at my car then back at him. This was a really bad idea. I looked at him again. He was in sweats and a dark gray shirt. *I loved that shade of gray.* What? I shook my head. I think I needed food and more sleep. Sighing, I nodded at him took a breath and followed him to the gate.

—ᴡ—

She's going to be the death of me. Thanatos almost laughed at the thought of him dying. It was a riot in his mind. Being sent (punished) to watch over a human was a joke for someone like him. But I guess the punishment fits the crime. After all he was there when Jane's world fell to pieces. But damnit it wasn't HIS fault! It was just his job. He flinched a little with unease. Well that's not exactly true. He wasn't supposed to rush his job, was supposed to be there when needed. But he was bored and sped things up a bit, not like the guy was going to last another month anyways.

His father didn't think it was funny though. He took his job **very** seriously. Training Than wasn't something on his bucket list of things to do. So because of his crime, Than was forced to now train Jane for her new job description. She just didn't know that. She had ignored the calling (stubborn his father warned him) that only a true *descendion* could have heard after the loss of a loved one. Personally it was a choice, the *descendion* could decide to hear the call or not. But because Than had rushed the fate of this, everything was not as it should be. Jane wasn't ready for the decision she was given and now two were sent to find her and sway her to one or the other side. He was sent as the *Lefate* or more simply the left hand man, left being symbolized as the wrong, evil, dark side. Another, the *Ritaya* or the right hand man, right being Gods hand, righteousness, and light side, was also sent down to sway the *descendion.*

Yes, they had a war going on and Jane was right in the middle of it. Why this one mortal was that important was beyond him though.

"So what do you do for a living?" She attempted at conversation behind him.

He just did what was best and ignored her until he reached the door to the many in the mansion he'd purchased for his stay here. Persuaded was a better word for it, but who was he to complain? Opening the door he held it open for her and watched as she seemed to be deciding if she was really going through with this. He looked at her in question and she nodded once and strode in ahead of him, just where he wanted her he thought.

—∾—

She couldn't stop gaping at the marbled floors and vibrant colors all around her. Than could not be responsible for the flower decor in the mansion. Somehow it just didn't seem his way. Actually she'd thought the place would look more like Frankensteins mansion on the inside, counteracting the appearance outside.

This was amazing. Before she could think she asked him who put up the flowers. He shrugged and continued down a long hallway probably assuming she'd follow. He was wrong. She couldn't get over all of the flowers everywhere. She LOVED bright, vibrant, sparkly petaled flowers. She really, really wished her phone was working. She'd be snapping shots of all these bouquets and flower arrangements like nobody's business.

Approaching a long rectangle box of tulips, she shoved her face near the petals and inhaled, not the best smelling flowers but she couldn't help the reaction. She pinched the petals in between her fingers and smiled at how smooth and soft they were. So perfect and so beautiful, Gods greatest creation surely.

Then something was pulling her away from the flowers, by her belt loop on her jeans. Walking backwards, she turned her head around to look at who was attached to the other end. Well duh, of course it was Than. "Do we have to leave so soon?" I pleaded almost sorrowfully. I glanced back at the potted flowers one more time.

"Do you want to get out of those clothes or not?" He continued to walk down the hall.

I blushed. I would never admit that I do, but people have told me I do so I guess I must. He must realize what he could have been implying at that point but I guess he decided not to mention it because he just kept pulling. Or he just flat out didn't care. That seemed to be his attitude. "I'm sure a couple of minutes wouldn't have hurt me," I mumbled.

Than looked back at me like I was crazy. "So you like flowers."

"I think like is a mild term for my affection towards God's greatest gift." I retorted with vehemence.

"I thought God's greatest gift was people, children and love?" He said sarcastically.

I looked at him puzzled. "Well, I suppose so but I was speaking for myself as an individual."

He rolled his eyes. I didn't understand what the attitude was for. I couldn't like flowers? He stopped at a door and opened it for me to go inside. Following close behind me, (honestly I could smell him, I couldn't quite place the smell but it was familiar) I stopped on the side to let him pass so that I could continue to follow him.

He opened another door and a bathroom was inside. Let me just say it was the most luxurious bathroom I'd ever stepped foot in. So my first one ever.

"The towels are in that cupboard. If you need anything don't bother calling for me unless you come out into the hallways in nothing but a towel, cause that's the only way I'll hear you where I'm going."

I gaped at him. He was just leaving the room when I had a question. "Wait! What about clothes? I can't put these back on that'd be pointless."

He looked at me. No he wasn't looking at me. He was . . . . well I don't know what that look was actually. Like he was . . . . "Ew, Than stop!" I threw my hands up around important spots to shield myself from his probing gaze. I realized afterwards how ridiculous this sounds but I mean if he was looking at you THAT way you'd either try to shield yourself OR if you're really depraved, strip on the spot. Since I wasn't close to depraved, I shielded myself.

"You're not hiding anything 'Azel." He just looked at me with amusement.

"Get me some clothes!" I only yelled back in embarrassment.

Sighing he just grunted and turned around leaving the room with a snick of the door. I honestly don't know if he was going to get me clothes but a towel was honestly better than the stink wet mess I was in now.

Stepping back into the bathroom I shut the door, locked it and stripped in record time. I played with the knobs finding the perfect temperature and hopped right in sighing and jumping around with giddiness at the warmth that was finally spreading through my body.

I got around to washing my hair and my face when I thought I heard something. I listened for a few more seconds until I continued to wash everything off ignoring the sound. It almost sounded like a door shutting. Shrugging to myself I stuck my hand out of the shower and grabbed the towel.

Toweling off a bit in the shower, I held the towel to my chest as I stepped out to enjoy the cool air on the parts of my body that were still wet. Wiping off the mirror to check my reflection, I grimaced at the dark circles under my eyes. Definitely need some more sleep.

I opened the door and walked into the bedroom nearly shrieking in terror at Than sitting on the bed with a bundled mess of clothing next to him. As it was, only a squeak left my lips. "Stop doing that!"

His only response of course was to raise his stupid eyebrow. Standing he just told me to dress and went to go stand outside.

I shook my head in exasperation. I should be grateful; I guess that ruled out the rapist theory. He could still be a killer I rationalized. Looking through the pile on the bed, I quickly realized it was all men clothes. I picked boxers I could roll up from the pile but nicked that idea quick. No skin showing, I guess I hadn't quite crossed out the idea of him being a rapist. I instead picked up sweats and a t-shirt that had a design on the front to hide my business.

Stepping out of the room Than was waiting there by the door. He hadn't changed and as soon as I closed the door he started walking. I guess I was supposed to follow again. This was getting really old.

CHAPTER 4

Than had led me to the jackpots of all jackpots. Yes. The KITCHEN. Of course it was as beautiful as the rest of the house. I was starving and there was food EVERYWHERE.

No I'm not exaggerating. There was food on the counters, normal. Food on the table, also normal. Food on the couch . . . What? "Why's there food on the couch?" I looked around noticing that Than was missing from the room.

"Than?" I started panning the area like a drone. He was so quiet I realized, I never really heard where he was at any one moment. *Sneaky sneaky.* I snickered at the phrase from one of my favorite movies, Mr. Deeds.

"What's so funny?" His voice came out of nowhere. I jumped about to the ceiling with fright.

"I seriously think you're starting to do that on purpose." He walked up to me with a phone in his hand.

I guess this was the part where I called my mom. Great. So not wanting to deal with this. Sighing I dialed her cell and started making my plate at the same time. She finally picked up when I sat down at the table with my bounty of food. "Hello?" Oh yeah, random number.

"Mom?"

"Jane! Where are you?" She was a bit irritated judging by her voice. I flicked my glance to Than who went to sit in front of the theatre home system he had. *Typical male.*

"I'm at a friend's house, my car died last night when I was at the mall and so he let me spend the night here." At this, Than turned his head slowly to meet my lying gaze. I gave him a what? look and listened to what my mom was asking me. Damnit, missed it. "What?"

She let out an exasperated sigh. "I asked who this friend is?"

"Oh, his name is Than. He's on Elm Street." Pause. "Um, so what should I do with my car? I don't want to tow it, it's too expensive. Should I take it to the shop that's there at the mall?

"Well I guess so. And who's paying for this? I thought we just had the battery replaced?"

You see what I mean? She is relentless!

"Well I don't know mom it's not my forte! That was dad's thing." After realizing what I said I had to take a breath. I'd always tried to get into cars so that whenever the boys weren't around I'd always know what to do. It never happened.

"Okay well do you need me to take you there? I was about to go shopping for groceries."

The phone was whipped out of my hand. "Hey! Than, give me the phone!"

He ignored me and spoke to my mom. "Mrs. . . . ?" He looked at me.

"Rivers" I supplied for him. Damnit he actually got a last name out of me.

"Mrs. Rivers, I'll take your daughter to get her car fixed. No, it's not a problem really."

He gave the phone back to me. "Hello?" I looked at him like he had three heads. Who *was* this guy?

"So be careful and what happened to your phone?"

I sighed into the phone. "I dropped it in a puddle at the mall on accident. I'm going to have to order a new one with my insurance I got on the phone."

There was a pause on my mother's side of the phone. "It was raining?" No, it hadn't been raining but you know how it may be raining in other parts of town? Yeah, used that one on her.

"It was at the mall. So weird, like serious freak rain out of nowhere."

Now Than was smirking at me. I glared at him. "Listen mom, I'll take care of this and call you when I'm done with the car business."

"Okay, see you later."

"Bye." I hung up and hung my head in my hands.

"Well now we know you're a liar."

I didn't look at him, not wanting to give him the pleasure of my attention. "I'm not a liar. I just don't want her to worry for nothing."

"Liar, liar, pants on fire."

I just ignored him. "Look, I don't need your help, really. I'll just call the business and have them bring my car around to the service department. I'll suffer the fees." I groaned inside. This was going to be a huge dent in my account.

Than just rolled his eyes and left the room. "What does that mean? You always roll your eyes; you're more of a girl than me!" Okay I mostly said it to get a rise out of him, but hey it worked.

"I'm taking you to get a battery so just accept it and move on with your life." He yelled this from wherever the heck he was at the moment.

"Insufferable man," I mumbled under my breath. I continued to eat my bounty. I mean I might as well get a free meal if Than was offering it, right?

After realizing that I'd eaten enough for an army, I followed Than to his garage. I'm sorry, that's a serious misconception. I followed him to his MUSEUM of cars and/or choice of motorcycles. *Who the heck is this guy?!*

I hadn't realized I was standing in the same spot for a full five minutes until Than cleared his throat. I glared at him. "Oh, shut up. You try living a simple life and walk into this without gawking at everything." I strode up to stand next to him. "Okay, which one batman?" I got nothing but his back walking towards a Maserati. "Really?" I asked in semi excitement and wariness.

"Would you prefer the Civic?" He retorted.

I scoffed at the option. "Just open the damned thing."

—∾—

You know that feeling you get on a roller coaster? The part when you're slowly getting to the top before that insane drop to the ground? Okay multiply it by 5, this is how my excitement grew at that point where Than pulled the car out of the garage and onto the highway.

I was gripping the 'oh shit' handle on the inside of the car. No, not because I was worried about his driving skills. Those (of course) were flawless. I was holding on for dear life because I felt like a woman on her period that walked into Godiva and was told everything was free. Flicking my glance towards Than, I couldn't help but notice how damned sexy he looked handling his shift. No emotion on his face what so ever. Just calm, steady gaze focusing on the road. I was almost afraid to speak to him.

"What?"

I flicked my gaze back ahead. "I didn't say anything."

"Still not going to tell me your name?"

Why not? I had already given away my last name which was more telling than my first. "Jane."

"Jane." As if testing my name out loud. It sounded like something one would moan during sex when HE said it. I shook my head. Jeez, when was the last time I took care of that itch? Hmm . . . I really needed to end my relationship since that was useless in that department. *You slut*, I thought to myself. Shook my head again.

"What now?"

I looked at him. Had I said something out loud? Oh my god I hoped not. I played the dumb blonde card just in case. "What? I didn't say anything."

"You sighed in frustration."

Oh was that all? Phew, I let out a breath I hadn't known I was holding. "It's nothing that concerns you, don't worry about it."

"Whatever you say . . . Jane." A shiver ran up my neck and goose bumps appeared on my arms. I crossed my arms against my chest. It's like he knew what saying my name did to me.

We finally made it to the mall. Thank God. Any more time spent next to him and I might combust into some deprived hot mess. Pulling into a stall, as soon as he placed the car in park I ignored all the oncoming stares from fellow mall goers and jumped out of the car, tripping of course with no grace. Did I mention my bag almost flew from my grasp again? Mhmm, record I think. How many times my bag runs away from me. Clutching it for dear life I swung it over my head and moved to the other side of the car.

"Real graceful 'Azel." I felt a blush coming on. I moved passed him, ignoring the ass. Let him eat my dust. I made my way through the mall garage to the doors that would bring me to the service department of the shop they had in a little nook of the mall here.

Opening the door, I didn't wait for Than. He was a guy; he could open the door well enough on his own. *Ass.* I was the first in line, thank Jesus it wasn't a busy day. Usually it was crawling with car junkies who needed something or other fixed. The customer in front of me moved on, done with his business. I moved to the counter. "Hi, I need . . ." Another chest was aligned with my eyes. What the heck? I looked up starting again to explain. "I need a . . ." It was then I realized I was looking into the eyes of an angel. A hot one at that. With man boobs bigger than most girls who get a job done on theirs. Christ almighty! Where were all these hotties with the bodies coming from?

"Miss?" Reeeally? That was his voice? Like milk chocolate drizzled over succulent strawberries. *So good.*

A smile blew across his impossibly kissable lips. Did I just sigh? Shaking my head I attempted this again. "Um, I'm sorry. I don't know what came over me. Sorry. Um, I—" Okay I had to pull it together. I took a deep breath and slowly blew it out. I opened my eyes and tried one more time. "Look, I need a battery for my car; it died on me last night."

"Was your car towed here? With a purchase of a battery we do free installation. I could have it done for you in a couple minutes if you'd like." Oookay call me crazy and sex deprived, but that sounded like some kind of proposition didn't it?

"Uh, er, no. See I was—" A chill crawled across my neck. I swiped at it trying to clear the feeling. *What was that?* It felt the same as when I was standing in line at B&N.

"I brought her here. Her car's at my place." I jumped a little at his voice. *Jesus!* Than was at my side, towering just as high as the hottie angel in front of me. The angel glared at Than and Than glared right back.

Woah. Testosterone levels rising.

"Than." The angel nodded once stiffly at Than.

"Don." 'Kay that was more of a snarl.

"Wait you guys know each other?" I looked back and forth between them. They were pretty much opposites. Than was darker, with his obsidian silver flecked eyes and a Damon Salvator haircut from Vampire Diaries. His build looked like he could be quicker, more flexible. I looked back at . . . what was his name? Don? He was like, a power house. There wasn't anywhere that wasn't packed with muscle; as if a flick would send someone flying. His eyes were the lightest of browns, almost glinting yellow. Wavy locks of a beach blonde was pulled back into a tail behind him.

Than snarled out something like 'acquaintances'. Yeah well whatever. If they hated each other that wasn't my problem. I didn't even know these guys.

"Yeah, okay, anyways. So how about that battery. Don, is it?"

He turned those light brown eyes on me, I swear I almost melted. The indifference in them melted away once they lit up on me. "Sure, if you'll follow me?"

I followed him but Than hung back. I shrugged whatever. We stopped at a wall of batteries. Different brands with different capabilities. Don explained them all to me and showed me the pricier ones. I winced and moved along to the not so high priced ones.

"Worried about the prices?" He looked at me with concern.

I looked back, looked away. In the middle of finding a job is a stiff position to be in, especially for someone who's so used to being a shopaholic. "I'm in the middle of job searching." I shrugged, I wasn't ashamed, and at least I was looking and had the experience to be sure of finding one soon.

"Ah, I see. Yeah that can be a difficult time."

I nodded in agreement. Well at least he wasn't a smart ass and actually had something agreeable to say. Unlike a certain person I was 'acquainted' with. I continued my walk along the wall and finally settled on one that wasn't so bad. Not like I had a choice really. Money was going out no matter what.

Don took the battery to the counter, scanned the bar code and repeated what I saw on the screen. That couldn't be right. It was under twenty dollars. I looked back at Don, was about to say something but he just winked at me. I looked around me; wouldn't he get into some kind of trouble for this?

"I don't want to get you into trouble Don. It's alright I'll just pay the full price." I started to pull out the sixty something I owed him but he placed his hand on top of mine, stopping me.

"We all need a break, don't worry about it. Really."

I swear he almost made me cry. A break, what I've been looking for since this summer. "Thank you Don."

I gave him the money, said goodbye to him and headed back towards the garage. This time I did look back, but he was already gone. My shoulders slumped in defeat. A break my butt. Oh well, I still had two more things to take care off. Phone and a best friend I had to let go of if I wanted to move on with my life. I felt like a new and fresh start was needed.

I saw the car and Than was leaning against the hood. That was irritating. Who plants their dirty ass on a Maserati hood? I glared at him, so disrespectful!

"What are you glaring at me for?" He unlocked the car and slid in the same time as me. *Irritating.*

"Nothing. I wasn't glaring."

"Could've fooled me. I swear there are twin holes in my head."

I remained silent. Why couldn't he have anything nice to say? Like Don? I pulled out the receipt for the battery to see how much he deducted off the full price. Instead of seeing that though, the first thing I noticed was seven numbers scrawled across the receipt. My eyes widened. Was that . . . ? It definitely, most assuredly was! Don wrote his cell number on my receipt! I quickly folded the paper before Than saw it and ruined this moment. I put the paper in my wallet just as we pulled up to Than's driveway and opened the gate.

He pulled the car into its place in his garage . . . ahem . . . museum, and I stepped out. He came around the car and extended his hand out to me. I stared at it blankly. "What?" I said dumbly.

He took his hand back to massage the bridge of his nose as if HE had a headache. Psh, as far as I was concerned he WAS the headache.

"I need the battery 'Azel, if you want me to put it in your car." Oh. I handed him the battery.

"Go use the phone if you need to or watch t.v., this may be awhile." With that he turned around to head back to my car. Wait, didn't he need my keys?

"Than! Wait, don't you need something?"

At that he stuck his other hand up in the air and dangled my keys for me to see. I seriously needed to keep those on me at all times. I made my way into his living room and picked up the phone from the counter where I had left it that morning. I called T-mobile to replace my phone without a problem. Just as I was hanging up I saw something move out of the corner of my eye.

"Than?" No answer. Hmm, that was pretty fast. He claimed it'd be awhile. But that's when I definitely heard something from down the hall. Like a chair being dragged against the floor to be moved.

"Than?! Is that you?" Still nothing. I got up to go investigate what in the world he was making all that racket for. Making my way down the hall I swear it was beginning to get colder. I paused to be sure I wasn't just freaking myself out. No, it was definitely getting colder, and I was wearing sweats and a t-shirt. Hugging my body, I had just made it outside the room I heard the noise from when I noticed the woman's voice.

He'll kill me. Once he finds out, he'll kill me. A sob escaped the voice.

What in the world? "Hello? Is anyone in there? I'm a . . . an acquaintance of Than's, sorry if I'm . . ."

I had pushed open the door and stood in horror at what I saw in front of me. A woman was standing on top of a wooden chair, a thick loop of rope around her neck.

He'll kill me for sure. Another sob escaped her looped throat.

I held my hands out in front of me. "Wait, listen! You don't want to do this." She actually looked at me with pale white eyes. Eerily I knew this wasn't what it looked like but I couldn't think of anything but saving this person from committing a suicide in front of me.

He's going to kill me. Kill me! I didn't mean to cheat on him but he's so cruel and Samael is so kind to me.

"I'm sure he was. But you can't end your life over this. Please come down. Please?" I didn't know what to say to someone who was this distraught and so up for killing themselves.

All she did was stare at me with that dead stare. *It's too late.* She kicked the chair out from under her feet.

"NO!!" I ran to grab her legs, ignoring the snap I heard that was clearly her dainty neck. It was truly too late. I fell to my knees . . . having run right through her? What? I looked up but she was still there hanging from the ceiling fan. Neck broken, dead stare now aimed at nothing.

Tears fell from my eyes. It took about three more seconds for me to black out in pain.

CHAPTER 5

Than had never come across someone so ungrateful. *I take her to get her battery, let her use my phone, my utilities, drive her there and back. Do I get any thanks?* No, he got glares. But the angel gets gah gah eyes. He should've known they'd send Abaddon. The newly appointed Angel of Death. They weren't going to make this easy on the son of Death. The only thing that was fair about this was that they were both new at their jobs. Self righteous fairies.

His head was currently under the hood of one beat to hell Hyundai. Someone had taken their fists a few times to this car. Undoubtedly to Jane's heart also. His fists bunched wanting to punch the dick down to hell for his minions to deal with. Shaking off the unwanted emotions she seemed to stir in him, he was pulling down the hood when a chill literally raked down his back. His hair stood on end.

Hmm. Spirits afoot, a guilty one today. This was the problem that Than had caused with his recklessness that fateful day. Spirits that wouldn't or simply couldn't find their way to where they needed to be were spilling out of the in-between like a bucket with holes. There weren't enough *descendions* these days. It seemed the more passion they had for life, the more powerful they were as guardians of these types of spirits. Because of him, it was taking longer for Jane to see what needed to be saved and guided. It wasn't a coincidence her last name was Rivers. Her unlikely descent was most likely from Charon. Ferry man to the souls crossing the river styx in the afterlife. He didn't envy her, Charon was a grumpy sonofabitch.

Something didn't seem right with the feeling he was getting though. Usually the chill came and went. The spirit would replay their end and move on until repeating the act or finally moving on, the latter highly unlikely without an appointed *descendion*. This chill however was remaining way too long. He waited a few more moments but it wasn't shaking. He started for the house, not liking this. Eerily, as soon as he reached the door the chill seeped out of him as usual.

Rushing inside he made his way through the kitchen and living room. He didn't see Jane anywhere. Didn't smell her faint floral perfume he noticed she wore either. "Jane?" He stopped running to listen. Nothing but cold silence returned his call. Cold? Of course, he mentally kicked himself. The spirits always left traces of ice cold air wherever they were. He usually stayed away from those areas. This time he followed it.

The coldest air was coming from a room down the hall from the kitchen. An easy vantage point from where Jane would've been had she been sitting where she was this morning. He followed the chill down the hall. The door was already open and that's where he saw Jane on the floor as if she'd fallen.

He rushed to her side and knelt down to pick her up. Carrying her, he made it to the living room where he placed her on the couch. "Jane?" He brushed the hair from her face, placing both palms on both sides of her face. He ignored how soft her skin was and knelt down to hear if she was breathing. *Yes, thank you.* She was still breathing. Had she seen the spirit that he'd felt? If she had, she was entering the scarier part of what her job was to be. Most often to humans, seeing violent deaths was a sight no one would ever forget.

"Jane! Wake up!" He shook her a little. It was then he noticed how ice cold she was. Her lips were even a light shade of blue. He grabbed the blanket off the arm of the sofa and draped it over her, rubbing her arms to warm her up. He decided to make a cup of hot tea for her so that when she woke up she wouldn't be so overwhelmed with the cold.

Making the tea, he walked back to Jane to check on her. Still out and lips were still blue. *Damnit! This is not in my job description!* He walked back to the kitchen and poured the hot water over the tea bag. He spooned some honey in there and walked back to the couch.

Glancing at Jane he almost dropped the cup of tea. She was pale as death, her lips now a full blown sapphire blue. She definitely did NOT look human anymore. He placed the cup down on the table and moved the blanket. *Shit, this would probably hurt.* He moved her to make space behind her to fit his body. She was freezing! Sucking in a breath he curled around her body using his unnatural body heat (from hell, duh) to bring her rapidly dropping temperature back up somewhat.

Pulling the blanket back over both of them he draped one leg over her and pulled her closer to him. "C'mon 'Azel, wake up for me." He lay there holding her, waiting for the outcome.

—~—

I was never so toasty in my life. But seriously? That outrageous snoring had to end. I thought my dad's snoring had been bad. Ha! Whoever this was, he was the king of snores. I opened my eyes slowly this time in case I was somewhere where I was going to be blinded again. The table in the living room was in my line of sight. I realized I was lying on the couch. Why was I on the couch? What happened to me? I swear I was last in the kitchen making that call to T-mobile about my phone. Then . . . then I went to that room. A chill swept through me at what I recall seeing in that room. A tragedy like nothing I've ever seen with my own two eyes before.

Snooooore!

Behind me? I looked over my shoulder and literally fell off the couch hitting my head on the table there. "Crack! Sweet baby Jesus! ARGH!"

"Azel?" He sounded worried. Why? I have no idea. I just wanted to know what the hell he was thinking sleeping behind me. Pervert! He poked his head over the side of the couch and looked relieved at seeing me. "Your better, I thought you were at the end of your road for a moment there."

What? Rubbing my head I sat up. "What do you mean? What happened? Why in God's name did you think it'd be okay to sleep behind me?"

He flinched at the word God oddly but other than that his face was emotionless. But she could've sworn she heard worry laced in his voice a moment ago. "What do you remember before you blacked out?" He brought my attention back to him.

"I saw . . ." Should I tell him the truth? He'd probably think she was kray kray if she told him. "I thought I saw something. But it was nothing. I scared myself." It didn't look like he believed her.

"Into a full blown black out?"

"Well—"

"Jane, stop. You were knocked out on the floor when I found you in the coldest room ever." He sat up on the couch placing me in a view I'd find a lot more interesting if I weren't in the current situation I'm in now. "Then I place you on the couch and leave you alone for at least a couple minutes and your lips are blue and you were pale as death when I got back. Hence the reason I was behind you, *keeping you warm*." Oh.

"Oh."

He rolled his eyes. "What did you SEE Jane?"

"You'll just call me crazy and insult me if I tell you. Why bother?" I started to get up but he grabbed my hands and pulled me down next to him on the sofa. Something in my stomach heated at the contact.

"Try me." He stared, giving me his full attention. It was too unnerving, I had to stare at my hands. But even those were unnerving since they were covered by his. I couldn't let go though. I was too freaked out. I needed the support. Taking a deep breath I told him what I'd seen after making a call to my mobile carrier.

His only reaction was to stare at me. No emotion as usual. "Well?"

"That's . . . interesting." I sighed in frustration.

"See! You think I'm crazy right? I knew it." I pulled from his light hold and got up to pace. "Look I know it's crazy and honestly this is the last thing I want to be telling a veritable stranger. But that's what I saw! I mean I heard her and she looked right at me! She SPOKE to me Than! She responded to what I told her." Than's head snapped to me then.

"She spoke back to you?" Why this was important, I'll never know.

"I think that's a little unimportant considering I just either had a talkative hallucination OR I've just seen a ghost."

"Mm, spirit not ghost."

"What?" I looked at him dumbfounded.

"Nothing, what did she say to you again?"

"Well I was asking her not to do what she was about to do and then in the end she said it was too late. Then she . . . she kicked the chair." I had to breathe slowly in case I knocked out again. Than simply grabbed me and placed me on the couch again.

"Thanks." I rubbed my temples trying to force myself to stay lucid.

"You're welcome."

Shocker, he knew words like that. I would've said so out loud but it was such a break through with our conversations I left it alone. I glanced outside and noticed how dark it was. Dark. Night time. Oh shit.

"Oh my gosh, what time is it?!" I glanced around looking for a clock around here. There under the TV on the cable box. "Oh jeez, tell me that's wrong Than."

He glanced over at the box. "I'm pretty sure it's set correctly."

Shit! SHIT SHIT SHIT. I haven't been thinking that maybe my boyfriend is freaking out trying to get into contact with me. Never mind my mother whom I'd promised to call when the car was fixed. I hopped up again running for the phone. "The car is fixed right Than?" I shouted from the kitchen.

"It's running." This time I didn't jump. Hmm maybe I was getting used to his silent techniques. I turned around and he was again standing right in my face. "Have you seriously never heard of personal space?" I started dialing my mom.

"I have. A useless term if you ask me." I raised an eyebrow at this.

"Hello? Jane?"

"Yeah, Hi mom. So the car is done." I grabbed the stool to sit on getting comfortable for the next conversation that was bound to be a long one.

"Are you coming home then? I made spaghetti for dinner." I hated that voice she used. The one where she really hoped I was coming home tonight. It made me feel like I was never home anymore. When in fact I was always home since I didn't have a job yet.

"Yeah I'll head home after one more call."

"Alright well get your butt home tonight."

"Alright, see you later then."

"Bye."

"Byee."

"So, who's the second call?" I stared at him. "One that was long overdue." I dialed my boyfriend's number taking a breath for courage.

"Hello?"

"Hey, it's me."

"Wow. Where have you been I've been worried."

"I know. I'm so sorry I haven't been able to call you. But look I have to talk to you."

Pause. "Okay."

Deep breath. "So I've been feeling this way for awhile. I just haven't found the words to tell you. Guess there's no other way though. I think we should break up." Release deep breath.

"Are you serious?" That's where the huge conversation came in and took about three hours. I had moved to the couch by then, now lying on my back. After shed tears we'd finally came to the conclusion.

"Okay, well I guess this is it. I'll see you around Jane."

"Don't worry we'll still be friends." God I hated this. But it had to be done. There were just no feelings left on my end of the line.

"Yeah. Sure. I'll see you around then."

"Okay. Bye."

"Bye."

I ended the call. Checked the time. No. There was no way I would make it home tonight. I sat up looking for Than. He'd faded into the background as was his way. "Than?" God was that my voice? I cleared my throat before calling him again. "Than?" I started walking but paused. I really didn't want to encounter what had happened only a handful of hours ago again.

"TH-!"

"Yeah?" He was behind me. How? Turning around I didn't even comment on the space issue.

"I was kind of wondering if maybe I could borrow the couch tonight. It's too late for me to be driving in this state and I think if—"

"You can borrow one of the rooms."

"-I drive I'll . . . Wait. Did you say okay?"

"Well you already borrowed my driveway. A room would be more polite on my end don't you think?"

A smile almost broke across my lips but it came out more of a grimace. I nodded at him. He made the motion to follow him. I dialed as I walked. Voicemail. "Hey mom, I had a break up conversation with my now ex-boyfriend. It took too long so I'm borrowing a room here at Than's. I'll call you in the morning. Bye."

Ending the call, I just kind of dragged myself behind Than. I was so exhausted. Relationships were ridiculously stressful. Why couldn't they be easy and wonderful like the movies or the books I read?

We stopped at a door in a shorter hallway. There were only three doors. Two on my side and one directly across from mine.

"My room is this one." He pointed to the one across from my door. "The one next to your door is the bathroom. If you need anything just knock."

I just nodded and opened the door to my room. I moved to shut the door.

"Jane?"

I opened the door again. "Yeah?"

"You okay?"

I wonder if he had been doing drugs while I was on the phone that entire time. "No, but I'll get through it. I always do." I moved to shut the door again, but he wasn't done yet apparently.

"You shouldn't have too." I looked into his abyss eyes. I could really get lost in those depths. "Goodnight 'Azel."

"G'night Than." I shut the door and moved to the bed. Shedding my borrowed clothes, I folded them up and placed them on the dresser that was against one wall. Pulling the comforter back I hopped up onto the enormous bed. It was too big and spacey for my tastes, lonely. But it was much better than my car seat.

Drifting off into exhaustion I really hoped against nightmares tonight. That was the last thing I needed.

CHAPTER 6

Running.

Why was I running? I don't know but that's what my body was telling me to do. The cold was just too unbearable. I had to get away from it. It'd freeze me to death surely.

Looking around me I tried to find somewhere familiar to hide. I couldn't run forever.

There were lights everywhere, not enough to light up the darkness however. People were talking and walking around me as if they didn't even notice me running through like a crazy person. So strange.

This place seemed familiar though. Great Greek gods stood around a fountain. Athena, Apollo, Hades, and Hermes, seemingly guarding the fountain. I ran past not stopping. That's not where I could hide.

I continued past, making it to a . . . casino? What? I just barely stopped running. Something trying to poke into my dream memories. I finally came to the end and stopped. I couldn't go anywhere else. It was a dead end. A huge fountain was in front of me. Behind the fountain you could see into the water through the glass. Fishes and sharks swimming about, living the life that was forced upon them.

That was the last thing normal that caught my attention. Sitting on the benches that stuck out from the glass part of the fountain, there was a . . . um, a headless man? I held back a terrified scream. He would be staring straight at me if he had a head. I turned away, couldn't bear looking at his body. What faced me wasn't any better. A couple was walking their dog, well, their skeleton dog that is, while they looked burned to a crisp. I almost threw up in my mouth. Their bodies looked as if they were placed in a fire until only burned flesh was viewed, and then taken out to suffer. I honestly don't know how they walked on their feet.

Where the hell was I? I had to get the hell out of here! Turning around to where I'd come in, I made for the entrance.

What?

Where the entrance had been, you can bet your sweet ass it wasn't there anymore.

"Jane." I froze where I was. Turning slowly unable to believe he was in this nightmare, I wanted him out! He shouldn't be here; he was too innocent though he was older than me.

Air left me in a whoosh. Not only was my brother here, so was my mother. "Jordan! Mom! What are you guys doing here?"

"What do you mean Jane? We all came to eat at Cheescake Factory. We were waiting for you while you looked around. We have our seats now, come on." I looked at them in confusion. They were waiting for me? I took a step but no, something wasn't right about my family. Something in their eyes was wrong. My mother's looked dead while Jordan's were plain freaky, a hard glint my brother's real jolly eyes would never have taken even in his pissiest moods.

"I need to—" I took a step back.

"Jane! Stop dawdling before we lose our seats. What is the matter with you?"

I took another step back from them. They took another step towards me.

I bumped into something behind me. Turning around I looked down at the man in the wheelchair behind me.

"Oh! I'm so sorry! I just . . ." The man grabbed my hand, not with malice but kindness. Familiarity ran through me. I knew that hand. The contours, hard worked hands that always knew what to do. A tear escaped me and I fell to my knees.

"Daddy?" I whispered as tears fell down my face unchecked.

He looked up at me, his face withered away from the strength used to fight his illness. Cheeks a bit sagging, hair still black though with white streaks running through. His wheelchair however was still sprayed with blood. The memory choked me. His hands though, those were always strong, showing through as the person he used to be before. Yeah, before.

"Jane, you leave this place. It's not safe for you here."

"But . . . you—"

"Listen. I don't have much time. You'll have to choose Jane."

Choose? I just looked at him in confusion, not believing I was getting to see him again. I grasped his hand willing him to never let go. I would be better! I would be a better daughter than I was when he was here. Just don't let go. I started to tell him so but he cut me off.

"You must choose. Take care of your mother and brother, and yourself Jane."

Everything around me disappeared into mist. I was left in a blinding white nothingness. "Dad!?" I turned around knowing it was hopeless. "Daddy!?" I wailed into the brightness that didn't seem to belong to what I'd just witnessed. Still on my knees I could do nothing but scream. Scream at my unfair loss and the unfairness of seeing what I've been missing all this time, then ripped from me again.

I curled into a ball and cried. Alone, forever alone now.

—ɯ—

"Jane! Goddamnit, 'Azel?! Wake up!"

Someone was shaking me. Quite vigorously at that.

I opened my eyes to darkness; a shock after seeing blinding white just before this. "Than?" What happened? Why are you shaking me, was something I didn't ask. His warmth was chasing away the leftover cold of that horrible nightmare.

"You had a nightmare. Are you okay?" I was not okay. The past day and a half has been an emotional strain. But far be it from me to whine to this man.

"I'll be alright." I didn't pull back from his hold though. He was so warm and I was still freezing. Yeah, that's the excuse I was using. It was as good as any right?

"What were you dreaming about? Just remember before you brush me off, you already told me about your spirit encounter." He was the one to pull back, releasing me from his warmth. I almost whimpered, going so far as to grasp his forearms so that he wouldn't completely sever contact. He just arched a brow at this. I ignored him. I looked around and found I was still in the room he'd let me borrow for the night. I next looked at the clock. It was three in the morning. I rubbed the exhaustion from my eyes.

"How did you know I was having a nightmare?" I looked back at him; he was no more than a few inches from me. It was . . . comforting I realized.

He looked at me like I was nuts. "You try to sleep across the hall and not hear the screaming that was coming from your room." I looked at him in shock. I'd been screaming in my sleep?

"It was the most sorrow filled scream I'd ever heard in my life." Had I spoken out loud? I guess so; I swear it was all in my head though.

A chill swept my body, spreading goose bumps all over my flesh. Wait a minute. I specifically remember shedding all my clothes last night. I looked over to the dresser. Yup, the clothes were still neatly stacked there. A horrifying realization crossed my mind, sending a full blown blush all over my body. My NAKED body. The nightmare and chill momentarily forgotten, I looked down at myself. Nothing but a comforter covering me up to just below my chest.

"EEEEK! THAN!!! CLOSE YOUR EYES, YOU PERVERT! WHY DIDN'T YOU COVER ME?! OH MY GOSH, **YOU** ARE DISGUSTING! CLOSE UM!" I grabbed for the comforter but his weight was keeping me from pulling the covers up and he refused to move so I fell to the mattress my back to him. I was mortified! This whole time he was talking to me he didn't say a word! Ugh!! This perfect God of a man was staring at my not so Goddess body and I hadn't noticed one wit! Another blush racked my body. I would never live this down, never.

"What are you freaking out about?" So calm, like my business wasn't all out in the open for him to see and stare at.

"I'm naked." I mumbled into the comforter.

"What? I can't understand you." Ugh, this guy! He was so insufferable. I lifted myself enough to speak clearly.

"I said that I'm naked!"

"So?" I grabbed a pillow and held it to my chest so that I could glare at him.

"SO," I growled at him, "I don't just share my business with any 'ol somebody who crosses me!"

"Well that's good to know I suppose. But why are you freaking out?" He truly seemed clueless. Maybe he was a doctor; it would explain his lush living and his apparent aloofness to my nakedness.

"Are you a doctor?" I looked at him suspiciously. He didn't act like a doctor before, but then how were doctors supposed to act?

He just gave me that look he gave me when I was acting like a crazy person. "No, why?"

"Well usually when a woman is naked before a stranger, she freaks out . . . ." I trailed off hoping he'd catch my drift.

He just waved his hand in the air like it didn't matter. "You have nothing to worry about. Besides your beautiful, you have nothing to be ashamed of." He looked at my chest and started looking lower. A blush (and I swear I must look like a cherry by now) crept up to my cheeks again. He was looking at me like he could see through the extremely plush pillow.

I slapped his cheek lightly. "Stop that! You don't have the right to look at me that way!" I must be crazy; I just slapped this beautiful man and told him not to look at me. **After** he told me that my body was beautiful, practically saying he liked what he saw. I must be broken in the relationship area, not to mention the sex department. I sighed inwardly. He looked a little shocked at my little love tap. "I'm sorry, I shouldn't have slapped you, I'm just not comfortable with all this." I hugged the pillow closer to me. "I just broke up with my boyfriend and this makes me feel a little guilty and weirded out.

"Why would you feel guilty . . . unless you liked me?" This last part was said with raised eyebrows.

My eyes widened. He was right. Why would I feel guilty unless I liked this egotistical ass? I shook my head, no. That was impossible. He was arrogant, mean, a thief, pervert, all this among other things.

"I don't like you. I just think there should be some kind of period after a break up where one recoups and thinks about things before hopping into another person's bed or starting another relationship."

Eyebrow raise. "You want to share my bed or start a relationship?" A smile was breaking out on his succulent lips I just wanted to . . . . grr!

OH! Sweet mother, Mary and Joseph! "Jesus! NO, you neanderthal! Would you STOP thinking with your dick and hear me? NO, I do NOT want to start any matter of those things with you! I don't even know you. Why you're new to town or what you do. Why would I hop into something so . . . so . . . ?"

"Adventurous? Dangerous?" He was really the most impossible man.

"No! Something so mysterious but yes dangerous. You could be a crazy lady killer whom you proceed to rape and chop up into little bits to hide in your refrigerator in the basement!" I was huffing and puffing from exhaustion at this point from trying to explain myself. I waited for his response, ready to defend my honor once again to this thick headed ape.

He just looked at me as if trying to process what I'd said. Seriously? It wasn't that hard to understand. "So . . . I have a shot?"

What? "A shot at what?" He lost me.

"A shot at a date." You're kidding me right? He wanted to go on a date with me? After he saw me naked, that just like a man, even though I didn't see myself as such a great catch. I deflated and dropped my face in my pillow shield.

"No!" I screamed into the pillow.

"Why?"

"Because I said no."

"Ah, but why?"

"Because you saw me naked!"

"So?"

"So if you saw me naked before asking me out on a date, how do I know you just don't want to get some?"

"Because I don't need to ask you on a date to get some."

This time I slapped him, hard.

"You arrogant ass! Egotistical, sonofa—" It was hard to get anything else out after his lips were slammed against mine. I struggled like any proper woman would have after being assaulted by a stranger. Honestly, I gave it my all. I even attempted shoving his face away from mine, but he just pushed me down into the mattress and held my hands above my head. Who the hell fought after that?

I allowed him to caress my lips with his own before he started lightly probing with his tongue. I opened and entered hell itself. His kisses were so hot I swear I was in a sauna. He switched both of my wrists to one of his huge hands and used the free one to move my pillow. I squeaked in protest pulling my hands automatically to grab for the pillow, but he held on firmly, it was useless. Of course once his muscle packed body aligned itself to cover me I settled down somewhat.

The kissing continued until my body was seriously getting restless with just kissing. I bit his lip in warning but this only seemed to rile him up more if his growl was any indication. He moved from my lips to my neck. Oh God, his beard was light enough that it didn't hurt but spread sensations all throughout my body. I was never a beard kinda girl, but if anyone told me it had felt like this? Ha, you'd bet your sweet ass I'd be rolling around with lumberjacks all day and all night.

I opened my eyes not realizing they'd been closed all this time. I undulated once against him and decided against it a second time. This was so wrong, what was the matter with me? I must seriously be sex deprived, I mean isn't four or five months long? I thought so.

I suddenly realized something was not right. I blinked my eyes a couple times, attempting to make the image disappear. The wings remained in sight. Black, razor tipped, leathery wings were attached to Than's back. They were HUGE. Like the span of the room, no lie. Instead of freaking out though as was expected of any sane woman, I just wanted to reach out and touch them. Let's just say I was curious George sometimes. I was able to pull one hand from Than's grip this time. He was way too busy with my neck, which, don't get me wrong was really turning me on. But hey, if you had the chance to touch some wings? You tell me which you would choose and tell me you're still sane.

I reached out to touch them, stroking from where the base was to brushing my fingertips across the span of them. Than shuddered over me. *Did he like that?* I did it one more time and he growled viciously in my ear. Woah, that was not a normal human sound. Suddenly as if he realized what I was doing, he flung himself to the side of my bed slamming into the wall. His wings were gone but his eyes no longer held the silver flecks, were indeed pitch black. And slap me silly but I swear I saw a peek of fang over one lip before he covered his face with his hands.

"Than! Are you okay?" I started to get up grabbing the shirt from the dresser and throwing it over my head.

"Stop." The way he said it stopped me dead in my tracks.

"Than . . . I'm sorry. Did I do something wrong?" I found the courage to crawl a bit closer to him on the bed.

He just had to look at me with those obsidian eyes and I stopped again. I didn't know what to do. Did he truly have wings? If so I was dealing with things I needed to talk to someone about, now. This was outrageous. If he had wings did I hurt him somehow by touching them?

"Just give me a moment." He growled this out, low and almost not understandable.

I decided to sit back down on the bed and wait. Wait this out and see what he had to say for himself.

"I'm sorry. I shouldn't have done that." He dropped his hands, clenching and unclenching them at his sides.

This only reminded me of a certain ex douche bag I had no pleasure remembering. I seriously didn't need this. Another violent man in my life was not on my list of things to attain. I looked away making my decision. "Maybe I should leave. Yeah." I got up and walked to the other side where the sweat pants were. "Look I'll bring these back or mail them to you, either way I'll return them.

"Don't bother, I've got a bunch." I turned to look at him but just nodded in response. Okay that was fine with me too, whatever. This was something beyond my power to control right now.

"Okay . . . well thanks for everything, I'll just see myself out."

He didn't say anything. Just stood there and didn't move. I nodded again and left.

—∾—

Driving was hardly possible but I had to get home some way. I was half way home not wanting to think about what

I've been through in only a day or so. Spirits, demon wings, crazy but hot person and a dead battery were a lot for a girl to take in all at once. Oh and a break up, almost forgot.

I scoffed at myself. Almost forgot? Woman you took yourself out of that relationship a long time ago, I told myself. I let a complete stranger/demon guy make out with me! Was I insane, desperate or both? Shaking my head I concentrated on the road. Looking at the clock it was nearly five in the morning. I seriously needed to get more sleep and I couldn't wait for my phone to come in. I wasn't worried about the law firm calling me; they'd told me it'd be a week or so.

I was finally on my street. I pulled up along the side of my house parking my car. Walked up to the front door and went inside. Good, everyone was still asleep. I went to my room and dropped all my stuff, my wallet falling out of my bag. Whatever, I was seriously not in the mood to clean up. I changed into my own clothes and slid into bed.

I was almost afraid to go to sleep. No one was here to hold me if I had another nightmare.

Oh get over yourself! You'll be fine, I chastised myself. Pulling the comforter up to my chin I closed my eyes and willed myself to sleep.

CHAPTER 7

I was standing over the stove hours later cooking some brunch for myself. I was dead tired. The last day and a half drained the life out of me. I just wanted to curl up with a book and lose myself in a world of fantasy. Or maybe continue writing and lose myself in both my own fantasy world and music.

Heaving out a sigh, I moved the egg to my plate and turned off the stove. Pancakes, bacon and an egg were the usual for me. I sat down at our dining room table and dug in. It was Saturday and no one was home when I'd woken up. It was nice and quiet for now. God new when my mom and brother returned it'd be virtually impossible to relax unless I holed up in my room and shut the door. I grimaced at the thought, my room got really hot in the afternoon and we didn't have air conditioning in this house like we used to in our old house.

I'd grown up on the west side all my life. We were born here in this house but moved by the time I was at least ten. I don't exactly remember why or how old I was. I just remember driving there at night, moving our remaining stuff. After the incident, we couldn't make the mortgage payments. So, suffice it to say we moved back to our childhood home behind my grandmother's house, getting a good deal along with the benefit of watching over her as well. I know you must be thinking I should be on my own by now in my own little apartment, but honestly I don't think my mom wants us to move out. I wouldn't want to bother having to come and visit anyways.

Now it was just me, mom and my brother. On the weekends his wife will bring over my niece while she works. They haven't exactly found their footing yet ever since they'd had little Shellie. But that's a whole other drama that I refuse to get into.

Taking one last gulp of my water, I took my plates to the sink and washed them. I dried my hands and went to brush my teeth. Staring at myself in the mirror, I didn't look alive. I looked pale and washed out. Not myself at all. Pulling my hair back into a tail, I returned to my room.

Noticing all of the crap that fell out of my purse from the night before, I picked up what had fallen out and started to put everything back into my bag when I came across the receipt from purchasing my battery. Big, fat sharpie stared back at me. Don's number was still there. *What? Like it was going to disappear?*

Maybe it wouldn't hurt. I couldn't exactly talk to my own friends about what had happened to me the past day and a half. Maybe a date with a seemingly nice person (who happened to be a hunk) was what I needed. What if he was pulling my leg though? What if the number was a prank? It was a weak excuse, even I knew that. I walked to the house phone and dialed the stupid number.

Riing. Riing. Riing. Riing.

See? Not even answering. Just another dumb ass ma-!

"Hello?"

Oh shit! "Oh, um, er . . . Hi?" I slapped my forehead. Jeez, could I be more blonde?

"Uh, yeah?"

"Sorry! Um, Hi, is this Don?" Real smooth Jane, suave is not my middle name.

"Yeah?"

"Hey, um I came by where you work yesterday to buy a battery?"

Pause. "'Kay . . . you know if you have a complaint you call the service department right? I'm not working today."

This time I hit my head against the wall I was standing by. "Ow! Jesus!" Oh crap I was on the phone and said that out loud. Male laughter rung out from his side of the phone. "I'm really sorry. I should explain this better. I could be wrong but I think you wrote your number, hence this call, on my receipt?" Please say yes, please say I'm not a stalker and somehow your number appeared on my receipt magically.

"Oh! Hey, yeah. I didn't think you'd call or maybe you threw the receipt away not even looking at it."

Thank God. "Um yeah I saw it the same day." Okay out with it Jane. "Well look, I was wondering—"

"Did you want to go out sometime today? Since I don't work and everything and . . . I take it you're not either?"

Was this guy for real? "Um, yeah, I was just going to ask."

"Okay cool, so where do you live? I can come and get you."

"I'm at . . ." Hmm, maybe not such a good idea to tell him where I live.

"You're at . . . ?" Should I tell him? He didn't seem like such a creep.

"Sorry, I'm at three three four Lakeside Lane. Got it?"

"Yeah, hey actually I'm really close by do you need time to get ready? Or should I head over there now?"

"I'll be ready in a couple minutes." Why was he so close? Did he live around here? I think I would have noticed a buff angel walking around these parts, it wasn't a large community.

"Great, see you soon." *Click.*

I hung up on my side. I wrote a quick note to my mom that I'd gone out with a friend and supplied his name and number in case she needed to contact me. I made my way to my closet wondering what to wear. We didn't even say what we'd be doing. I looked outside where clouds filled the afternoon sky. I decided on some skinny jeans and a tank. I didn't want to get all dressed up for nothing. The most effort I did was put on some shadow and gloss and put my hair in an up down style so that it wouldn't be in my face but still be left down. He was gorgeous, I had to put a little effort into it I decided.

My phone buzzed. **Outside. You ready?**

Butterfly's fluttered around in my stomach. "Stop that." I placed a hand over my stomach willing them to settle. Slinging my bag over my head I locked up and walked to the front.

I got to my gate and paused. Seriously? Don had more in common with Than than I thought. Sitting across the street without a care was Don. Don on his Yamaha R1. Again, seriously? I walked up to him motioning for him to take his helmet off.

"Um, should I grab my helmet? I didn't know you were riding."

He just stared. "You ride?"

I turned around and motioned to my own Honda cbr 600rr, covered by an old comforter in place of a cover. I turned back to him shrugging. "Yeah, not frequently though. Let me just grab my helmet 'kay?" He just stared at me.

Okay, yeah I had a bike. I was in a rebellious stage and did everything possible to make sure I proved everyone that I could get my license AND get a bike. Sure my brother helped me as a co-signor but hey, I still got it didn't I?

Unlocking my door again I had to hold my dog back from escaping the house. I ran to my room and grabbed my helmet and a light sweater. Locked up once more, I ran back out to the street, those damned butterflies were punching my insides. I'm not gonna lie, I was excited. I haven't ridden on the back of a bike for maybe a year or two now. Been riding solo ever since.

Don was still staring at me like I had three heads. "What? You don't think a girl can ride?" I lifted a brow in question.

He shook his head as if coming out of a daze. That long hair swishing across his broad back. *Mmm, mine for the entire ride.* "Uh, no. It's actually hot as hell." Okay, was not expecting that. A blush crept into my cheeks. Oh boy was this going to be another blush day?

"One more thing."

"Yeah?" I looked at him in question.

"What's your name? With all the business and Than around I never got it yesterday."

Surprisingly, I laughed. God, something must really be wrong with me. He was right; I never told him my name yesterday. Settling down I told him, "It's Jane. My name is Jane. Sorry, but you never did ask me."

He looked up contemplating my point. "Huh, your right I didn't. Well, now that that's out of the way. Hop on." I pulled my helmet on and readjusted my bag. Stepping up on the back peg, I grabbed his shoulder to steady myself and hopped up behind him. I placed my shield down and placed my hands on the tank in-between his, ahem, jean covered, muscle packed thighs. *Blush.* I sat there anticipating him to make his move onto the road, but all he did was sit there.

"Are you waiting for something?" My voice was muffled but he heard me somehow.

He didn't say anything but looked back at me. Those light brown eyes were killers. He grabbed my hands and repositioned them around his waist, entwining my fingers. "Don't want you falling off Jane." I could only see his eyes but that's all I needed to see to know he was smiling. *Blush.* I just nodded at him. Who was I to complain? He finally put it in first and pulled out onto the road.

By the time we made it to the freeway I was relaxed against Don's incredible back. That is until he had a free shot out of traffic. I nearly fell off the back of his bike; ignorant of what he had intended to do. He grabbed my hands with his left though, feeling me fall away. No lie, I squealed like a little girl. I knew he was laughing, could tell from his entire back shaking from it. *Sneaky guy.* He released my hands after I had renewed my grip on him and continued to speed like a demon out of hell down the freeway.

I started to anticipate how he moved and before long I was one with him. It was invigorating! I would never go this fast on my own bike, afraid of all the crazies on the road around me. The speed he was gaining was incredible! This was exactly what I needed, to feel free. To feel like I was flying away from all of my problems. God it was great! I smiled behind my helmet. Who knew today would end up like this? Behind a gorgeous man on his gorgeous bike, flying on the freeway to wherever the hell he was taking me? Loved. It.

Something so normal was the cure to all the crazy that was happening to me lately. Maybe it had all been just a bad day. I nodded to myself; yeah that's what it was. Just a bad day.

Coming off the freeway, we were in town now. Where was this angel taking me? We pulled into a parking structure behind what I knew to be probably the most expensive theatre around these parts. A movie then? He parked in the designated bike stalls and cut his engine off. Pulling off his helmet, which by the way I'd like to say ironically, was a dark avenging angel with the wings on the side of the helmet, blazing sword in hand ready to deal justice to some poor soul in his sights, he looked back at me. "So? You still alive back there."

I glared at him halfheartedly and gave him a little slap on his shoulder. "I'm perfectly fine. You shouldn't jump the gun like that though. I nearly became a smear on the road!" I grabbed his shoulder and hopped off the bike from hell.

His laughter was dying down as he swung his massive body off the bike as well. "I would never let you fall."

Somehow I believed that. I took my helmet off and hung it off one arm. "So what are we doing? Movie?" I expected a simple yes from him. However I only got an eye roll.

"Nah, that's for normal people. C'mon." I followed him completely stumped. Now I really had no idea what to expect. He weaved through the parked cars and led me to the security office in the corner of the lot. Knocking on the door we waited for someone to answer. I found myself thinking who the heck *this* guy was now. Who was I making acquaintances with these days?

A well rounded man opened the door. "Oh, Don, hey my man wassup?" They firmly grasped hands in a handshake and did the whole man half hug thing.

"Hey Paul, this is my friend Jane. Was wondering if it'd be too much trouble to leave our helmets here?"

"Of course man, no problem. I'm outta here at four though for the next shift, so just be back before then alright?" Don thanked him, grabbed my helmet and handed it to Paul.

I put my own thank you in there and moved on with Don. "So how do you know the local security?" Don side eyed me and looked forward again.

"A while back, I did a favor for his family." That's all he said, quick and to the point, no more. I wasn't having it today though. I was tired of half ass answers.

"What kind of favor?" I looked up at him expectantly. He didn't look at me this time. Surprisingly he answered with no hesitation.

"I happened to be around when his daughter Abby had just ridden her bike out into the street. A bus was not far from where she'd popped out of nowhere seemingly to the bus driver. I ran in front of the bus and grabbed her before she was hit. We both nearly ate it." I had stopped towards the end of the story in shock. I jogged to catch up to him.

"That's a big favor!" I can't believe anyone would do that. Maybe yell out a warning surely. But to run in front of a bus that was nearly on top of the girl? Not many people would, none that she knew anyways.

He just shrugged. "It was a reaction kind of thing." Yeah, maybe to a cop or someone with some kind of expertise. I dropped the subject following him to the small shopping mall across the street from the theatres.

"So what made you want to get a bike? It takes a certain person, let alone a woman who'd ride a bike." He glanced at me curiously.

I shrugged this time. "I can't really say what made me go through with it. It started out as something that seemed interesting to me. I did the classes and passed. Why shouldn't I have gotten a bike afterwards? I guess I was also competing, in my mind, with my two friends I'd gone with. After about a year I went to one of the local bike shops and there she was. Screaming my name, even after the salesman told me the bike I was looking for, they didn't have." A small smile appeared on my lips at the memory. All I had to do was look to the right and my bike was sitting prettily waiting for my attention. "There were a bunch of fools looking at her. But I pressed the issue to Vincent, the guy helping me, that I really wanted her. I made a million and one calls trying to find a co-signor and my brother graciously signed on. She was brought to me as soon as I got insurance. I love her and mom will never convince me to sell her."

"She wants you to sell your bike? Why?" He literally looked aghast at the idea. I chuckled and impersonated my mother's rants that came and went.

"*There was another motorcycle accident! You better not be going over the speed limit! That's all you're going to wear? Put on pants missy!*" I looked at Don, "The list of problems she sees with my bike are literally endless." I shook my head as we came up to a bikini shop. "Um, not to judge or anything but I think this is for women Don."

He shot an exasperated look my way. "Ha ha, real funny. We are here for you. I doubt your wearing a bikini under those skin tight jeans." *Blush.* "Where we're going you're gonna need one."

Well he should've told me that! I don't have the money for this! "Okay, well why didn't you tell me? I could've thrown one on before we left. I can't afford this, you know I'm job searching. Can't we do something not so wet?" I looked nervously from him to the shop and back again. I really hated owing people, truly, deeply hated it.

He turned and faced me. "Listen, the manager owes me. Just go pick something out and I'll go talk to her, alright?"

"Why are you using all these favors up on me?" He didn't even know me, let alone need to be doing all these things for me. It was completely unnecessary in my mind.

"I don't need them."

"Well neither do I. Let's just do something else Don. A movie is simple; let's go back to the theatre." I pleaded to him with my eyes. It didn't work. He took my hand and dragged me into the store. I attempted to pull my hand out of his light hold but he only gripped on tighter.

Walking up to one of the ladies on the floor, he asked her if Flor was working today. The woman went to find her.

I glanced around, this looked really pricey. It was one of those Brazilian bikini shops. Every piece was at least forty dollars or higher. With my luck, the one I wanted would be over that amount.

A woman with hair as black as night that fell to her lower back came strolling out from the back with a smile plastered to her face. She looked to be about thirty five and around my height. "Don! *Mon ami*, it's been too long. Come to collect that favor I see." Her accent was light but she sounded French to me. She smiled serenely at him and glanced my way, that smile fading slightly. 'Kay, I guess she didn't expect Don to be in company. I sniffed in my mind. *Too bad ya old hussy.*

"And who is this? Your sister?" My eyes widened. Why I ought a . . . . My hand gripped Don's in anger.

"Flor, this is Jane, my date. We need a bikini for her. Where I'm taking her she'll need one. Please help her with anything she needs." He emphasized the word 'date' and looked at me the entire time he spoke to her.

You could practically feel the sneer she directed my way. "*Oui*, if zhat is vhat you vish." In her jealousy, her accent was thick and ugly now. Don simply ignored her and nudged me to look around. It seemed the simplest choice to head over to the sale rack. I jumped a little at Don's exasperated grunt.

"C'mon legs, find something you really like." I glared at him, legs? Really? What was with all these guys and their pet names for me? I had a perfectly suitable name. Jane. *JANE.* Was it so hard to use?

I've almost had it with men. I rolled my eyes heavenward and moved on to a rack that was regular priced, and preceded to have my eyes fall out of my head. Fifty dollars for one piece of two?! These people were nuts! I'd rather swim naked!

Don chuckled next to me. "That can be arranged."

Oh my God, did I seriously say that out loud!? I needed to watch my mouth; I'd look like a strawberry in no time if I kept this up. I ducked my head down and shuffled away from him down the rack.

Making my way to the small section, I finally came across a simple black bikini top I approved of. Moving to the medium sizes, it didn't take me long to find a bikini bottom that would keep my tan line in check. I smiled at the color, black light purple, fave choice. I made my way to the counter to have the worker check me out, Don trailing behind me. The girl was obviously already told that this would be on Flor, ringing me up but not bothering to tell me the amount. I really didn't want to know.

Thanking the girl, we finally left that thieving shop. "Don't ever make me go through that again Don."

He just stared at me in question. "Go through what? I didn't know it was such a hardship for a girl to shop. Thought you guys were pros."

I seethed at his intentional obtuseness. "You know what I mean. It's simple, if I can't afford something, it doesn't leave the shop with me. I rarely go anywhere knowing I won't be able to buy anything." I glanced away not wanting to ruin this date, but seriously this was one of my pet peeves. I hated feeling like a charity case. Sighing I looked at Don. "Alright so where are we headed?"

"Just follow legs, just follow." I didn't let it slip my mind that he hadn't responded to my outburst. I must be churly because of lack of sleep I decided. Taking a deep breath I did a mental set down and did what he asked. I followed.

Walking for what seemed to be forever, we stopped in front of the local Sea Park they had here by the beach. Why did I need a bikini for this place? Unless . . . no, really? I looked to Don in excitement. "Reeally?" I asked him like a child being told they were going to a candy store.

He looked at me with a chuckle on his ridiculously lickable lips. "C'mon." He grabbed my hand again to pull me along. I didn't pull away this time.

He walked up to the window and again asked for someone he apparently knew here. The boy behind the window nodded once and went to the phone to dial someone in the park. "Who are you collecting from now?" I asked exasperated.

"Don't worry about it." The boy told Don where he could find his friend . . . . Sharon? Apparently by the dolphin arena and he dragged me along. The park wasn't such a big place. I'd only been here a couple times before when I was still in elementary school on field trips. It had changed a bit since then I suppose, not that I'd remember everything anyway.

We finally made it to the arena where we met up with Sharon. She couldn't have been more than the same age as me, this time I didn't get a glare though, but a kiss on the cheek once Don introduced us. "Oh, Don she's adorable!" Okay, did I mention she looked like a hopeless romantic? I mean so was I, but this girl had it BAD. She continued to ogle me with awareness that we were on a date. "Oh, I would be more than happy to get you guys ready to play with my boys." I apparently missed the entire conversation, doing my best to overcome a body blush coming on at her scrutiny and a hundred questions to Don about how we met and all that junk people asked a new couple.

Chuckling, Don had to calm her down. "Sharon listen, it's our first date alright? No need to fuss, I think you're making Jane uncomfortable judging by the twitching and shuffle dance she's doing over here."

I gasped. I was not! "Shut it!" I whacked him on the chest. Sharon did nothing but gush some more over how cute we were. Lord, help me but it would be a long day.

We finally got Sharon to settle down and bring us to the area where employees had volunteers to swim with the dolphins sometimes. "You'll be swimming with Jack and Domino today. They're our strongest of the boys, and the most playful. I'll join you in the water to get you started and then they're all yours 'kay?" I only nodded. I'd never swam with dolphins before. This should be interesting.

I changed into my bikini and joined the other two where we agreed to meet by the enormous pool. Stepping out into the sun I really hoped I didn't fry like an egg, Mr. Sun and I were not friends. I walked along the pool when Don came walking out from the other end of the pool where my jaw preceded to fall to the floor. Aw c'mon! That was so unfair, I almost turned around to run back and hide in the dressing room. I would've really, but I was glued to the spot watching him walk along the side of the pool.

A perfectly sun kissed tan wrapped up all those muscles like dove chocolate wrapping up the delicious vanilla hidden inside. Strictly an all chocolate girl, this was for descriptions sake. Being a sucker for nice calves (I know, weird) I glanced at those first and his were flawless. Everything else was pretty much a part of the package. He was seriously packing, I felt bad for Jack and Domino. Whoever was pulling him was seriously going to be tired at the end of the day.

"Like what you see Legs?" Startled, I glanced up and had to shade my face from being blinded. No, not by his angelic features you twit, by the sun. Duh! I said nothing, I couldn't say anything, tongue tied as I was.

"Jane? Hello, earth to Jane." I blinked rapidly, had he asked me a question? I'm sure he had. What was it again?

"Er . . . what?" He just laughed as Sharon joined us.

"Well look at you two! Hotties with the bodies! Match made in heaven I'd say!" God, shoot me now. *Please.*

Sharon had a bucket of fish in her hand and that's when Jack and Domino also joined us in the water. I've been this close before, but now I'd be in the water with them. So exciting! After feeding a couple fish to the two, we followed Sharon's lead into the pool cautiously, not wanting to fall in. I decided not to look at Don when he was wet, it wouldn't bode well for my complexion.

Sharon proceeded to teach us how to hold onto them, not to fight them and what they were trained to do. It reminded me of riding on the back of a bike so I used that theory to put to the test when the time came. She finally deemed us worthy enough to be on our own and stepped out of the pool, staying nearby to treat the dolphins when necessary and to be of any assistance to us if something should happen.

Both me and Don grabbed hold of our ride. I got Domino while he got Jack. I let my hand glide over Domino's skin, firm and powerful. As soon as I gripped his fin he took off. At first I was shocked but held on for my life. I could hear Sharon cheering me on from the poolside and calmed letting Domino do his thing. He suddenly ducked underwater and I only had a few breaths in before I was underwater with him. Holding that precious breath, I let him lead me to Jack and Don. They twirled us around each other and I had to laugh at how magical it was. Doing so, I released precious breath and my boys fin to kick to the surface for air. I didn't make it far. Something slimy and hard gripped my ankle painfully.

What the . . . ? It was only then I noticed how freezing the pool became. I was jerked violently down, back into the pool. Looking down I was horrified to see a man, his body rotted as if he'd been in the water for an unknown amount of time. One eye was missing and a crab crawled from the INSIDE of his skull. I wanted to vomit. Now. Kicking as hard as I could, I tried to kick free from the man's hold. No such luck, he had an iron grip on my ankle. With the little air I'd had, black spots appeared in my vision. *I was going to die. Here in this pool.* Losing consciousness I sank to the bottom of the pool, the light from the sun blinking out with my last breath.

—ᨓ—

"Are you crazy?! She could've died you dumbass!"

"I didn't know she was going through it already! Maybe if YOU hadn't forced it on her this would never have happened!"

So LOUD, why did men always have to be so obnoxious? Why were there men shouting above me anyways? Why was I freezing? The sun was beaming down on me earlier when we got into the pool. *The pool.* It was coming back to me. Creepy, zombie guy dragging me down, then me Losing consciousness. It was almost enough to send me over again.

"Shut up!"

"You shut up you selfish ass!"

I couldn't take this anymore. "Both of you—" my body chose this moment to have me coughing up the water in my lungs. Hacking, I did my best to clear my lungs and throat while two pairs of hands patted my back. "Shut up." I finally got out on a ragged breath.

"'Azel are you alright?" Than? What was he doing here? I thought that other voice was familiar.

"Are you okay Legs?"

"Legs? Really, you're SO original." This sneered from Than. God, they were worse than two bickering cheerleaders.

"You're not any better. At least—"

"Stop!" Seriously, what was with these two knuckle heads? I opened my eyes to see a light glaring down at me. Where was I? "Where am I?" I tried to sit up, laying back down when my vision swam. So, this is what a real hangover felt like. Did I die for a little while? Who rescued me from the pool? I blushed. More than that, who gave me cpr?

Don raised his hand. "I did." Than glared at him.

Oh, well at least it hadn't been Sharon. Where was the lovesick girl anyways? I looked around again, gosh I was cold. My teeth even started to chatter. "C . . . cold. Blanket?" Than moved away to pull a thermo blanket from a shelf and placed it over me. His hands were warmer than the stupid blanket. Wish he would lay those on me, but then I remembered where I was, who I'd come here with and what had happened last time Than had laid his hands on me. This was so awkward. I tried to sit up again, this time Don helped me up and wrapped the blanket around me, tucking the ends against my chin where I held it in place with my frozen fingers.

"What happened?" Than asked angrily. I started to answer automatically when Don cut me off.

"Can't you see she's recovering? *God*, let her take her time." Than flinched and if possible, glared harder at Don. Don just smirked knowingly back at Than. Weird, these two were going to drive her insane.

I looked at Than. "What are you doing here? Did you follow me or something?" He just scoffed.

"Follow you? I didn't even know you'd made it back home alive from my place last I saw you. Why would I follow you?" Ass. Hole. Totally forgot. Being with Don made me realize that there were SOME nice guys out there.

"Fine. Whatever." I looked to Don. Sharing my ghostly experience with Than had been a mistake. Sharing them with Don would be disastrous. I played dumb to get his story and play it from there. "What happened?" I asked him.

He seemed to be pondering my question before he answered, looking at Than before he did so. "I was underwater with you and saw you kick to the surface. I did the same but when I reached the top, you weren't there. I dove back down and saw you drifting to the bottom. I don't know what happened but I grabbed you and brought you back up. You were unconscious before I even got to you.

Than snorted and turned away pacing the room like a caged animal. What was his *deal*? Could he not be a jerk for one second? It seemed that Don was on the same wavelength as me "Would you stop being an ass for five seconds?"

Stopping dead in his tracks, he cranked his head at an angle that creeped me out, to give a chilling glare Don's way and reminded me of the last time I was with him. Though instead of remembering the demonic pieces of that memory, all I thought of was his lips caressing my neck, his hands gripping my body as if it were life itself. I shuddered, creating goose bumps on my flesh. Don mistook this for a chill and rubbed my shoulders to warm me up. Than glanced at me with a knowing smirk. I looked away. *Arrogant ass.*

Okay so it was safe to say no one else was seeing what I was seeing. Why? This was the second chilling encounter that's happened within the span of two days. I didn't miss the significance of it only beginning since I've encountered Than. I didn't know yet if Don had anything to do with it as well. I never got a clear answer on how these two knew each other, only Than's mumbled response. I was inquiring again now. "How do you guys know each other again?" I rubbed my head as a serious migraine started to take in my right temple.

They looked at each other before Than, again, answered for them both. "I told you. We are acquaintances." I looked at Don who seemed to become very interested with something on the ground. Something wasn't adding up here. I decided then to pack them together with the encounters I'd been having. Alright, if these two wouldn't fess up, I was out of here. I didn't need this drama or any drama for that matter. A break up was bad enough. My brain couldn't compute how they were connected to my hallucinations (I refused to believe anything else right now) but I knew they were somehow.

"Where's my . . . ?" Shit I didn't have a phone yet. Damnit. "Can I borrow your phone Don?"

He made to grab for his phone as he asked me why. "I'm calling my mom to pick me up. If you two are just going to lie to me, I can think of other ways to be insulted without damaging my intelligence as well." I flicked my hand at Don for his phone. I was so irritated with all the non answers I've been getting that I was ready to throw a bitch fit. Or throw someTHING at someONE.

Don paused at handing over my ticket out of here. It was more than likely my mom wouldn't pick me up but they didn't have to know that. "Don?" My hand still hovering in the air, Don made to put his phone back in his pocket.

"That's unnecessary, I can take you home myself." I narrowed my eyes at him. Oh, that was it!

Hopping off the table, someone had brought my clothes and bag here. I grabbed my tank first and proceeded to throw it over my head. I pulled my jeans on, grabbed my bag and exited the room without further ado. Both of them followed me but I was far from paying attention to them both. The whole way back to the parking garage they tried time and again to get me to see reason of Don taking me home. Well, Than kind of just remained silent, grunting here and there. My legs were exhausted by the time I reached the security office and knocked rapidly on the door.

"Jane, please I'm sorry. You don't have a ride home, I'll—" Don was still pleading his case.

"I'll catch the bus, thanks." I didn't turn around to cut him off.

A snort on my right. "With what money?" My shoulders slumped in defeat. Than was right. I don't know how he knew that but he was right. I'd used whatever I had left for the battery. Why were all these things happening to me?

Paul opened the door before I could say anything. "Well hello Jane! Don." He nodded to Than, not knowing him. He handed me and Don our helmets, once in hand I began to turn around before I had an idea.

"Excuse me? Paul?"

"Well, yes Jane?" Please, please, I prayed silently.

"Would it be possible for me to use your phone?" I couldn't help but notice that both men behind me stiffened at the request. But Paul's face only deflated.

"I'm sorry, that phone doesn't dial out anywhere besides on the premises."

I deflated also. "Oh. Well thanks anyways." I turned and strode out of the structure leaving the boys behind.

There's a lady who's sure all that glitters is gold. And she's buying a stairway to heaven . . .

One of their phones was going off to Led Zeppelin's Stairway to Heaven. I'd put my money on Don.

"Yeah?" Point one for me. Don answered. I didn't stick around to catch the conversation. I kept walking away from them both, trying to think of a way to get home.

CHAPTER 8

One of Abaddon's fellow angels was telling him to hightail it out of there, now. "I don't understand." He replied, confused that the complete about face of the plan.

He'd been so close to drawing Jane away from whatever frightened her at Thanatos' horror mansion. He had been watching from beyond the gates. Unable to interfere with each other, he was not allowed onto the property in any way or form. He'd gritted his teeth in frustration the entire time an unseemingly thing for an angel to do. But a whole day and a half with death's son was more than enough for Than to dig his claws into the girl and brainwash her.

The night she ran from his place, she looked like a ghost herself and exhausted. He didn't know what Than had done, but it'd damaged her whatever it was. He followed her home to make sure she made it there alright and waited out the night for his chance to claim her to his side.

It wasn't until they were in the pool that he'd noticed the water turning frigid, signaling a violent spirits presence. He hadn't felt something like that in a long time. Being the Angel of Death, fresh from training at that, he didn't witness the presence of those types of spirits. He took care of the natural deaths. Almost peaceful ones, if you could call death peaceful.

His fellow warrior did not have a response to his subtle inquisition. It was not his place to question, though being among the top echelons of heaven had its perks, it was his duty to do as he was told. Frustrated though he was he nodded to himself and glanced at Than. Than looked back at him in understanding and jerked a nod in the direction of his bike. Don's only satisfaction was that Than didn't look like he wanted to deal with her at the moment either. Something had the demon bristling, Don just wished he knew what had happened the night before to give him an idea.

He hated to do it but if he wasn't supposed to be there, he'd leave. No matter that the very thought of Jane in Than's presence one more second made a nerve tick under his eye. Nodding back, he didn't say anything but walked back in the direction of his bike. If he were in a secluded area, he'd have taken to the sky until flashing to the heavens. As it was he had to act mortal. Once he had the privacy he'd contact the heavens their normal way and discover to the best of his knowledge why he'd been retracted from his mission for the time being.

—~—

Than didn't know what that call had been but was nearly grateful for the interference. He hadn't planned on seeing Jane again so soon after what'd happened in her borrowed bedroom last night. He wasn't stupid, he knew he'd have had to encounter her again but she got under his skin in a way that made him uncomfortable and wary.

He'd punched himself mentally a thousand times after she'd left. How could he have lost control so easily like that? He was twice the fool for letting his guard down. Why he kissed her? At the time he'd just wanted her to shut up. *Liar.* Okay, okay so her lips called to him. So What? If a guy didn't notice her plump, wet lips at all, he'd call him a liar. They were hard to miss and had been moving a mile a minute in her heated argument. He'd admit only to himself that she was cute as hell when angry.

He smiled at the memory of her slap. A tickle to him, but she didn't know that. She'd been furious at his claim, and in her fury she'd never looked more beautiful to him. Fire, he was used to fire, liked it, breathed it. Reveled in it. How could he not have kissed her with all those temptations in front of him?

Again, he was twice the fool. Now that she'd seen his other form, she'd be aware of it whether he hid it from her or not. Whenever his emotional state was high, she'd see it. Or at least sense that something was not right with him. This, as you can imagine, made his job a level harder than what it should have been.

The reason he was where she'd been on her second spirit encounter? A mystery to her, surely. But to him? Almost dying, her own spirit had called to him. Didn't matter where he was, what he was doing, or who he was doing. Inconvenience? Yes. His very being was ripped from time and space to her dying body for his collection of her soul to take to Charon. Painful? Meh, he'd gotten used to it over the centuries.

What he hadn't expected was the knowing of whom it was he was being called to. He still couldn't figure it out, but he recognized her . . . . essence, her very aura. That'd never happened before. With anyone, no matter if he'd had a type of relationship with them and later picked up their waiting souls at their time of death. So it hadn't been the kiss. So what then? He'd thought of asking his father, if you could call him that, but nicked the idea. That was only asking for problems.

He brought himself back to the present. Don had already made it out of sight into the garage. Now, where was . . . .

Turning around, if he had a heart he swore it would have stuttered at the sight playing out before him. *Damnit!* Running at full speed for his mortal body, he'd never make it in time. Taking the risk he shifted, immediately changing forms and grabbed Jane before she was hit. His last thought was that she was surely going to be his undoing.

—w—

BEEEEPPP!

I only had a split second to turn my head at the oncoming car before I froze like a deer in the headlights and let out a scream.

BANG! . . . Ha, just kidding. I didn't die. I would have though if it weren't for Than.

Alright rewind.

—w—

BEEEEPPP!

I only had a split second to turn my head at the oncoming car before I froze like a deer in the headlights and let out a scream. Or at least I would have let out a scream if I wasn't pushed out of the way. As it was, it was more like an 'Oomph'.

I had been trying to make my way across the street while the hand signal was up. I know, dumb. But I mean it's like a one in a million chance that from the last time I looked at the entirely deserted road, a dumbass would come from out of nowhere. Typical that I'd be that one in a million.

The next thing I knew the idiot was blaring his horn instead of slowing down like any smart driver would do. I thought that for the second time in one day I was surely a goner. What I didn't think was that Than was that close to me. Close enough to push me out of the way? No. The last time I looked both Than and Don were at least ten feet away from where I'd been. Don on his cell and Than brooding with his lean arms crossed across his impeccable chest.

However, that's not what my brain was telling me now. Expecting to eat cement I braced myself for a sure face plant that was seconds away. It never came. I did eat carpet though. *Better than cement.*

Wait, carpet? My brain was malfunctioning at the confusion.

Than's heavy body was pressing me down into the carpet and I was having a difficult time breathing. I mumbled into the carpet for him to get off. God, he must've had at least another hundred pounds on me. He lifted off of me slightly but only enough for me to lift my face out of the carpet for air. I sucked it in greedily.

After getting enough oxygen to be sure I wouldn't faint. I realized we were in a bedroom. How was that possible? Where were we?

"Than? Where are we?" Was that my voice? I sounded like a woman who had been kidnapped and blindfolded until now. Scared and unsure. His only answer was to breathe measured breaths, as though concentrating on something.

"Than?" I was afraid to move. Something wasn't right. The hair on the back of my neck stood up. Yeah, something was definitely wrong.

"Don't. Move." Was he eating something? I almost didn't hear him. It sounded like he was playing chubby bunny with marshmallows in his mouth. And where'd he get the food anyways? Who could be eating at a time like this?

I tried to wriggle my way out from under him. "If you'd just . . . ." I froze at the low growl at my ear. Okay, or not. Don't move, he'd said. Check.

I remained where I was while he did whatever it was that he was doing above me. Don't shit me, this had to look awkward but I mean what would you do if there was a crazy, two hundred or so pounded man (maybe demonic) practically on top of you, growling in YOUR ear? Never mind the crazy fluttering going on in my stomach. Yeah. Let me know, be more than happy to use that option.

Riing. Riing.

Neither of us moved. Wasn't he going to get that?

Riing. Riing.

Still no movement. "Um, you gonna get that?"

Riing. Rii-

The call went to voicemail. I started to refocus on a way to remove Than from my back when my mother's voice rang out over the room.

"Jane? I called your friend's phone and he said that I could reach you at this number. Call me back. Bye."

Great. Just great. She'd be questioning me for hours on my whereabouts. Terrific. God my back was killing me. Than slamming into me to save me wasn't exactly a perk right now. I probably had a huge bruise somewhere back there. I shifted to try and soothe my pain.

"Jane." A rumbling noise above my head. "If you keep moving like that, I won't be able to control my actions."

Oh, really? If it'd get him to at least turn me over it was worth the risk. I moved again, my butt brushing against him. He growled in frustration and flipped me over. "Stop moving woman!" A small giggle left me, I couldn't help it. Who said that? I sucked it back in to keep myself from a full on laugh. I must have lost my wits by now. A god was hovering inches above me, who may or may not be something other than human, saved my life, drove me nuts and I think was a little attracted to me judging by a certain piece of anatomy that seemed to be firming up down there. Unless he kept a rock in his pants for some reason.

"What's so funny?" I sighed. In actuality nothing was funny in my situation. I sobered immediately.

"Nothing. Get off me." He didn't move, impossible man.

"Why? Thought you liked to play games?" He dropped the lower half of his body, confirming my suspicion about the rock he kept in his pants.

"Ugh, puhlease. My back is killing me from your supposed rescue, thank you very much. I needed you to flip me over! Now get off!" My back did feel better, but he still didn't move.

"Hmm, no." What? My eyes widened. His face was getting closer to me as his gaze dropped to my lips. Oh, no. Not again, I was not about to be this man's plaything. Girding myself for what I was about to do, I took a deep breath and threw my head at his.

Sweet Mother! Post head butt, he rolled to the side cursing every entity in the sky. I rolled away from him massaging my own temple. Not the brightest idea but there wasn't another way to remove his weight. I had to do it, I reasoned to my pounding skull.

We both stood in similar poses, hand to head. "Are you *trying* to piss me off?" No, not exactly. I couldn't trust my reaction to him if he'd kissed me again. His kisses turned my brain to jello. I ignored his question and looked around. This was the room I'd borrowed the night before! We were back at Than's house. How? I looked around for the nearest weapon in a frantic rush. This was nuts. Everything was NOT okay in my life right now. Something with these two men and the hallucinations was all wrong!

Looking around I took the advantage of Than nursing his pounding skull to fly across the room to the fire place where a handy poker stood at the ready just for me. Swinging around, poker at the ready, I fired my questions.

"Alright! Who . . ." It took a second but hey what the hell? "Or *what* are you?!" Everything within the past forty eight hours and counting were impossible, unthinkable to my mind. "Well? How'd we get here? We were just out on the street, *miles* away. Who are you?"

One eye on me, he dropped his hand and cracked his neck. His shoulders dropped in apparent relaxation and returned his full attention to me. "What? Are you gonna stoke my fire?" He started walking towards me in a way a kid might try to persuade a kitten to come to them. Preparing myself, I renewed my grip on my weapon. "Come, you're not going to hit me Jane." Huh, little he knew, I was jacked up on enough crazy to spare a swing at the creep.

"Yeah? Try me—" In the time it took me to complete my sentence, Than had me up against the wall, gripping my weapon wielding wrist just hard enough to make me drop the poker. *Damnit!* "Ow! Stop!" I brought my right knee up for his crotch but he only grabbed my entire thigh and flipped me around, dropping me unceremoniously on the bed. I bounced once before attempting one more time for the poker on the floor. No such luck, he grabbed me again banding his arms around my torso, locking my arms to my side. My mind raced to any defense I might still have against him. I flung my head back. He only laughed after dodging my second attempt at a head butt.

"Really? You thought that'd work twice?"

Huffing and puffing from exertion, I didn't bother with an answer but continued to struggle. I was NOT going to be raped or whatever end he had in mind for me. I would NOT! I struggled to the point of passing out, he was gripping me too tightly.

"For crying out loud, you'd think I was going to kill you or something." This only made me struggle harder now that he'd voiced one of my greatest fears. "Jane! Stop struggling!"

"No! Let me go!" I kicked and screamed for help though I knew no one would here my cries. It was better than lying down nicely. I'd go with a fight damnit! "Please!" I half yelled, half sobbed out my pitiful plea. "I don't want to die. Please!" Than froze behind me and loosened his hold on me. Not enough however for me to escape.

"'Azel, shh. I'm not going to hurt you. Just calm down and I'll answer your questions the best I can." It was my turn to still. My shoulders shook with the tears I refused to shed. Was he telling the truth? I hardly knew what to think of the man behind me, or whatever he was.

He made me feel so many things, it was impossible to claim he was any one thing. Psycho, an ass, kind at times, but the one that bothered me the most was when he looked at me the way he did just before, when he was planning on kissing me. It was enough to drive anyone nuts. I turned my head to look at him. I noticed his eyes were back to normal, those silver flecks glinting against the light pouring in from the window.

Staring at him a while more, I didn't know whether he was telling the truth or not. I sniffed. "Really?"

A heavy sigh of defeat left him. He stared hard into my eyes before answering. "Yes. Okay? Just don't cry."

I lifted my chin and looked away. "I wasn't going to cry . . . much." His arms loosened further and he finally dropped his arms to his sides. I turned to face him to catch the ending of an eye roll. I stuck my tongue out at him in defiance.

"Unless you want that tongue somewhere, I suggest you put it back in your mouth." I sucked my tongue back into my mouth immediately. He just smirked and sat down on the bed, patting the spot next to him. I was wary about being on the same bed as him; it hadn't went well last time.

He just sighed in exasperation this time. "Sit down, I won't touch you . . ."

I began to sit before he finished that sentence. "Unless you want me to." I shot back up into the air.

He laughed at my skittishness. "Oh 'Azel just sit."

I sat. At the very end of the bed. Remembering I had a call to make I made a sudden move to grab the phone. I dialed as fast as possible not wanting Than to change his mind about answering my questions.

"Jane?"

"Mom! Hi, I'm sorry about the confusion on phones. Yeah I'm with Than now. Things didn't work out getting a ride back with Don."

"Oh? So how come your not here?"

"Uh . . ." Shit. Well she had me there, I couldn't very well tell her that I'd almost gotten fly swatted by a car and proceeded to be teleported back to Than's house. OH, and did I mention he's something other than a human being? Yeah, crazy stuff mom.

"Look we just started a movie. Can I finish it? I'll have him either bring me home or just crash here if necessary. Don't worry, I'll be fine either way."

Sigh on her end. "Alright, remember though tomorrow's a weekday. Don't think you're on holiday. You have job searching to do missy."

"I know. I will, I'm really hoping on the last one though."

"That's good but you still need to search. You have bills to pay."

It was my turn to sigh. We've been going through this everyday of the week since I got canned, rather rudely from my last job. "I know mom. I got it."

"Okay then, I'll see you later."

"Alright, bye."

"Bye." *Click.*

I tossed the phone to the side and refocused on Than. God, he looked so damned edible. He was lounging against the pillows with his hands behind his head. His eyes were closed, seemingly looking relaxed. I knew better though. He was wired like a warrior, if I had to describe his reaction time. I took his inattention to let my gaze travel down the rest of his body. His chest was covered with a simple t-shirt but didn't hide all the corded muscle behind it. His torso led down to thick muscled legs encased in jeans that could probably crush another man's ribs. I was working my way back up when a noise cracked the silence of the room. *What was that?* I looked up to Than's face and the noise sounded again. Was that . . . him? It certainly looked like it came from him. His eyes were hooded and focused entirely on me. *Damn, caught staring.* Ogling more like. *Double damn.*

I cleared my throat, avoiding his all too knowing gaze. "So? What are you?" After taking a breath I looked back at him. I had to see him when he answered, see the truth behind those obsidian pools. He just stared for a while. Probably thinking of a way to lie no doubt. It seemed like he couldn't help it at times. For what reason, she didn't know. She'd heard of compulsive liars but had never had the unpleasure of meeting one.

He looked away when he answered. "It is . . . difficult to explain." Sighing in defeat he sat up and crossed his legs in front of him, hunching over. How hard could it be?

"Just lay it on me. I'm a big girl, I think I can handle it." He snorted at my claim. Maybe I needed to start smaller. "Okay, let's try a different approach then." I paused, sorting through the different questions I had. "What about what I thought I saw the night we were . . . er, making out?" So awkward bringing it up. I started tracing patterns in the comforter. "Do you truly have, um, wings?" I looked up at him.

Looking at the far wall he was still as stone. "I was really hoping there was still a chance you hadn't seen them, touched them no less." The last he said on a sigh, as if remembering my touch. He turned to face me, waiting for my reaction no doubt.

Well, okay then. He had wings. The next question I blurted on impulse. "So how come I can't see them now?"

"I have to lose control of my form in order for you to see them. But it'll be easier for you to notice them, now that you've seen them, *touched* them." I flicked my gaze to just behind him where indeed, I could see a faint outline if I really focused. My mouth opened in a little oh. This was unreal!

"What about these hallucinations?" I took a leap, thinking he knew about those too. I was really hoping I didn't have to face those alone anymore.

He got up off the bed with a release of frustrated breath. "Look I can only tell you certain things. I'm not at liberty to share everything with you. It would—" He flinched in what looked like pain. "I just can't. I'll answer what I can."

"Why don't you just tell me what you're able to then and that way it'll be faster and less . . . painful for you." He looked at me, seeing that I had seen him flinch at almost mentioning something he shouldn't. He began pacing a slow trek in the carpet beginning an unbelievable tale.

"You are having what you call hallucinations, because you've seen someone die." He paused for my reaction to see if I wanted him to continue. How did he know that? I held back the instant tears that always rested at the back of my eyes when this tender topic came up. I just nodded once for him to continue. He obviously knew more about me than he let on.

He nodded in approval of my endeavored strength. "Because of this and because of the passion and pain you continue to show for him, you've been chosen by unseen forces for a job." He paused, choosing his words carefully while I waited for him to continue. I was hanging on his every word now, there was no going back. I decided to hold all my questions until the end of everything he had to tell me.

"*Descendion* is the term we use to describe your kind. Mortals chosen throughout the centuries to guide spirits to where they need to be, whether it be the gates of heaven or hell. The problem is that the mortal is to choose whether she or he remains answerable to Him," he pointed upwards, "or the other." He pointed down. Shock tried to take hold of me at what he was telling me. These beings existed? Truly? Raised as a Christian, I never believed in my religion, only giving it a wary respect. I was more of a fate type of girl. Everything happened for a reason, I'd always say. I tuned back into Than's voice as he continued.

"It's not 'hallucinations' your seeing." He shook his head. "Though it took awhile for the *sight* to take place since your loss, you are seeing the replays of these beings dark endings." He stopped pacing to look at me. "Their deaths." Convinced I wasn't going to fall off the bed, he continued his pacing. "Your job is to communicate with these spirits and persuade them to continue on." Okay, this was all I could take before my questions spilled from the collection that was rapidly building.

I placed my head in my hands rubbing out the pounding in my head. "Alright." I let out a pent up breath. "First question, I get the reason or the how of my chosen person. That would mean that I'm not the only one out there. Millions of people have seen and felt the same way I have. Are there more of my . . . kind?"

He smiled. Deciding to sit next to me, he leaned back on his elbows warming up to the topic. "Ah, this is true. Most are missing a crucial piece to the puzzle that is a *descendion*." He looked at me like I was supposed to guess. I just shook my head in wonderment.

"You have to be a descendent of a Greek God or entity. Hence the title, *Descendion*."

I'm pretty sure my jaw hit the bed. "How . . . ? What . . . ?" I looked around the room as if the answer would jump out at me from somewhere. "I'm not Greek though." He just shook his head.

"Being the very last until you have a child someday, you will hardly resemble someone so ancient."

"But it would show somehow surely!" I kept shaking my head in denial. "A relative or my last name. Something!"

He slid a sly smile my way, seeming to enjoy this way too much. "Your last name Rivers. Do you know any Greek mythology?"

"Sure, some. Why?" I didn't know where he was going with this one.

"There is a river in the underworld, where the ferryman Charon, ferries souls to the other side. Anything about that ring a bell?"

Not really. "Should it?"

"Your last name is Rivers . . ." I just stared at him blankly. So? There were a lot of Rivers out there. "Your job is too guide spirits to heaven or hell . . . ." OH. I see now.

"You've got to be kidding me. I'm a descendent of Charon?" Saying it sounded ridiculous. But Than only nodded in agreement.

"I can't believe this." My eyes widened. "Am I adopted?"

He shook his head. Phew. At least I was really the daughter of Anne and John Rivers.

Next question. "Are these beings deaths always going to be violent?" Please say no . . .

"Yes. It's not your job to deliver regular spirits to their resting place. That belongs to some other poor sap." I looked at him in question, that seems way easier than dealing with my type of spirit. He just shrugged. "Those types are lighter and harder to travel with since they are on the edge of already knowing they want to crossover somewhere. They get lost sometimes." This seemed to amuse Than. I didn't catch the reference so I moved on to my next question.

"What determines my decision on who I'll answer to?" This seemed the most important question. Her nightmare came back, her father telling her that she'd have to choose. Was this what he'd been talking about?

"I can't answer that." I stared at him in disbelief.

"Why? That is a crucial piece of information!"

"It's a decision that cannot be tampered with. My answer, if I were even able to utter it would create a whole new set of problems. Next question."

Damn him.

"Alright, fine." Let's see what he had to say about this one. "How do you know my father died? Let alone, the feeling I have for that or that I was there when it happened?" I set my focus completely on him. This was bugging me the most out of everything else. I would have seen him, remembered him surely if I'd seen him before. Then again, I'd been so distraught over what had been happening at the time, no one else mattered at that moment than my dad.

He sat up and returned to his pacing. I was wondering if he'd ever answer me. This was the big elephant in the room. If he decided to tell me, I had a feeling it wasn't something I'd like.

"I was informed about your background when he had died." I flinched at the word 'died'.

"Don't use that word." I glared at him. My dad wasn't an animal. He was a human being. "Use another word."

He arched a brow in question. "Passed alright with you?" I nodded in agreement. That was kinder, much gentler than the term often used to describe a dog that got hit on the road.

I refocused on the answer he'd given. It was possible. Something about it lacked truth though. I let it go for now. "How am I to make these things listen to me? To follow me? After that, how will I know where to take them and how to get to . . . heaven or hell? I don't have wings like you." I gestured to the outline of his massive wings behind him.

"The first time you had an encounter you had said that she heard you. Actually looked at you and answered you. Correct?"

I nodded remembering when I had told him about trying to calm the woman down; to keep her from swinging. I remembered his particular interest in the fact that the spirit had spoken back to me. "Yes. That's right. She told me to my face it was too late after I'd attempted to persuade her to come down."

He nodded, just looking at me like I already knew the answer. "So that's it? I just have to persuade them?"

"Not persuade. Convince. You must convince them that this is not the afterlife they want to continue. That there's another peaceful place to continue on to. Their being here unbalances things for your world. I'll never understand why Themis allowed it." I snorted in disbelief. Could they have made this any harder? It was no small feat, convincing a spirit to move on from the world of the living. Full of grief as they were, and regret, it'd been a wonder I'd ever gotten that lady to focus on me.

I fell back onto the bed in exhaustion. This was too much. Than laid back beside me. My reaction would've been to skitter to the far side of the bed. As it was, I was too tired, to shocked to move. I just lay there.

"You're taking this surprisingly well." He broke the silence. Yeah, well it was better than thinking I was a nut case. I turned my head to look at him. The one thing I couldn't figure out was what he had to do with all this. I didn't bother asking since it seemed like something he couldn't answer.

"Is Don a part of this too?" He nodded. I didn't elaborate on that one. So they had both lied to her. Why? They hated each other I knew, but seemed to always keep a certain distance. Where did Don fall into all of this? It seemed he had some answering to do of his own.

"What's the difference between who I serve? It seems that a *descendion* would always choose heaven."

"You'd be surprised." That was his only answer. I guess he was right. People did make dumb decisions all the time.

"Can you see them? The spirits, I mean."

"No. But I can feel them. The bitterest cold you'll ever feel. The reason you're always in a frozen coma I'd gather. I have never encountered that reaction before in a *descendion.* For some reason your reaction to these spirits take a fatal turn if not handled correctly." Great, so not only was I to become a personal guide to dead people, I could die from it too. Wonderful.

"But I didn't die. Why?" I tried to think back on what had saved me. Then I realized, it was Than. Than was holding me when I'd woken up. His unusual warmth was the reason I wasn't dead right now. I turned on my side to confirm my suspicion.

"It seems my body temperature keeps you in check and returns you to a normal state. Lucky you." He grimaced as though this wasn't something he was looking forward to. Jeez, was I that distasteful? It didn't show when he kissed me. Maybe it affected him somehow?

Well it's not like I had asked him to save me. I was grateful though, that was a loss my family didn't need. Two within a year? Mom would be a wreck.

It occurred to me that if Than wasn't around when I dealt with these things, who would save me? I shot up off the bed and started pacing. "Oooh noo." I groaned out loud. Than sat up staring at me in question.

"What?"

I just kept walking. I had to, otherwise I'd lose my mind. No. This couldn't be happening. This *couldn't* happen! I had a life! I had a possible career ahead of me! How was I supposed to focus if I had to be chaperoned all the time? "Don't you see?!"

"No. I don't 'see'. What are you on about now?"

Hands on my hip I gestured wildly at him. "YOU are the only thing keeping me from dying when I encounter these things. YOU bring me back. I can't be on my OWN." I let out a feminine growl of frustration. "This can't be happening! I have a possible job opportunity; I can't be chasing spirits all over the place, then passing out to almost DIE. What am I supposed to do, bring you to work with me?!"

"You have to learn how to deal with them the right way. It's the only way to stop the black outs. Other than that problem, there's nothing else you can do about your situation. You'll have to multitask if it's a normal life you want to live." He shrugged those big shoulders. "Well, semi-normal anyways."

"Is there another way to live my life?" I asked in sarcasm.

"Well, it wouldn't be what you have in mind."

I paused. There actually was another way? "How?"

"Trust me Jane, you'll never agree to it."

Damn the entire male species! "Damnit Than! Just tell me how!"

He lay back down on the bed resting his head in his hands, showcasing those biceps of his, all male elegance and prowess. Like a tiger who seemed relaxed but would rip your arm off in an instant.

"You'll have to die after making your decision."

CHAPTER 9

Little did Jane and Than know, a world away from where they were, there were three who watched with avid interest at the destinies playing out by their hand.

The Moirai, or the fates, gazed on in their fountain of visions as the two conversed on the mortal girls' fate as *descendion*. Lachesis, the allotter of threads, looked on in fascination. This was no small feat for a fate. Alive seemingly from the beginning of time, Lachesis and her sisters have seen it all. Nothing surprised them anymore. But then why should it? They were the creators of beginning, middle and end. They could change any humans' fate with the flick of their wrists at any given moment, on any whim that may please them.

They, of course were not without their own rules. Some things it seemed were even out of their control. The fate of the Fates she thought grimly. She'd only just prevented the girls' death again. Atropos, the unturnable, had been having a bad day of ambrosia addiction. Unwittingly, she'd been about to cut the thread that held Jane's life, going on and on about how her dearest cousin, Thanatos, 'did not deserve such a girl as that one'.

Shaking her head now, times have changed her sisters and herself. Picking up on the 'lingo' as her first sister

Clotho, the spinner, liked to call it. They adapted to time and change as no other being could. If she'd had the luxury to describe them, Clotho would have been blonde, Atropos a raven haired witch, and herself, an even tempered brunette. As it was, they all had hair spun of gold, and bodies to rival any goddess on Olympus.

They were often misinterpreted as old hags. Mortals, their ill temper against what was, had given the true fates ill faces. They indeed never heard the end of it from the other deities. Though it only took an ill placed word on their threads of life to silence them quickly enough. Atropos always took it too far, cackling madly and snipping her shears almost too close for comfort to the golden, almost unbreakable threads that belonged to the Gods. They had special shears for those, hidden away where no one would find them for misuse of course, but the Gods didn't know that.

Refocusing on the vision before her, it was found curious by the three that Thanatos, a known bastard and selfish prick, was found to have *feelings* for the little mortal. Something that was not foretold in Clothos' thread of life for him. Fate was a fickle thing. They could weave, guide and destroy, but that free will humans seemed to have often misguided the thread they spun so strictly for a specific purpose. As she'd said before, the fate of the Fates. That was why they had to be ever careful when dealing with mortals, always watching, to counter or progress a decision.

"I tell you, give me the sight to find the shears Lachesis! This flea I call cousin will destroy the poor girl. He's already ruined her life beyond repair! Look at the grief she suffers!" Atropos was still going on about ending Death's sons' life.

She only scowled at her sister. "You care not about mortals, why is this one so special to you?"

A careless shrug. "The lesser of two evils. A chance to end his worthless life? It's almost too sweet to pass up." She turned away to go do whatever it was she did on her own time, Lachesis didn't know. Besides coming together to decide the fate of one mortal or the other, they were all private women, enjoying their independence when they had it.

She shook her head at her sister's back. She knew very well that crossing Death, however little he could do to them, would not bold well for many on this plane or Earth. If he could not get to them, he would go for others. That was the way the world turned. They knew this well. Ever careful.

These two had a painful future ahead of them. The only way, she thought. It was the only way, to save them both.

Holding Jane and Than's thread within both her fingertips, she went to her weaving room to begin entwining the two.

—∾—

"Die?" I asked in disbelief. "I don't see how that would help my situation.

He rolled his eyes. "Well of course there's more to it. But I can't say."

Of course he couldn't. Still standing by the bed I crossed my arms and dropped my head in aggravation. Alright that was enough for tonight. "I have to stay here tonight." Cold indecision. I had to be cold, I'd never survive otherwise. If this was my fate, I didn't see any other way around it. I definitely wasn't going to 'die' as Than so eloquently put it. I could do this. My father hadn't said to run, he'd said I had to choose. Choose who to work under? Probably, so I would do so. After successfully learning how to bend these beings to my will.

"When the next episode happens I'll do my best to get them where they need to go." I was talking to myself, but was doing it out loud for sanity purposes. I didn't want it all bottled up in my head. There wasn't any more room for crazy in there. Turning to Than was the hard part. I needed his help.

"Will you be there to help me? You know, if I . . ." I mimicked me falling to the ground unconscious. "Splat."

Than seemed to think it over. I couldn't believe he'd be this selfish. To bring this up and leave it to me to do on my own. He finally looked at me. "Was that a request? Or are you telling me?" He arched his stupid sexy eyebrow in question.

I just stopped short of stomping my foot and throwing a hissy fit. "*Please,* Than, will you help me learn how to do this job that was thrust upon me?"

Smirking he said, "I don't appreciate the sugary sarcasm, but sure, I'll help . . ."

I deflated in relief. "Thank yo—"

"Ah, ah." He held up a finger, cutting off my thanks. "On one condition."

"What?" I couldn't believe this. "Is this really necessary?"

He shrugged. "Fine. Do it on your own."

This time I couldn't hold back the little pout and stomp of my foot. "Fine! What? What is this stupid condition?"

The only way I could describe his smile, which sent chills down my spine, was evil. "I get at least one kiss a day, when I want and how I want."

My answer was immediate. "No."

He shrugged and lay down on the bed. Curses on his grave! This man, this *demon*, could not expect me to uptake that condition. I'd be putty before the end of the week but I looked back at him warily. "Just a kiss?"

"Just a kiss."

"Nothing else?"

"Nothing else."

Damn, damn, damn him! I massaged my temples going through the ramifications of this if I said yes. I knew the games he'd play. I ran them through my head. No touching, probably unless I allowed it, and even then I knew he'd take it to an entirely different level. I could still date and stay away from him. Whenever he wanted though, he could interrupt me anytime, anywhere with anyone.

Damn the man! He could teleport, that wouldn't be too hard on his part. What about me? How did I feel about this? His kisses weren't the worst thing that ever happened to me. But, as I'd mentioned earlier, I was a hopeless romantic. I put up a good front and aloofness from time to time, but what if he turned out to be this bad ass with a soft inside? I almost snorted, that was doubtful. I've only seen that in movies and in my books, they knew how to reel us in. It worked too. I always found myself healing boyfriends and solving their problems instead of actually working on our relationship together. Only to suffer for it later. Take my car for example.

Alright. Fine, I could do this. Just had to stay aloof to him. Ignore his deliciousness. *Stop that!* Taking a breath I faced him to give my answer.

"Alright. One kiss a day on your terms in exchange for your help."

Sitting up to lean on his elbows, that chilling smile crossed his face once again. "Deal."

I nodded and began to leave the room. But not before he grabbed my arm and twisted me around to face him. His lips landed firmly on mine before a protest could leave my lips. He stroked the inside of my mouth with his tongue and

I could do nothing but surrender to the total conquering of my lips by his. My hands gripped his broad shoulders when I had mean't to push him away. Even worse, a little moan escaped me when I'd actually mean't to curse him to hell. It was always a weakness of mine to be manhandled sexually. Most men couldn't and were too afraid of my in your face, independent nature to attempt it.

His strong hands alighted on my hips and gripped. Hard. Any little simpering miss would probably have disliked that. I, however, was no simpering miss. I only came up against him all the harder. A little roughness was a turn on in my book. Feeling my willingness he pulled me the rest of the way to be flush against his hard wall of a body. The mad kissing continued to a fierce battle for dominance. I bit his lower lip hard in warning but he only growled that animalistic growl and pushed harder against my own. His hands were everywhere, caressing, squeezing, stroking. A girl would lose her mind! I know I was losing mine fast and should stop this before it went any further. While it was still seen as two people, who wanted what their bodies wanted, nothing more.

My body screamed at me when I broke the kiss finally. Than only ducked to my neck, to lick and nibble. God it felt so good. I let my head fall back, reveling in the attention he was paying to my body. But that's all it took. That one thought, to pull me out from under the wave of lust. It was only my body he wanted, nothing else. Not that I cared of course. I just got out of one relationship, didn't need another. Than finally stopped, noticing the stiffness in my body. I pulled out of his burning touch, continuing until my back hit the door of my borrowed bedroom.

I tried to catch my breath as he stalked me to the door. "Stop." Barely a whisper and huskily unconvincing. I didn't even hear myself and neither did he. He stopped right in front of me, breathing my air. I looked up into his eyes. Eyes that had gone black with a fever to conquer, to control, to pleasure. "Than, please . . ."

"Please what?" He placed his hands on either side of my head and leaned down to breathe in my scent. "What do you want me to do?"

I nearly went back under but caught myself and forced myself to say more firmly, "Stop. I want you to STOP. Please."

"Hmm." He grazed my neck with his teeth, sending goose bumps all over my body. Resisting the urge to grab onto him from falling over, I placed my hands behind me, trapping them from mischief. "If you say so." He licked my neck once more then turned the knob of the door, effectively making me stumble back into the hallway. The last I saw of him until morning was his back walking down the hall, practically emanating pent up sexual aggression.

Next Morning

I was sitting in the kitchen alone with a cup of water, contemplating what to cook for myself since there was no one else here to do it. Sighing, I rose from my seat and I went to scrounge up everything I would need to make a decent breakfast.

I didn't mean to think about it, but there was really nothing else to think of. I'd just get it out of my system now and be done with the whole thing.

Yes, I'd reveled in the kiss I'd shared with Than. Loved the way we seemed to battle for dominance on who controlled it. Loved his hands on me. Loved the sounds he made in the throes of his lust. He was like a sleek panther, all dark elegance and ready to pounce at any given moment. No, I didn't know what he was. Didn't know what part he played in my future. He could be tricking me for all I knew. Trying to make me choose the wrong side. He'd said that my kind have chosen the wrong side before. Now I had to wonder, which side *was* the right side?

I had a couple pancakes done and just laying the egg inside when I decided to call my mom. She needed to know what was going on about where I was today.

She didn't sound happy when she answered. "Hello?"

"Hi mom." I didn't sound any better. I had a hard time sleeping last night.

"So what?"

Always straight to the point. "I stayed over the night, as you know obviously. I am aware of my job search, Than happens to know a few law offices that are looking for people so he's going to help me out with that today."

"Are you ever coming home? Your brother's birthday is coming up you know."

I did know. Had been dreading it since I would be unable to get him anything. "I know. I'll be there don't worry. I'm coming home tonight. I give my word. I'll be there."

"Yeah. Alright, well I have to go into a meeting. See you tonight."

"Okay, bye mom."

"Bye." *Click.*

I placed the phone on the countertop. Pushing my hair back and turning back to my cooking, I flipped the egg. I finished in silence and went to sit down to eat. It all went down like lead, landing hard in my stomach. It seemed I was picking up on Than's lying skills easier than I thought.

Shaking my head I just sat there for awhile contemplating my future. Picking up my dishes I took them to the sink to wash and decided a walk outside might help clear my head.

Closing the door behind me with my free hand, I sipped the fresh coffee I'd made, making my way down the steps and heading in what looked like the direction of the estate's garden. Flowers always calmed me and were such a peaceful sight.

Coming around the house, I found I'd been right. Stepping onto the large rocks placed strategically as a path to the garden, I followed it delightfully. Feeling like I was seven again, I added a small skip to my step smiling to myself. An even bigger smile bloomed across my face as I finally reached the garden.

What a garden it was too. My eyes were feasting on the different assortment of colors, the perfume clouding my senses. I followed the path of tulips, proudly standing at attention, leading me to the thick of their forces. Seeing a strong willow in the center of the grass that was planted around it, I made for the swinging bench attached to one of her limbs.

I sat down and took a deep breath. Oh, it was so wonderful! I closed my eyes to take in the peaceful moment. This is what life should be for someone after a loss such as mine, I thought. Quiet, easy, helpful. But no. Life only provided harder tasks for you to conquer. As though in her way, she was helping you to force your mind onto other things to keep you going. For she knew, oh how she knew, the bottomless pit I'd fall into if I were ever given the time and peace to think.

Now, I didn't think. I only took in what life was giving me. I gazed around at the mums, carnations, hydrangeas; even a small sunflower field to my right was placed in the ground. I took a sip of my coffee again before placing it carefully on the grass at my feet so that I could push myself into a slight swing.

I only noticed now as I swayed on the bench, that the garden was an entirely separate section off of the estate. The rock wall around the estate was at least eight feet in height. I hadn't noticed the path had led me to a opening where the gate was left open, so engrossed I'd been in my trek through the garden. I wondered solemnly at the soul placed in charge of this piece of art.

At that moment I felt the hairs on the back of my neck stand. Knowing this for what it was, I slowed my swinging to a stop and glanced around. Someone was watching me. Before it had always been Than. I couldn't help but wonder though if it was another spirit coming to torture me. I searched for the tell tale chill of their presence, but I felt only the warm sun on my skin.

Turning this way and that, I didn't see anyone. Maybe I was just being overly sensitive. Beginning to relax, it was then that the voice broke the peace in my soul.

"Hello."

I jumped off the seat and put distance between me and the being standing before me. She was almost too beautiful to stare at. Her hair was like the finest gold, with a body of a supermodel. I took one more step back for good measure. If she'd asked me, I'd say she were in her twenties. Her eyes were her only give away. Ancient eyes stared back at me in curiously.

She smiled at me and shook her head as if saying 'silly child, I'm not going to hurt you'. Forgive me for not believing that smile. She wasn't human, I knew that for what my eyes told me and what I knew existed after Than's confession.

"Do mortals not greet each other?" Her voice was another give away, also ancient, tired. Not to mention she just confirmed herself as other than mortal.

"That'd be true, if you were a mortal." A delighted laugh escaped her pink lips at my claim.

"I've seen and experienced many things throughout my centuries alive child." Her eyes were still laughing when she continued. "I've yet, however, come across one as cheeky and strong as you." Turning away from me, she paused as if just thinking of something. Turning back she asked me, "Will you walk with me?"

"Where? Who are you?" She only smiled serenely and tilted her head towards the rest of the enormous garden before us. She didn't let me answer but moved on.

I wasn't sensing anything dangerous from her but what did I know of what she was? I looked back at my escape but discarded the idea. I'm sure if she wanted me dead, it'd only be too easy for her to block my path. I caught up to her just before she hit the first stone of the path leading out farther to more of the garden.

"Do you believe in fate Jane?"

"How . . . ?"

"Please, do not ask me such benign things child. You are much smarter than that; let us not waste more time, hm?"

Whoever she was, I already liked her better than Than. "I do. It's the only type of belief I let myself take on honestly."

She nodded as if already knowing what my answer would be. "And do you believe, knowing what you now know, that you will succeed in your journey as a *descendion*?"

I looked at her in trepidation. I was almost glad to be speaking with a complete stranger about my worries in the new task handed to me unfairly. She laughed as if hearing my every thought. "Life is rarely handed to us on golden dishes little mortal." Though I bristled at her nick name for me, I had to smile at her tinkling, bell like laugh. It was like listening to wind chimes.

"You mean silver platters?" I smiled at her misuse of a common human phrase.

"Ah yes, but gold is worth much more don't you think?" I shrugged.

"You say Potato, I say Potahto." That tinkling laughter again. I smiled, backtracking to her previous question.

"I honestly don't know. I dread my next encounter every second of every day, knowing it'll come when I least expect it." I answered soberly.

"Ah, but you know they are coming now. You are not unprepared, and you have help no less."

I snorted. "For a price."

She gazed wistfully ahead of us as we passed some rose bushes. Pausing by one, she leaned to one and sniffed delicately. "Doesn't everything come with a price? Whether in your world or mine?" She looked at me, looking much older then she had only moments ago.

I stared into her eyes, only now noticing she had no irises but a solid white. However eerie they were, I couldn't look away. "I suppose everything does." I plucked a rose from its place on the bush, pricking my finger in the process.

"Ouch, stupid bush." I glared at the bush but the woman only smirked at my carelessness.

"Take responsibility for your own actions Jane." She turned away and continued down the path. I wiped my finger onto the jeans I was wearing and followed.

She gracefully sat on another bench, this one on solid ground and surrounded by lilies. I dropped down next to her. She touched my knee sensing my worry no doubt. "What troubles you little mortal?"

Picking my words carefully, I didn't want answers that didn't help. Looking at her I unburdened myself. "I'm worried that if I choose, as I'm told I have to do eventually . . . . I will make the wrong decision. That I won't be able to see my mom, my brother. I can't put my mom through that, a second loss, whether I be dead or alive. It won't matter to her, I will be gone, and she'll be alone but for my brother and our faithless dog for company." She brushed the tear away before I even knew I was crying. I looked away, waiting for her answer.

"We all have decisions that are hard pressed to make. Some that even seem impossible. But we must make them."

"Why?" I sniffed, staring at the ground stubbornly. "Can't I just ignore it and do what I want? Look the other way? Not make the decision at all."

She tipped my face to look her in the eye. "But then you would be ignoring your fate. Your destiny. That is no way to live Jane."

I sniffed as I realized what she was trying to tell me. What I've been doing all along since my loss. Ignoring reality, responsibilities and decisions. I wasn't moving on, I was just existing. A shell of the person I used to be.

She suddenly got up to kneel before me. I rubbed the wetness from my face. "My time here is up. Listen and listen well. You must make every decision that comes to pass from here on with the utmost care." She placed her hand on my chest, over my heart. "Listen with your soul, guide your actions with your heart, and only let your mind control the reaction." With that she disappeared right in front of me.

I don't know who she was, but that was a lot to ask for a 'little mortal' girl. I sat on the bench until the quiet tears left me completely; my only company the beautiful flowers around me.

CHAPTER 10

The road before us was deserted. I guess it would be since it was almost midnight.

So I'd missed another night at home I thought wearily. I reclined my chair slightly and watched the forest pass us by in a blur of black and hints of green. Than was driving me home and it'd taken all of my strength to force myself to leave the safety he'd provide me if anything happened. I couldn't stay with him though; I couldn't lie to my mom anymore. I had to try and take care of this on my own.

I hadn't said anything to him about my visit in the garden. Wouldn't have mattered anyway, I didn't even have a name to give the ethereal being that'd given me advice I didn't know what to do with. Closing my eyes I concentrated on the loud roar of the engine. We were in Than's Bugatti Veyron tonight, you can imagine the noise that thing made with a mid-engine. I didn't understand why he'd taken another exotic out but he'd said something about going out afterwards.

I ignored the twinge of 'feelings' I had about that. I refused to name that green monster. It was impossible to feel that way after so short a time being together and not even liking each other's company on top of everything else. I didn't ask any more and he didn't elaborate. Fine.

"You remember what I said right?" Than's deep voice crossed the small space. I sighed inwardly. We'd been over this ever since I'd put my foot down on me leaving to be home with my family.

"The part about how to take the spirits where they need to be? Or the part where I kiss my 'lovely behind' goodbye if I fail again?" He'd used the phrase to make his instructions stick in my head. At least that's what he claimed. No wonder I'd felt like my ass had been on fire the last handful of hours.

He just scowled at me. "Are you taking this seriously?"

I answered in exhaustion. "Yes! It's just that after going over it a hundred times, I'd rather die just so that I don't have to listen to you Than!"

"Ungrateful mortal." Funny, he'd never called me that before.

Sighing again, I just stared out the window in silence.

"Remember when you get your phone, put my number in it immediately."

I just held a thumb up letting him know I understood. I dropped my hand back into my lap.

"What's wrong?" This he said somberly, the edge out of his voice. Hmm, almost like he even cared.

"Nothing." Not like he would *really* care anyways.

Heavy sigh on his side of the car. Whatever, it was my turn to be the silent one. I was tired and had a lot of things to contemplate. Things to remember if I were to survive. Thrive at what I had to do. I didn't need any interference.

We had finally made it to my street and Than pulled up slowly to my house. "Thanks for the ride." I grabbed my helmet from the ground and stepped out of the car. I was about to shut the door when Than called my name.

"Yeah?" I ducked my head back in. He looked like he had something to say but decided for something sarcastic.

"Don't get yourself killed alright?" I nodded hesitantly then shut the door. He peeled off into the night without further ado.

I shook myself out of my daze. I hadn't known I'd been watching until his taillights disappeared. *Ridiculous.* I opened my gate and walked up to my door. Gently pushing our dog out of the way, I gave him a little rub down as he jumped up onto my bed with his incessant breathing. We had a pug, he was only adorable when he was sleeping. Otherwise I liked to believe he was Satan's dog. Maybe I could have Than take him back where he belonged I mused.

Still smiling to myself, I took a long hot shower rubbing the tension from my shoulders and neck. I was in desperate need of sleep. Tomorrow was my brother's birthday and I had to at least get enough shut eye to function properly.

Stepping out into the fogged up bathroom, I dried myself and threw on my pj's. My dog was no longer in my room but that was regular. Mom was his favorite person in the world, so he was most likely in her room again. I turned on the ceiling fan and turned off the light. Pulling the covers over me, I wondered when my next encounter would be. I didn't know but I really hoped I was prepared for it.

—∞—

"Happy birthday Jordan!"

My brother didn't wake up. I poked his leg with no reaction.

"Jordan? C'mon, wake up! Mom's going to be back from her walk and we need to get ready."

"Mmm."

I huffed out an exasperated breath. Walking away, I made my way to the bathroom to get ready. I'd try to wake him again on my way back to my room.

After seeing my reflection, I hung my head in defeat at the dark circles under my eyes. I really needed to get over it; it didn't look like I'd be getting any sleep soon anyways. With all the spiriting away I'd be doing, I'd be lucky to keep my slight tan I'd scored over the summer.

I finished up in the bathroom just as I heard the front door close and the tell tale huffing and puffing from my dog after his walk. Mom had taken a half day so that we could all spend the rest of the day together for my brother's birthday. Stepping out of the bathroom, she had just placed his leash and harness in the designated bowl on the kitchen counter. She was holding a small rectangular box in her hand. My heart skipped a beat in excitement.

"Is that my phone?" I skipped over to her and held my hand out. She dropped it in my hands and I tore into it. Ah, sweet life, back in my palms!

"It must be, I didn't order anything and it's from T-mobile." She moved on to wipe the dog down in the living room where he liked to perch himself on the couch.

Finally having the phone out of the package, I inserted all the necessary parts and plugged in the charger to my bedroom wall. I returned to the couch where my slug-a-bed brother still lay.

"Jordan! Mom is here. C'mon do you want to go to lunch for your birthday or what?" Taking a new tactic I said in a sing song voice, "I guess you don't want your present I was going to buy you when we got to the mall. Oh well." I walked away to go change. There was a hint of shifting noises on the couch as my brother heard the tempting call to wake up. My job done, I continued to go through my drawers and pull something simple out to wear.

I decided on forest green shorts, a black tank and black converse. Grabbing my bag, I looked at my phone I'd left on my bed. It wouldn't be charged nearly enough to bother bringing it so I left it there taking my chances. Shutting my door to keep the dog out of mischief while I was gone, I moved to sit at the table to tie my laces.

"You ready?" My mom had come out of the bathroom.

"Yeah, what about Jordan?"

"He's in the bathroom now."

"Okay." Well he wasn't the fastest moving person. Food and free anything's usually got him moving though.

My mom had moved to the kitchen now sipping on her coffee and waiting like me. I was just tying up my left side when she asked me, "So, what's going on?"

I only spared her a glance. "With what?"

She gave a sniff of disapproval. "Who is this person you're hanging around with all the time now? Than? Is that short for something? How do you know him? I've never heard his name before."

I took in a breath. Here we go. I'd do my best not to lie. Hugging my bag to my legs I faced her to answer her questions. "He's just a friend as of now. I don't know if Than is short for something. I met him at B&N and you've never heard his name before because I just met him myself."

"You just met when? You're staying over stranger's houses now? You better be careful Jane. I don't want to find myself in a situation where you end up dead at a stranger's house."

I sighed. Loudly. See how dramatic she is? This is ALL the time. Not some of the time. Every. Time. Maybe Than wasn't the reason I was lying to her, maybe it'd been this way all this time just to keep the inquisitions at bay.

"I met him maybe a couple (last week) weeks ago. Don't worry! You're always worrying about the worst that could happen to us. I think I have some semblance of a brain to make decisions for myself."

"Hmph. Yeah, like in Vegas?"

I brushed this off. I had just turned twenty-one, who wouldn't go insane on their birthday? "That doesn't count mom."

She flung around from dropping her cup in the sink, annoyed now. "Don't tell me it doesn't count Miss Jane! I've could've come home by myself after that trip. I'm lucky to have one of you left after that damned trip."

This sobered me. She was right. "You're right. I'm sorry."

She sighed heavily. "Go check on your brother, he's taking too long. It'll be dinner time by the time he gets out here." I went to knock on the door but there wasn't any need, he opened the door as soon as I rose my fist to knock.

"'Kay I'm ready. Let's go."

—⁂—

Okay, I'd just like to say that as a woman, I have expensive taste at times. My brother? He's the same. He may even get it from me since we were only two years apart and hung out all the time when we were younger. So I ended up buying him gauges for twenty something dollars. Ridiculous? I like to think so. But it was his birthday so I mean, he was happy and that's all that mattered right?

Right. I had to chant it in my mind a few times for it to stick but all I kept thinking about was no job, no job, and no job. I really needed those people to call me immediately. My account was dwindling precariously on the low end of the spectrum and the stress that came with it? I was definitely beginning to feel.

We decided to eat at Ruby Tuesday's since it was in the mall and mom didn't feel like driving all over the place. We didn't expect it to be so busy on a . . . huh, Tuesday. Ironic? So, that's how we ended up in a spot where the air conditioning blew directly on us and how this embarrassing conversation started.

My mom was in the middle of a tirade on how freezing it was and why they couldn't turn the air down. I was in a tank so I'd appreciate the climate control also, but you don't understand how my mom goes about it. Loudly and with a pissy tone.

"Why don't they just put us in the freezer if they're going to make it this fricken' cold?!" She was shaking her head and crossed her arms over her chest, rubbing her arms in an attempt to warm up. Her glare sharp enough to cut a diamond.

"It's nöt so bad mom." My brother was totally oblivious to the gasket that was about to blow if we didn't find a different seat. Now. With that, all mom did was give my brother an 'Are you kidding' look.

"I need my winter coat for crying out loud!" I rubbed my temples at this point. I really didn't need a migraine right now.

"Mom," I looked at her pleadingly, "do you want to move? I'll just flag the lady down and we can ask for another seat." Anything to make her shut up, I thought. People were starting to stare.

"Why? This whole place is freezing, I doubt moving will he—" That was when our waitress interrupted her rant.

"Hi there! I'm Jessica and I'll be your waitress today. Can I start you off with some drinks?"

"Could you tell your manager to—"

"Jessica, is there another seat in the house? It's kind of chilly here." I cut my mother off before she gave the poor girl a bad day. I looked at the ceiling where the vent was to make my point.

"Um, well let me see what we have open and I'll see what I can do for you, alright?"

"Thank you." I sent her on her way with a small smile. Then glared at my mom once she was out of sight. "Could you be a little more subtle?" I said in my sugary-sour tone.

"Well if the air conditioning wasn't on full blast, I wouldn't have a problem." She raised her eyebrows as if challenging me. I ignored the challenge and opened my menu. Not that I really had to look, I was going to get the same thing I always got when I came here.

"What are you gonna get sis?" I looked at Jordan then back at my menu.

"Probably my Alpine Swiss Burger, you?" I looked back at him to catch his answer. At that moment the chilly air. decided to take a swift drop that was NOT normal. Goosebumps broke out across my skin.

"See? It's freezing isn't it?" This from my mother who'd noticed my skin's reaction. *Could she feel it too?* No. Couldn't be, she must still be referencing what she was feeling. God knew if she felt what I was feeling, she'd leave the restaurant immediately.

Crap! Was this seriously happening right now? I automatically started looking for my phone to dial Than as I frantically darted my gaze around the restaurant looking for ghoulies. Then I remembered my phone was on my bed, useless. Not to mention I hadn't synced any of my contacts OR added Than's number. Shit! I kept scanning the restaurant looking for anything out of the ordinary. How was I supposed to approach it with all of these people here? Would they be able to see what I was doing? Saying?

"Sis? Hey, you alright? You look a little jumpy."

I looked at Jordan with a tremulous smile. "Jumpy? What? I'm not jumpy; I guess I'm just hungry is all." I tried to focus on my menu but it was hardly possible. It was arctic now, what was the spirit waiting for? A Go sign? I tried to glance around without seeming too fidgety but I didn't notice anything. What was going on?

"So I was thinking about this steak burger they have here. What do you think? I don't really care for the bleu cheese though. Hmm. Jane?" I barely heard my brother through the pounding that was my heart beat.

"Hmm? Oh, the burger? Well one of my friends actually had that once, it looked awesome to me and he said it was good. I think you'd like it. The fries were awesome too." Was that rushed out? I hoped not.

My brother stared at me like I was on pills or something. "Are you sure you're alright?"

"Mhmm, why wouldn't I be alright?" I gave a silly smile and laughed, gave him a little slap on his arm for good measure. I refocused on my menu as the air remained in a frigid state. Still, no spirit.

Then as if it had never been there. The air turned warm. Just like that. I was stunned and looked to my mother for confirmation that I wasn't crazy.

"Well finally! See? I knew they could turn the air down." She looked at me pointedly. I could care less at that moment.

Was it really all the a.c.? Or did I just encounter something of a near miss? The waitress returned to us.

"Is the air better now?" She looked to me then my mom.

"Much better!" My mom beamed at our waitress now.

I was speechless so I just nodded. I didn't trust myself to speak.

"You guys ready to order? Or do you need a few more minutes?" Jessica just looked at us like a happy puppy ready to serve.

We made our orders and she moved away to send them to the kitchen.

I stole the moment to go compose myself in the bathroom. "I'm going to use the restroom guys." I got up and went ahead before mom could offer to go with me. That's the last thing I needed.

Pushing open the door, I swiftly glanced under the stall doors to make sure no one was in there. All empty, great. I moved to the mirror to check my appearance. A ghost stared back at me. I needed to pull myself together; else I'd never make it on my own. I'd be dead on the Ruby Tuesday floor before anyone could scream out, 'ghost'!

Letting a breath out I repeated to myself, "You can do this. You CAN do this." Breathe in, breathe out. I closed my eyes for a five count before getting ready to walk back into the restaurant.

My eyes were still closed when a chill swept up my legs and curled around my body, sending a shiver cascading down my back.

My eyes flew open and I stared back into the eyes of a girl no more than ten years old next to me in the mirror.

I jumped back from her ethereal form and tried not to scream, to breathe. Just breathe. Okay, it was more like hyperventilating, but I couldn't scream, I couldn't alert the other customers to anything amiss in the ladies room.

I assessed the situation the best I could. The girl hadn't moved from her spot, was staring at herself in the mirror as if I weren't there with her. I attempted to sidestep, made it one step over and she still didn't move. So I slowly made my way to the door and turned the lock to keep anyone from wandering in on me.

I know, crazy right? The person I was about three days ago, would have said I was an idiot; that I should be running back out the door, not locking myself in with the damned thing.

Slowly making my way back to my original spot I tried to look the girl in the eyes. Compared to the last two ghosties, this one was peculiarly normal looking. There was nothing wrong with her, well besides the fact that she just kept on staring at herself.

I cleared my throat. "Hello?" Nothing, she didn't even flinch or react.

"Um, can I help you? Can you hear me?" I moved closer. Everything in my being was screaming for me to get the hell back, but I had to fix this or I'd end up dead on the floor. Me and Than had gone over the option of just running away from the situation, but we didn't want to chance it that the end result would be the same. If I didn't help the spirit to move on, I would go into a frozen coma until I was dead. My garden visit also came into mind when she'd told me to start living my life instead of existing in it.

I nearly missed what the girl said, so lost was I in my own thoughts.

No one can help me now. I can't live this life anymore. They don't love me. Nobody loves me.

Who was she talking about? I took a look at her dress. She seemed to come from sometime in the fifties. She wore pristine white stockings with her muslin dress, puffed sleeves and black buckled shoes. Her hair was half up, half down, pinned with a beautiful jewel encrusted barrette.

"Hey, it's okay, someone loves you alright? Um . . . What's your name?" I thought maybe if I got down to what was bothering them and gave them attention to their needs, they'd focus on me, respond to me.

Nobody cares. Why should I care then? Her voice was so depressing. I literally wanted to plug my ears it was so bad. This girl has had it rough, that I definitely was getting from her.

"What's your name?" I tried again.

That's when she pulled a knife out of her dress, hidden away in the folds. She must have grabbed it when, in her time, she had been in the restaurant herself. Shit, shit, shit. Time was running out, subtlety was seriously not working.

"Hey! What's your name!?" I yelled it at her this time.

WHY DO YOU CARE?! She flung back at me, actually looking at me this time. Her eyes were ablaze with sorrow and hate, her long hair flinging around her shoulders in her vigorous turn to me. I was so stunned she'd responded I almost forgot to speak, her energy had even knocked me back a step.

Standing my ground, I stared back at her, hands fisting at my sides for strength. "Because I want to help you. Tell me your name." For a ten year old she had a sneer that belonged on a jaded woman's lips.

You can't help me. No one can help me now. I've decided.

She was going into repetition again. I had to pull her back. "What if you could go somewhere where people loved you? Where girls like you are held precious in the eyes of friends? Family? Would you want to go there? I can take you there."

Her attention remained on me. She stared, as if waiting for more. More for her ears that have heard nothing but abuse. That's when I started hearing the other voices. Voices she must be projecting to me.

WHY CAN'T YOU DO ANYTHING RIGHT SOPHIE?

DON'T TOUCH THAT SOPHIE!

YOU DISGUSTING RAT, WAIT 'TIL I TELL YOUR MOTHER WHAT A BAD LITTLE GIRL YOU'VE BEEN!

GET OUT OF MY SIGHT!

I DONT CARE! GO TO YOUR ROOM AND DON'T COME OUT UNTIL I TELL YOU TO.

THAT'S IT! I HAVE HAD IT WITH YOUR IMPUDENCE, NO DINNER FOR YOU TONIGHT, GET UPSTAIRS NOW!

I winced and covered my ears. It was terrible! What child had to go through such things at ten? Women and men both were a part of those screams. Screams at a child who knew little better than wanting to play and enjoy life like her friends at school did.

You can't help me. She turned back to face the mirror.

"Sophie! Wait! Yes I can, I can take you to the nice place, the people there will adore you, and they'll make time for you. I swear it."

She completely ignored me, raising the knife to her wrist.

Just as she put the knife to her small wrist I lunged for her. "Sophie, NO!" I reached for her wrist not thinking that I'd grab anything, but I did. I grabbed her wrist and at that moment a searing pain shot up my hand and into my arm, traveling into my body. I wanted to release her; I'd compare the pain to something of a shock of a bunch of volts into my body. But I couldn't, I wouldn't let go.

My body felt as though it was being pulled in different directions next. It was enough to make me want to hurl. Gripping harder, I made sure Sophie was still in my grasp.

She was, I don't know what was going on but the pulling suddenly stopped and we landed, or at least I did, hard.

"Jeez." I rubbed the pain out of my bottom and sat up. Realizing my eyes had been closed the entire time, I opened them and instantly lost my breath at what I was witnessing with my own two eyes.

Everything was white, or some shade of it anyways. I was staring through what some would call the pearly gates. I wouldn't exactly call the color pearl, more of a pearlescent hue that shimmered as if to entice the eye, to convince one to enter. They were closed at the moment, two statues of what seemed to be angels standing on each side of the gate, one with a deadly looking spear and the other with a sword angled at the ground. *Guardian angels?* I snorted at the irony.

I looked down and expected to see clouds at my feet. I was only half let down. I was on concrete but there was a sort of fog or mist swirling around my feet. I felt a sudden tug on my arm and realized I was still holding onto Sophie. My eyes widened at her. She wasn't a spirit anymore. She was flesh and blood. Her skin was of the most perfect ivory, brown long locks and her clothes were all in color instead of the faded white-blue of her spirit form.

"Where are we?" Now she spoke instead of mind projecting her words and feelings.

I didn't know if we were really in THE Heaven so I gave her a version of the truth. "Remember that place I told you about? This is it."

Her eyes widened as if she hadn't believed me. Heck, I hadn't even known what I was talking about at the time, only that I had to try. Sophie attempted to walk towards the gates but I held her back. Something striking me as odd about this whole situation.

No, it couldn't be this easy, I still refused to let go of her arm. What if she reverted to her spirit form? She never really agreed to come here. I had had to grab her to stop her from completing the act that would end her episode. Was I in some way showing her what she could have if she would only let go of all her pain and sorrow? That this was what was waiting for her if she wanted someone to love her the way she hadn't been in her human life?

She tugged impatiently again. "Sophie, wait." I glanced at the gates untrustingly.

"What? You said you would take me to this place to be loved. Why can't I go?" She pulled a bit more forcefully on her wrist. I held firm not believing the sight ahead of us. I narrowed my eyes in suspicion and faced Sophie for one last try.

She turned reluctantly away from the gates to look at me in question. The sorrow was still there in her eyes, the hate. Somehow in my heart, I knew this child would not be able to enter heaven's gate with a hateful soul.

I knelt on one knee before her, on eye level to make sure she listened to every word I had to say. I don't know how I knew, I just did. "Sophie, listen to me. Are you listening?" She looked once again to the gates and back at me, she nodded slowly.

"I need you to forgive your family for the pain they've caused you." She was ready to balk, her eyes widening but I cut her off.

"No. Listen to me. They were in the wrong, but you can't move on with your life," I stared meaningfully at her, "if you hold so much hate and sadness within yourself." I arched my brow to make sure she understood, she had to, else I'd be dead and she'd be a spirit again.

She stared at the ground, her wrists in my hands. "How? How can you ask this of me?"

My lips pulled down in the corners in distress at losing this beautiful little girl to repeat her suicide over and over again. Still holding onto one wrist I tilted her chin back up to look at me and put on a little smile for her confidence. "Because you will be in a better place, with people who love you. They won't be able to hurt you anymore." A single tear left her eye before she thrust herself upon me in a hug I knew she needed more than anything.

She pulled back to look up at me and smiled a serene smile. It was then I knew I'd done it. I'd saved this little girl, there were no more shadows in her eyes. I smiled back at her as she disappeared within my arms. I dropped my arms to stare at the gate. Sophie reappeared there as they began to open. An angel in the form of another little girl appeared next to her. She leaned over to Sophie as if to tell her a secret. A giggle left both of their lips at their shared secrecy. Sophie turned back to me and waved before turning back and taking the angels' hand to pass the gates.

I didn't bother waving back, she was gone before I could even raise my hand. I didn't even get to take a breath before I was sucked backwards from the gates in front of me. The same pulling sensation returned and I closed my eyes holding back the vomit that was rising against the back of my throat, fighting for release. I was just thinking there had to be a better way of doing this whole traveling deal when I landed once again, hard, on the floor of the Ruby Tuesday's bathroom I'd just been standing in.

"Ow." I was on my back, lucid and staring at the ceiling. I was in awe of everything that had just happened. Did time pass the same while I'd been doing all that? I guess I'd find out when I left the bathroom.

Someone was pounding on the door. Wonderful, this would be hard to explain. Sitting up, I got up off the floor and went to unlock the door.

A middle aged woman stared back at me, a bit irritated by the looks of her.

"Do you mind? This is a restaurant restroom; you can't just go around locking the doors! Excuse me!" With that she shoved past me and slammed one of the stall doors shut.

Huffing out a breath, I made my way back to my table. Our plates were there and my brother and mom were digging in without further ado. I sat down and unwrapped my utensils as if nothing had happened.

My brother nudged me with his elbow. "What'd you do? Fall in?" Smiling he turned back to his food and took a disgusting bite of his steak burger.

"No, I was having a tampon situation." This shut my brother up immediately. No guy liked talking about feminine products at a table full of food. I smirked back at him.

I cut my burger in half and dressed my fries with ketchup as I went through in my mind what I'd just accomplished. I had done it, really did it. Maybe I'd really be able to do this on my own. No Than, no Don. Just me and my slightly awkward life.

After we finished eating and talking about benign things, my mother paid for the food and we left the mall to head back home. I was sitting in the car staring out the window, watching all the unsuspecting souls walking around minding their own business. I smiled and closed my eyes to take a nap.

Maybe things were finally starting to look up for me.

CHAPTER 11

I was sitting in the living room about a week later when I got the call. Yes, that call. Parker, the woman who'd interviewed me that day at the law firm, was telling me when I was starting and what I'd need for the first day with them.

I was currently doing a happy dance around my living room area while silently screaming out in triumph at landing this job.

"Jane?"

Crap, okay Jane, breathe. "Yes?"

"Okay so don't forget to bring those things. Our HR guy needs that information for your medical and other paperwork he'll be having you fill out when you get here."

"Of course. I'll see you then!"

"Alright, bye."

"Goodbye!" I hung up the phone and immediately dialed my mom.

"Hello?"

"Mom! I got it! I got the position at the law firm!"

"Great! When do you start?"

"Well she wanted me to come in Friday, but I thought Monday would be best and she agreed that that'd be fine." I rushed out in a breath, I was so excited.

"Thank God it didn't turn out any longer than a month or so."

I sighed in relief, dropping onto the couch in the living room. "I know me too. So I guess I'll see you when you get home?"

"Yup, see you later."

"'Kay! Bye."

"Bye." I hung up

Things were really starting to look up. It'd been a week since the Ruby Tuesday incident and since then I hadn't had any recent encounters. Actually I've been relatively normal and bored at home since then.

I haven't seen Don or Than since the last times I've seen them either. Nor have I contacted Than by phone. That way he couldn't contact me either. I smiled to myself; keep up that wall Jane and you're smarter than I thought you were. Shaking my head at myself I grabbed the remote and started flicking through the guide, searching for anything interesting I'd like to waste my life away on today.

Hmm. Sex and the City? Hell's Kitchen? Ah, there we go. Wedding Planner. Pushing select, I dropped the remote on the head of the couch and hunkered down for a long afternoon of doing nothing. Then later I'd get up, make lunch and sit back down to watch some other mundane movie or show. If I was really lucky I'd end up falling asleep until mom got home or needed me to start dinner.

After about an hour into the movie, it'd gotten so hot in the house I had to bring over Jordan's smaller fan to plug into the wall and point directly at me. Somewhat satisfied I positioned myself back onto the couch to catch the ending of Jennifer almost making the biggest mistake in the movie by marrying that icky euro guy. What was his name? Masimo or something? I don't know, but before I knew it I'd fallen asleep.

I was running again. Damnit, I was really getting tired of running all the time.

I stopped and realized where I was. The blasted casino again. Looking around, I seemed to be the only one here this time.

"Hello?" I walked around the glass aquarium that held all the tropical fish inside but still no one was there. I turned around and started walking towards the Cheesecake Factory. There was no one in here either. I was alone.

Moving to the table where my father had his last meal, I sat exactly where I'd taken a seat that afternoon. Hell, I still have the pictures in an album at home of what we ate, drank. That evil drink my father shouldn't have had. Heck, all the drinks he'd been having that he shouldn't have had on that trip.

I felt my anger rising and tried to calm down. I was so angry at so many people that couldn't help what had happened to him. No one could help. It was fate, fate for him to be taken that day.

"Dear child, why do you cry so?"

I sniffed back the threatening tears as that same chiming voice greeted me. Flicking my gaze to her, I wiped the tears that had fallen unbidden down my face.

"I'm angry and frustrated."

"Ah, tears of anger. Why?" She pulled the chair opposite me and sat gracefully, like she was floating.

I flicked my angry gaze to her. "My father was ripped from my life! It wasn't his time to go, he still had time!" More tears streaked my cheeks. I didn't wipe them away this time.

"How do you know?"

I looked at her, hating how calm she was. She didn't understand and I didn't expect her to.

"I just do. How can anyone just rip a loved one away in such a fashion?"

"Death hardly cares what others think about the fashion of death of the one he's to take away, little mortal."

I looked away, knowing she was right. But I didn't care. It was too sudden, one minute enjoying a wonderful lunch, the next laying in a pool of blood on the shiny marble floor. Damnit!

I started to babble, I was so frustrated. "If I had just known! If I'd known, I would have done things differently! Been ready to call the ambulance instead of stand there in shock! Useless! We were useless to him! Everyone was that day!" My shoulders were shaking with the violence of my tears. She stood up and moved to my side, leaning over me to hug and to soothe. Whispering things in my ear I didn't hear through my racking sobs.

"You need to let it go. There is nothing you do for yourself by blaming yourself and others for his death."

I sniffed, rubbing my face across my sleeve. How? How could I let it go? We made up excuses for ourselves in the beginning, trying to make it better. But we knew it was all lies. It would never be better if it weren't the same as it was when he was here.

"Child, his fate was sealed long before you came into this world." She brought my gaze to meet hers. "You know this, and yet you blame yourself? Why?"

To her it may seem simple. Black and white. But I knew better. My family and I could have done something! Made him stop smoking more forcefully with threats or some other means. Start making him eat healthier. Anything!

She just tsked at me and went back to sit in her chair. "But would he have been happy?" I didn't care that she'd somehow read my thoughts, only that there was always a way.

"He would've been alive! Here, now. With his family! With his wife and kids who love him! ***That*** *would have made him happy! I stood up angrily and swept my hand across the table. The dishes crashed to the floor, echoing into the emptiness that was the tomb of my father.*

Enjoying the sound other than the sorrow beating in my heart, I moved from table to table. Upturning some, breaking more dishes, overturning chairs, hell even flying some.

I was exhausted and alone again when I threw a final wine glass at a nearby pillar. Heaving in breaths and releasing them, I moved slowly, dragging my feet to sit by the aquarium and just cry.

No matter how I looked at it, there was no use trying to reason it out. It is what it is. But I still felt the raw pain that gripped me.

I felt a new wave of tears coming at the helplessness of the situation when a hand was placed on my own. My eyes widened at the familiar lines and coloring. Hard worked hands I knew as well as my own.

I whipped my head up to stare into the dark eyes of my father. This time he wasn't in the wheelchair, but standing as proud and tall as he used to before. The wave of tears broke, but of happiness. I grabbed his hand with my own and stood to hug him.

I sobbed at the second chance I was given to see my father. Not just as he was when he'd passed but how he used to be when he was healthy. I inhaled his familiar scent hoping to burn it into my memory, Brut cologne and leather. I gripped his broad back that had always felt so strong to me. As if he could hold the world on his shoulders without a care and shrug all the while.

"Jane, she's right. This isn't you or your mother's fault." He pulled out of my hold and I unwillingly let him. "You have to let it go." His deep baritone soothed some of the strain from my sobs.

I just shook my head, dropping my gaze to the floor. I watched as my tears dropped to the marble floor, creating a small pool at my feet.

For the second time my chin was lifted to meet the gaze of my peer. "Shh." He wiped the tears from my face and I leaned against his hand for comfort just as much for strength. He held my face between his warm palms and I took the moment to remember the feeling, I may never be able to again. I could get trapped in my own head, dreaming endlessly about seeing my father.

"No. You can't do that, so don't even think about it. Think of your mother and Jordan. Would you leave them alone too? You can't be selfish Jane. My time was done; it was coming sooner or later. We all knew that."

I wanted to, God knew I wanted to just quit. Just drift off and forget all my responsibilities and be with him. But he was right, if that was what he wanted for me then I'd make him proud, I'd do it for him.

Taking a deep breath I finally carried my own weight and looked at him, covering his hands with my own. "I'm not leaving them, but you can't ask me to forget."

"You don't have to, but you need to live your life Jane. Stop wasting it on thoughts that'll get you nowhere but in circles." He broke eye contact and looked up as if his name had been called. I gripped his hands knowing what was coming.

"No . . . No! Please don't go yet. Please." I hugged him willing him to stay, just a while longer.

"I love you."

A sob escaped me. "I love you too."

Soon I was hugging air.

I woke up gasping for air, shooting straight up off the couch. When I realized where I was I dropped back onto the couch, still trying to catch my breath.

Then I realized I was so hot that I'd been sweating and I was lying in a pool of it.

"Eew . . ." Getting up I moved over to the kitchen to grab a towel. I went back to the couch to wipe off the sweat when the most obnoxious knocking started up on my front door. Looking at the clock on our cable box it was only two o'clock. Way too early for my mom to be home and there was no way my brother would be back from work either. The knocking started up again and I finished frantically wiping up the sweat from the couch. It really was quite disgusting.

Moving to the kitchen, I threw the towel in the sink to be washed later before moving to the door. I unlocked it and swung the door open.

Than was standing on my doorstep. He looked a little pissed. Okay, okay he looked really pissed.

An evil smile took place on his lips before he took a step towards me.

"Hello Jane, been skipping out on our deal hmm?"

Deal? What deal? I barely remembered what he was talking about but was too late to react when he forced himself the rest of the way in and grabbed my waist, roughly pulling me flush against his incredible body. A small growl sounded in his chest at the contact.

God I missed his body. No! Shh! No, you did not! Get a hold of yourself. Push him away.

I got as far as placing my hands on his chest to push and only encountered hard, unresisting, male chest. My resolve must've softened because a smirk found its way onto his luscious lips, leaning his head down to claim my mouth.

The door slammed and locked on its own. That's the last thing I remember before a feeling of falling caught me off guard. I gripped Than's shirt and stiffened for a hard fall but my back only met softness. I broke the incinerating kiss to see where I had fallen. I don't remember placing anything quite this soft on the floor.

What the . . . ? We were laying in what had to be the most luxurious looking bed in the history of man. It must have been a Cali King because I could literally place my entire family on this bed. Pillows were everywhere, small and large, even those little wiener looking ones. A sheer black canopy made the top of the four poster bed, falling down all around us.

Still breathless I asked him, "Where are we now?" I was seriously exhausted with all these teleporting tricks.

"My bed."

"*This* is your bed?" I squeaked out. I started to struggle and get up. No, no, no. So not happening. I got as far as the head board and pulled my legs tightly to my chest. I realized I hadn't changed my clothes before answering the door and so that left me in my vicky secrets panties and a old ACDC shirt. Curse Than's timing.

Than started to crawl towards me, muscles bunching in his arms. His eyes were entirely focused on me, making me tighten my hold on my legs. It was then I recalled exactly what our deal had been.

"Stop! You can't touch me if I don't want it and you said ONE kiss a day." He froze and didn't look pleased at my sudden recollection of memory. Then I realized that was his intention the entire time! To distract me with the one kiss and make me want him in that moment. I glared at him in realization. The scumbag!

Still glaring I moved to the edge of the bed. I was the one who was pissed now. How dare he? I was in no mood after that nightmare, waking up in my own sweat. Then he comes out of nowhere expecting me to just fall at his feet? Disgusting! I stood to the side of the bed and flicked my angry gaze to him.

"You disgusting, inconsiderate . . . MAN!" I grabbed a pillow and threw it at him. He just caught it and put it down. That only made me madder. So I threw another one at him and turned away to start pacing, not watching the end result of the pillow throw.

"That's a little rude Jane, don't you think?"

I stopped in my tracks to stare at him in disbelief. Rude? Walking back to the edge of the bed, I placed my hands on the bed intending on giving him a piece of my mind.

"Rude? You think I'm rude? I had just woken up from a nightmare, you start pounding on my door like a crazed lunatic, come in uninvited, assault me, teleport me-

"Shift."

"Shut up! Take me from my home without my permission and had planned to rape me! YOU are rude Than, YOU are the epitome of . . . of . . . !"

"A man?" He supplied so graciously.

"Yes! I mean no! Yes, but no! You're like a little boy who can't get what he wants by asking so you force and manipulate people into doing what you want them to do. Just like how you got that deal out of me, or how you got me to follow you in the first place all over that damned mall. I bet you even had something to do with my car battery dying!" The last was spit out in anger.

He scoffed. "I'm hardly *that* powerful Jane, and rape is a very strong word for something you wanted."

I let a frustrated scream escape me. "You're impossible!" Why did he even come? I was doing fine on my own. No encounters like I said and had taken care of the last one.

"Why are you even here?" I crossed my arms over my chest, somewhat shielding his all too penetrating gaze.

He seemed confused and only looked at me questioningly. "In my own bed?"

I rolled my eyes. "No you obtuse man!" I placed my forehead in my hand to massage. "Why did you come to my house?" I tried again.

"Oh." He repositioned himself on the bed. He leaned back on his right forearm, grabbed a pillow and stared off to the side. This gave me the chance to observe him unnoticed. His thick, black hair looked damp, probably from a recent shower. I pushed my thoughts away from what he must look like in a shower and moved lower. His eyes were lost in thought while his mouth was set in a grim line. Continuing down I couldn't help but notice the no nonsense feel of the regular black tee and dark blue denim he had on his statuesque body. His shoes were what looked to be . . .

He sighed loudly, distracting my perusal of the exquisite male form. "'Azel, if you keep staring at me that way you'll end up in the same position we started in . . . ." I met his penetrating stare. "You know that right?" He said it as if he were talking to someone who wasn't quite all there or slow.

Anyway his shoes looked like they'd kick someone's ass somewhere. There I was done. I stared back at him, giving him a what? look.

He rolled his eyes. "I came to inform you of some going ons that have to do with you."

I arched a brow. "Oh?" *And?*

He looked at me, seemingly deciding how much to tell me. Using his left hand he patted the spot in front of him, asking me to sit. I shook my head, I didn't like what I felt when I got to close to him. It screamed of something I couldn't keep, something forbidden. I ignored how right it felt though.

"Tell me or take me home." I only stared back at him in challenge.

He looked peeved but went on to say, "Someone doesn't want you saving these spirits."

I looked away. So, he knew I'd saved one. I was a little hurt that he hadn't congratulated me but shrugged it off. What was he? My boyfriend? Like I needed praise from him? I blushed at the word boyfriend.

"What?"

Shit. "What?" I asked flippantly.

"You're blushing." He said slowly. "Why?" He sat up a little to catch my answer.

"Nothing!" I shot out. Too fast and loud. Damn it. I cleared my throat and tried again. Looking him straight in the eye I said again, "Nothing. Why? Who is this person or who are these people that want to stop me."

He looked as if he'd argue the subject change but seemed to think better of it. He fell on his back mumbling something in an exhausted tone.

Leaning forward I asked him, "What?"

Lifting his head he responded. "Erebos."

A shudder racked my body at the name. I don't know why, maybe something instinctual. Whatever it was, I didn't like it.

"Who is Erebos?" My skin broke out in goose bumps. I grabbed a small blanket from the bottom of the bed and wrapped it around myself. I still shivered, my teeth starting to clatter. Why was it so cold?

"Damnit girl." Than came up from his perch and grabbed my arm. I resisted but he only used his male strength and pulled me down next to him. Cradling me to his chest, he wrapped his left arm around my middle and held me. I have to admit his abnormal warmth had no rival.

After a pause and some shifting on both of our parts to get comfortable, Than continued to explain. "Erebos is a primordial deity. Made from the very fabric of space and time, before even the Titans and Gods. We are all children born from these deities." He spit the last word, anger coloring his words.

"You don't like them?" Obvious answer, but I wanted to hear it.

"Let's just say these deities aren't any of our favorite family relatives." He had started to draw circles on my hip, even through the fabric of the blanket and shirt I had on, I felt the burn as if we were skin to skin.

"He is the god of Shadows. He reigns in Erebus, the part in hell where the dead have to cross before making it to the underworld. Sort of a metal detector like at the airport." He looked down at me. "Even before Charon ferries their soul over."

I just waited in silence, taking in everything he was telling me. Waiting for the inevitable punch line.

"His job used to be to search the spirit for light or darkness in order to determine whether to send them to Charon or to a more heavenly direction. Anyway, he's somehow found a way to collect spirits, making them repeat their deaths. This in turn made them even darker, more violent. It seems the more they go through, the death escalates the darkness, in turn making Erebos stronger."

I burrowed deeper into Thans warmth not liking where this was going. "Why does he need to be stronger?" It seemed to me that being a primordial deity would entitle this being to one of the most powerful alive, an immortal to boot. More power stroke me as a bit off balance, not to mention selfish.

"Too rule the underworld, naturally." I felt Than shrug, like this wasn't new to him. This Erebos must have been trying for a while then.

I worried my bottom lip. Here came the punch. "What will he do to stop me?"

The circles stopped, his grip on my hip seemed to tighten. "Whatever he's using to collect these spirits and bend them to his will. He can use on you too."

My heart dropped into my stomach. Oh. This just got more complicated than I thought it was going to be.

His sigh was heavy on my neck. "Jane, there's a reason why there aren't many *Descendions* left. One I failed to mention when you'd asked before." He paused, choosing his words to say to me. As if anything after that would be worse than some primordial being after my ass.

"He killed them."

Oh how wrong I could be sometimes.

CHAPTER 12

Somewhere in Heaven . . .

You must protect her Abaddon.

Don had been going over this as respectfully as he could muster, being ripped from his mission so suddenly and not to mention rudely from his date with Jane a week ago. But He would not listen, always coming back to this protecting her bit. He was! At least he had been trying until that call, leaving Jane to Thanatos' evil clutches. He ground his molars trying to regain control.

"Sir, I've told you, I'm protecting the mortal as you've wished. Until having to return to you unexpectedly."

You question my motives?

Power thrummed behind those words, on the brink of being unleashed on him for his insolence no doubt. He may be giving, loving and forgiving, but never think twice that he could not punish with a vengeance.

"No sir." Don was standing in a white abyss of nothing, soft rolling mist at his feet. This was where His followers were to converse semi-telepathically with Him. Only the highest and trustworthy on the hierarchy of angels could speak with the creator face to face, no exceptions.

Don refocused on his current predicament. "What would you have me do for the mortal sir?"

There are forces after this child of shadows. Forces we would naturally have nothing to do with.

He paused. Don waited, feet apart, hands clutched behind his back military style. The only peace he found here was having his wings extended for long periods of time. Keeping them subdued was not his idea of a spa day.

Coercion is no longer an option. You must go to the child, tell her all. This does not interfere with the other side if you tell her all of our side of course.

Don was stunned to hear this. This had never occurred to him as a mission that had casualties. However from what He was asking, something was afoot.

"If it would please you, sir, what has happened to cause such a drastic step for such a subtle mission?"

A weary sigh broke over the link he shared with Him. *The Greek pantheon has lost control of one of their own. He seeks to control realms he does not have the power, or authority to control. The child has ruptured his plans and to him must be stopped. He will go for her.*

Don's face scrunched up in confusion. Who? Who would destroy such a girl as Jane Rivers? He seemed to know what Don had been thinking for he answered his questions with one word.

Erebos.

That bastard, primordial God? Rage overtook Don.

You know why I've chosen you for this task Abaddon. Be sure to correct the situation.

Don growled out a 'Yes sir,' had turned to take flight but stopped when He had a few last words to say.

If you do not save and protect her Abaddon. I cannot begin to explain what will happen to Earth's realm.

Nodding grimly, Don took off, flashing to Jane's house.

Erebus . . . .

In the depths of the underworld, just before the gates to Charon, there stood a being of raging hate in the realm he'd named Erebus. Taken of course from his own name. One couldn't begin to describe the crippling fear that shown through one's eyes at encountering Erebos.

The realm was not as it once was, though how it was before couldn't exactly be called comfy, situated in the underworld as it was. The everlasting smell of decaying spirits, souls and bodies filled his nostrils. He inhaled the glory of the fear and sorrow that encompassed those who were trapped here.

In what he would call the sentencing hall, he sat high on a dais, in a chair made of the essence of spirits. One would think this was impossible to sit on. Being the god of shadows, it wasn't a great feat for him. His chair consisted of ethereal bodies controlled into broken, contorted shapes to fit his body perfectly. If something didn't feel right, he simply controlled the spirit to break and shift no matter the pain he brought. It was led to believe that spirits weren't aware of their body once they left their host. That was a strong misconception.

Spirits could feel everything a *god* did to them. He smirked as he took a finger that was out of place on his throne. Taking hold of it between his thumb and index he simply broke, and ripped it from the hand that controlled it. Holding the finger he paused and listened as the screams broke out across the hall. He shivered, reveling in it. *Delicious.*

He carelessly threw the finger over to Cerberus, currently chained to a pillar. The finger returned to a form of meat Cerberus could eat. The enormous beast licked up the small treat, lying back down.

He'd stolen the guard dog to Hades a few days ago without much of a fight. But then again Hades wasn't nearly powerful enough these days to defeat him. He chuckled at the absurdity of a claim even being mentioned on another's lips.

All a part of a plan he thought, standing to move to the key to all of his success in taking over the underworld. Clasping his hands behind his back in thought, he stared at Charon's Orb. Purposefully misleading, the Orb didn't belong to Charon at all. It was created by a goddess who had fallen in love with a mortal man ages ago.

Erebos peeled his lips back in disgust, it was a wonder the entire Greek pantheon hadn't collapsed in on itself eons ago.

He'd heard that the goddess, one of many children between Zeus and Aphrodite, had created an orb that could collect spirits and souls alike. Her purpose behind it was to collect her beloved before he could be passed on to Charon to take into the underworld. Ah, but the orb was tricky as all things created by gods were. She collected her beloved, only to discover that spirits and souls were very different entities. Souls could be returned to the corpse, reanimating the body to live and thrive. Spirits on the other hand, could exist only in ethereal form.

Erebos had wished he'd been around to witness the ridiculous attempts the goddess had made. In the end she'd collected the spirit instead of the soul and was left with a spirit who repeated his death countless times, becoming what Erebos thrived on.

Of course, he released a frustrated breath; this didn't come without consequence from the young goddess. Angry with the outcome of the orb's purpose, she went to deal with Charon and the primordial god Chaos. Between the ferryman of souls and the god of nothingness which all else sprang, she gave birth to the very first *descendion*. She taught her child to save those spirits who would live to repeat their violent deaths and guide them unto heaven or hell.

Not many know about how these mortals came to be. Many god's and goddesses only knew the updated short story, that being a descendent from Charon was what it took to be a *descendion.* Being a primordial god, he knew almost all that was the beginning of time.

"Sir, you requested my presence?"

He turned to confront one of his many loyal shadow servants.

"You've found her then?"

"I did sir, yes."

He nodded. Being aware of all the repetitive spirits in his realm, it'd come to his attention that one had been saved. Never in so many years since the last *descendion* he'd collected, had a spirit been saved. He'd gone into quite a rage, killing half of his servants and destroying the west wing of the hall.

He waited for his servant to complete his report. The shadow demon shifted uncomfortably.

"What is it?" He growled in warning that if he didn't like the answer, this could very well be the end of another servant.

"She is heavily guarded sir."

"By whom?" Erebos didn't like where this was going.

The demon gave a none too subtle gulp. "The Angel of Death and the son of Death." Before he could react, the demon shifted from his sight.

It was just as well, there would have been a smear on the ground had he waited around.

Erebos roared his displeasure and there went the east wing of the hall. Cerebus snapped and growled at being disturbed by his wrath. More shadow demons were called to him at once. This would not stand. One puny mortal was not interfering with decades of planning. He had three of his most vicious and conniving shadow demons before him. Fear, Jealousy and Sorrow. The two males and female would be equipped enough to deal with this and remove the problem this mortal presented.

He only stood with his back to them before snarling one word. "Go."

—∞—

After that exciting tidbit you can imagine I wasn't in the happiest of moods. I felt run to ground, trampled on and tired. Why was everything getting harder? I thought that'd been it, save the spirit and move on to the next and my life.

But no, things were never that simple.

"We just haven't been able to discover what he's using to collect spirits."

I faded back into the conversation. "What?" I was still tucked away against Than. I didn't think I could move if I wanted to, frozen as I was with fear of what was to come and what I'd have to face.

"Are you listening?" If I looked, there'd probably be a scowl on his face at my inattention.

I nodded. I realized it was probably late and mom would be wondering where I was. "I need to get home." I didn't move and neither did Than. No, really I did need to. I soaked up a little more of his body warmth and sat up. The blanket fell away and the cold intruded on my skin. I rolled off the bed and waited for Than to follow and take me back. He looked as if he'd refuse but just rolled his eyes and moved to stand before me.

I looked up, up, until I met his eyes. Something was there, something I responded to. I just didn't know if it was my brain or my heart that led the inquisition though. I looked away as Than wrapped his arms around me and 'shifted' us to my gate. He held on a moment more before releasing me.

I wrapped my arms around myself looking at him then away. "Well, goodbye." I turned to open my gate.

"Forgetting something?" His deep voice rang in my ears.

I turned around. "What?"

He dug his hand into his back pocket and brought my phone out. I gave an eye roll, used to the trick already. "Give it here." I hung my hand out for it.

"Next time I have to do something I ask you to do, our deal anti's up Jane." My name was a purr on his lips. In the next moment he was gone.

I stared at the empty place where Than had stood. That was exactly the problem with giving in to my feelings. He could disappear, just like that. I shook my head at those empty thoughts, trying hard to remember that important fact.

My dad was right, why the hell was I wasting my time thinking of things that kept me going in circles? Walking up the path I noticed my mom's car, crap. I grabbed for my keys but remembered I didn't have anything on me. Damnit, how would I explain this to her? As I contemplated the ways I could lie to her, I heard the faucet running in the sink and knocked on the door.

Before I could think of anything clever, my mother was standing before me, not looking to happy I might add.

"Where have you been?" She asked in a low whisper.

"Why are you whispering?" I responded in a regular voice.

"You have a guest." I did? She nodded in the direction of the living room.

I pushed passed her before she could question me further and wonder at my state of dress. Turning the corner of the long hallway, I heard the door close behind me before I felt my heart drop to my stomach.

"Hello . . . . legs." At the last word, Don stared at my legs, bare to everyone and their grandmother.

"Jesus Don!" I walked away from him into my room to throw on some shorts, cheeks flaming with embarrassment. Really? Two of them in one day was really bad for my heart rate. I stalked back out and put my hands on my hips. I glanced to the kitchen, which was open to the living room, spared my mom a glance and motioned for Don to come with me.

"Mom we are gonna take a walk."

"Hey, be back for dinner!"

"I will!" I called before I shut the door. Turning around I spared Don a glare and walked on without waiting for him.

"What are you doing here?" I called out to him. He caught up and was now beside me before he answered.

"I came to see how you were doing after I saw you last."

I snorted. "A little late don't you think?" I looked askance at him.

"Sorry, I was called away that day and have been occupied since." He said sheepishly.

I sniffed disdainfully. "So what was with the whole disappearing act?"

He glanced around at the other people on the street. I looked at him questioningly. He grabbed my arm, but not in a menacing way or anything.

"Is there somewhere private we can talk?" I didn't take it as a threat, but I had my doubts about being alone with Don. Being with Than was starting to make me loyal to him, even if I thought he was a jackass most times.

"Sure. C'mon." I led him down the street and around the next corner to this empty lot that a car service department owned during the week but was open to the public during the weekends to park at.

I moved to sit on one of the huge concrete pillars they had laying around the lot to make sections for the cars to park in. There were a few empty cars there so I thought this would be fine for him to say whatever it is he wanted to talk to me about. I remembered he also had some questions to answer for me as well.

We sat in silence for a while until I had to break it. I had to be back for dinner after all. "Well?"

He seemed to take in a large breath before turning to look me in the eyes. He was still gorgeous, but there was just something about him that didn't make me sizzle like Than did. If I were smart, Don would be the one to go for. Apparently I was an idiot.

Don took my hands in his and rubbed small circles over my skin. "Look there's really no way to break this softly and don't be scared or anything alright?" He looked at me worriedly.

Okay. I mean maybe a week or two ago when I first met him and he said this I'd be freaked out. Now? Not so much.

"I'm all ears." I waited, drawing comfort from his strokes on my hands. With him it was comfortable, with Than I would probably get flustered and pull away because of how my body always lost control with him. I shook myself mentally attempting to focus on Don.

"I'm an angel." He paused, waiting for my reaction.

I just stared back at him. Seriously? You mean when I'd described him I was right? Serious kudo points for me. When I didn't respond he continued.

"Are you okay?"

"Yeah, is that all?"

Groaning in frustration he got up running a hand through his hair. "You don't believe me."

I shook my hands in front of me, pulling from his gentle hold to get that notion out of his head. "No, that's not it. I do, I'm just waiting for an explanation is all."

He looked as if he didn't believe me. I held my hand out and gestured for him to explain.

"My name is Abaddon." He crossed his thick arms over his broad chest, looking down at me. "Don for short. I'm the Angel of Death." He arched a brow in expectation. Of what, I'm not sure. I continued to stare, allowing him to continue. I thought I'd just ask all the questions afterwards as I'd done with Than.

When he didn't get a reaction out of me he seemed to relax and move on.

"I was sent here at first to guide or convince you to our side of the spectrum as a *descendion.* What that is—"

"I know what I am." I cut him off before he could go into it. This seemed to surprise him.

"You do? How?" It was his turn to wait for me to explain.

I shrugged. "Than told me." This seemed to darken his mood.

"He did huh?" He mumbled something under his breath, but I didn't catch it.

"Okay, so it's safe to say you know these things exist and what your background is?"

I nodded.

"How long have you known?"

"That day I was almost hit by a car—"

"What?" I looked back at him. His face was contorted in rage.

"I give him one chance and he almost blew it! Idiot! I knew I shouldn't have left you with that incompetent dickwad! Fuck!" He had started to pace frantically. I guess it was okay for angels to swear?

I stood to stop him by bringing my hands to his chest, almost getting trampled in the process. He grabbed onto my arms to keep me from falling. I grabbed onto his shoulders, feeling the warmth seep through and give me the fuzzies. Clearing my throat I righted myself and looked away before explaining that Than had saved me in time but had had to shift me in order to keep curious eyes away from the scene.

"That's when I had to ask him what the hell happened; because there was no way I believed he was human anymore."

Don seemed to laugh at a private joke of his. "So you know what he is also?"

I was going to answer in the affirmative when I realized I didn't actually know what he was. Don recognized my confusion. "You're kidding me." He barked out a laugh. "Of course the bastard would try and seduce you without actually letting you know what he was." He shook his head.

"Well, what is he then?" I ignored the whole seducing bit. He didn't need to know exactly how in it I was with Than. Don obviously knew what he was. Now I wasn't so sure of where I stood with Than. Don was looking like the better bet now. I mean I wasn't a fool, I knew he was a lying scumbag but if this was important I had to know.

He looked at me sheepishly. "I can't tell you."

I only stared at him dumbfounded. "You're defending him!?" I screeched at him

"No! I just can't interfere. Never mind. There are more important things I need to tell you."

I rolled my eyes. These two were definitely not my favorite people. "Well by all means, tell me what matters to *you*." I snarled sarcastically and went to sit back down on the pillar.

He ignored me. "Look, a powerful being is after you and it's my job to keep you safe until he's stopped. So it's most likely I'll be around more, just thought I'd warn you." He stared and waited for my reaction.

"You're talking about Erebos?" He nodded, seeming surprised again but knowing Than was the source of all my knowledge now.

"If he's primordial, how can you or Than stop him from killing me."

He scoffed. "First off, just because he's immortal doesn't mean there aren't means to subdue him or make him weaker. I'm not saying it'll be easy, but it's possible. Secondly, he's not trying to kill you Jane. He's trying to *collect* you. Collecting your spirit will make him stronger. It's why we try to convince *descendions* to a side swiftly, as they become easier to guard as opposed to being alone and on their own. You'll come into your own powers soon after choosing."

My eyes widened, well that was something I didn't know yet. "Powers?"

"What? Than didn't tell you that part?"

"Out with it." I was a little hurt I'll admit. Just the way he'd been acting earlier . . . . *What did you expect?*

"Every one of your kind has powers though they seem to vary depending on the mortal. We won't know until you do though, neither do we know what triggers it. From what we've gathered over the years is that strong emotion is a common trigger, but not always. Once, there was an incident where a male discovered his powers after getting attacked by a dog. I guess his trigger was fear because fido wasn't too alive after he was through with him." He shrugged as if it was natural for a mortal to have such powers.

I tried to escape the images of all the ways a dog could've been killed by a paranormal human. Shuddering I opened my mouth to ask another question when my phone signaled a text message. Opening the message, I was annoyed to find that my mother was telling me to come home and eat. Sighing I pocketed my phone before turning back to Don.

"This isn't over." I poked him in the chest. "Not by a long shot."

He grabbed my hand, pulling me flush against him. "No, it's not."

Warmth flowed through my body. I was comfortable being around Don. He wasn't always lying and finding ways to break me down. We stayed that way a while longer until I broke eye contact first. "I have to go."

Don nodded and released my hand. The warmth receded from my body. "I won't be far." He surprised me by leaning in to place a kiss on my forehead before turning to walk in the opposite direction.

I was in a daze as I walked back home alone. This was seriously one great, big, mind fuck. Than made me feel like butterflies danced in my stomach and wanted out every time he stared, touched or spoke to me. Don made me feel relaxed and calm whenever he did those things. I felt protected with both of them, fiercely. Now one was lying and the other was pretty much my personal stalker.

As I walked through my gate, I felt like I was leaving the old me behind. I didn't think things would ever be the same again.

CHAPTER 13

You know those nights when you drink too much? Imagine it, and then remember you wishing for a fitful sleep into the next morning, without interruptions of any kind? Yeah, that wish never came true for me this morning. I woke up to the sound of a lawn mower.

"Could you just get that corner over there by the fence Don?!"

"Sure thing Ms. Rivers!"

I cracked my eyes open then shut them again, my eyes watering at the bright sunlight shining through my windows. *What the devil!?* What time was it anyway? I tried another attempt at opening my eyes, a bit slower this time. Glancing at my cable box it wasn't even nine in the morning and these idiots were cutting grass?!

I growled into my pillow, scrunching my face in anger and irritation, calling my mom and Don all kinds of stupid in my head. Wait, Don? What was he doing here? Okay, yeah he said he'd be hanging around, but I didn't think that meant he'd be our new gardener.

Sitting up I stretched and cracked a few choice joints that wouldn't give. "Ugh, gods give me patience." Scratching my head through my tangled mane of a head, I dragged my legs over the sides of the bed and stood up stretching more. At five eight, I wasn't exactly a good crunch sleeper. Rubbing my eyes I moved out of my room to the bathroom.

I decided to take a shower since I felt disgustingly sweaty from the heat that had festered in my room from the overbearing sun. Humming to myself, I washed the exhaustion from my face and enjoyed the cool water flowing over my body. If I could just stay in a bit longer I'd be in heaven. Taking the extra three minutes, I heard the bathroom door open and just expected it to be mom.

"Jane, your mom wants to kn—"

I shrieked a piercing scream and covered crucial pieces of my body. Our shower stall door was clear, yes marbled, but still! "DON GET OUT! GET OUT, GET OUT!"

"So is that pancakes?"

"GET THE F OUT OF THE BATHROOM!"

"Ookay pancakes it is." He replied cheerfully. God! Seriously?

Beyond pissed and forgetting the three minutes, I slammed the water off and grabbed my towel. Drying off I stepped out, threw on my clothes and moved to the kitchen to give these people a piece of my mind.

I looked around for my mom but she wasn't in the house. "Mom!?" I went to go look out over the sink window in the kitchen to see if she were still outside. "MOM!"

"Would you stop yelling? She went to walk the dog." I turned with a snarled response on my lips.

"WHAT in all that's holy, are you doing *here* Don?"

Leaning against the refrigerator with his arms crossed, he scanned his eyes over me in one sweep. I crossed my own arms, cocking a hip. Oh no, he would not make me flinch. If this was a stare down I was going to win it. I was in no mood this morning.

"Well?" I reiterated.

He only shrugged. "I saw your mom working in the yard trying to remove a tree. I came over to offer my assistance."

I sneered at him. "Oh? And I suppose that gives you the right to barge in on me while I'm showering does it?"

"How else was I supposed to make you breakfast?

"I thought mom was making breakfast?" I arched a brow at his obvious lie.

"She was but I offered to help her with that since she wanted to walk the dog." A careless shrug again.

"Well, aren't you just Santa's little helper this morning." I rolled my eyes and moved to grab a glass for water. Going to grab the pitcher, I waited for him to move from the fridge.

"Think it might be possible for you to move?"

"If you say please, I may consider it." He shrugged his enormous shoulders again, this time he caught me looking because I was so close. He smiled knowingly.

"Move please, or I'll move you myself!"

He laughed, it was so deep and masculine, my jaw dropped a little at the beautiful sound. I shook my head quickly before he caught me staring and placed my hand on his chest to move him. He grabbed my wrist before I could apply any pressure.

"As amusing as that would be to see, I have to move anyways. Your eggs are burning." Winking he moved me to where he'd been standing and took my place by the stove.

Shaking off the warm tingles where he'd grabbed me, I opened the door and reached for the pitcher, pouring half a glass. I turned to peruse this angelic god in my kitchen, cooking MY breakfast. So he could cook, I'm not going to mention how hot that is. Any man cooking is hot, but a man such as this? Smoking hot.

"Jane you're staring." He glanced over to me, placing my egg over onto a plate that also had a couple of pancakes and two strips of bacon.

I sighed. "Sorry. I'm sorry for staring and for yelling at you. It's just you guys had the lawn mower going so early and I'm exhausted from you and Than telling me different or incomplete stories. It's all so confusing trying to piece together." I stepped to the side to look out the window, checking if my mom would be returning any time soon. I couldn't let her overhear this. That was a disaster I could not handle at the moment.

"It's okay, just try not to snap my neck off in the upcoming weeks." He threw me a dazzling smile bringing my plate to the table. I moved to sit when he pulled my chair out.

"Thanks." I put my cup on the table and waited for him to sit at the head of the table. I have to admit he was rather too large for this table. I stifled a laugh at how ridiculously huge God had made him.

"What's so funny?" He asked with mirth in his eyes.

"What? God couldn't have made you guys any bigger?" I responded sarcastically.

He just smiled good naturedly. "Nah, I just came out wrong."

He had me laughing at his joke. I haven't had a good laugh like that in a while.

"Your laugh is beautiful." I cut off my laughing at the awkwardness I felt at that statement and smothered it with a cough. Clearing my throat, I moved to eat.

"So what exactly are you supposed to do with me? Follow me around like a puppy?" I didn't look up from my plate but continued to eat my breakfast.

"Not exactly." Of course he'd give me a non-answer. I rolled my eyes, continuing to chew.

"Alright, well I'm feeling drastic change coming on here. I'm going to the mall." I was hoping there was a slight chance that mentioning the mall to a man would turn him in the other direction.

"Alright, I'll drive." Damnit.

—w—

I was in my room while Don waited up front in the driveway. What to wear? I had my hands on my hips as I stared into my closet. This was the reason I was going to the mall, other than going to the salon to whack all my hair off. I was going for a Rihanna look, post abusive boyfriend. I also needed new clothes since I just filled up three trash bags of clothes as old as the hills.

What brought about this change? I shrugged every time I thought about it too hard. Why not? Since my life was changing so much, I might as well go for a full features change too. Thumbing through my hangers, I finally settled on a black tube top then dug into my drawers for skinny jeans. I finally placed my feet in my wedges and grabbed my bag. I sent mom a text on my whereabouts and shut my gate behind me.

I remembered Don's bike and stopped to look up and see what he was driving today. I breathed a sigh of relief when my eyes locked on a regular charcoal grey Tacoma. So, the angel had a brain.

I ignored his once over and walked around to the passenger side. Hopping inside, I looked around to gather in my surroundings. *Just in case I need to initiate a tuck and roll.*

"Where to boss?"

I snorted as he started up the truck and I pointed him around silently.

"You gonna be mute the whole time?" He stared straight ahead.

I didn't bother looking at him either. "Is there something to talk about?" I asked bitterly.

"Well, no. Do you mind if I ask you questions then?"

I finally looked at him suspiciously. "Why?"

"Well I think I should be entitled to knowing a bit about the mortal I have to protect."

"Don't you know all there is to know?"

He shrugged. "Not really."

I shrugged back, I guess it'd be harmless. "Fine, ask away." We'd be there in twenty minutes anyway.

"Where's your boyfriend?" My eyes practically bugged out of my head.

"Really? That's your first and most important question?"

"Nah, I work my way from bottom to top." He spared me a glance and a wide grin. Insufferable man. Insufferable but cute.

I huffed out a breath, turning back to face the road. "I don't have one. Next question."

"Why not?" I looked heavenward for patience.

"Things weren't getting better so I didn't want to make them worse."

He finally dropped that one. "What's your favorite color?"

"Purple. Or anything bright and neon." I said the last as an afterthought.

"Really?"

"You sound like that's unbelievable." I looked askance at him for verification. Why should it matter if I like neon colors?

"I just didn't peg you for a happy and colorful girl."

I shrugged. "It really depends on my mood, but right now I'm doing purple." Sorry, that's how it goes buddy.

"Alright, I know your bike story already." He paused, seeming to think on a question before a smile broke out on his face. *Suspicious.*

"Where's the most interesting place you've had sex?" He arched a brow but his eyes remained on the road.

"I'm so not answering that question. Next." His face fell at my noncomplacency to play his game.

"Aw, c'mon legs! You need to lighten up!" I just shook my head, refusing to answer his stupid teenager question.

"Please?" He turned and gave a puppy dog pout. I couldn't hold the laugh that escaped me. The problem was that it actually worked.

"Okay! Alright, the most interesting place . . ." I thought long and hard about this one.

"Oh! I know! One time I was majorly drunk at this new club that we'd finally gotten into. I'd run into one of my more favorable exes, things led from one thing to another and well we, um . . ."

"C'mon out with it. What happened?"

I bit my lip. "We ended up on the roof . . . and . . . well you know." A furious blush formed on my face.

He busted out laughing.

I glared at him. "What!? We had to climb down to a lower level and my knees were so sore from the gravel they'd put up there. We almost couldn't get back up over the ledge we dropped over!" He was laughing uproariously.

I had to admit it was pretty funny. I joined in on the laughing.

He finally calmed down enough to ask me another question as we pulled in to the mall. "Did anyone ever find out?"

I looked at him aghast. "No! I've never spoken about it after that. It was just so ridiculous afterwards when I thought about it. Probably the most daring thing I've ever done. If you ever tell anyone I'll stab you where it hurts with a blunt knife!" I looked pointedly at his package.

He cringed but nodded and pulled the truck into a stall close to an entrance. I unbuckled my seat belt and hopped out of the truck, still smiling from the hilarity of that predicament. Don joined me as we moved to the entrance of the mall. He held open the door for me and I made my way to the salon.

"Look I'm going to be a bit at the salon alright? Come back in about an hour."

"Alright, see ya later." I turned away and entered the salon for my makeover.

—∞—

After an hour of sitting in the chair and talking mindlessly about random subjects I finally met up with Don who was waiting patiently just outside in the mall. My head felt ten times lighter.

I walked up to him looking down, I refused to look at him. It was such a drastic change from my usual long hair. All I could see was his feet as I stood there waiting for his response.

"Um . . ."

Oh no, he didn't like it. I had shown the woman working on me a picture of Rihanna with some fringe and a bowl cut up to her shoulders. She did it and straightened it at my request. My hair was naturally kinky; there was no way I was walking around with a bush on my head.

My shoulders slumped at his response to my hair. "It's ugly?" I mumbled.

He grabbed my chin in one hand and tipped it up to meet his gaze. "You look amazing Jane. What are you talking about?"

My heart fluttered a little at his approval. I don't know why I needed him to approve, I just did. "Really?" I looked at him pleadingly but suspiciously to see if he were lying.

He just laughed and wrapped his arm around my shoulders heading in another direction. "Where to next?"

His weight was comfortable and warm. I brushed some of my bangs off of my eyes. "Well I need some clothes." I lead us to a forever21 and took his hand off of my shoulders to explore the store faster.

It was about twenty minutes into my shopping adventure when I noticed a slight burning sensation in my fingertips. Since my left arm was occupied with a few pieces of clothing I had to try on, I brought my right hand up to inspect. It wasn't too intense, more like if I touched a lava lamp when it had been on for awhile. I rubbed my finger and thumb together, ignoring the sensation I continued to browse.

Passing the jewelry section, I looked up to locate my angel friend. He was over by the jeans wall, talking to another girl who looked a bit older than me. I shrugged moving on down the wall of jewelry, picking a few choice rings and bangles.

I finally moved to the changing rooms to try on my bounty. Once in the room, I started bouncing to Taylor Swifts song, we are never ever getting back together. I threw on the clothes and did some turns to see how they fit and repeated this a couple more times. There was a slight volume change of voices out in the store, maybe a group of girlfriends who had just entered.

I put the clothes back on the hangers and opened my door to place the ones I didn't want on the rack that was provided in the dressing room. Smiling, I was satisfied with the three tees, one white jeans and some of the rings I'd plucked off of the wall.

Walking towards the cashier to pay I noticed that burning sensation in my fingers had gotten worse. Now it felt almost as if I'd placed my fingers on a heating stove. I hung my clothes over my arm; it was too painful to put pressure on my fingers. What the hell? Looking up from my fingers, which looked normal other than the burning, I looked around the store for Don.

I narrowed my eyes in irritation at the gaggle of girls that'd gathered around him talking all at once. I strode over to him and the flock, dumped my clothes on a side table carrying more jeans before clearing my throat behind the girls. None of them turned to look at me, Don finally met my gaze. He didn't have any one expression on his face, if anything he looked bored and exasperated by the attention. None the less some of the things these girls were saying made my eyes widen.

"So how much do you actually bench?" This from a girl with raven black hair and exotic, angled, green eyes.

"Do you have a girlfriend?" From a strawberry blonde.

"Are you free tonight?" Another blonde, except this one had enormous jugs that she insisted on brushing his arm with.

"How big is your—"

"LADIES!" They all turned around to stare at me. I had about two or three inches on all four of them without my wedges on. I was practically a giant compared to all these mini twits. I crossed my arms, staring them down.

"What's your problem?" From raven hair.

I narrowed my gaze on her. "Can't you see he isn't interested?"

"Well if you weren't interrupting, this would be a whole lot easier." Sneered Jugs.

I couldn't believe the audacity of these chicks! "Listen here you little—"

"Jane." Don cut me off and I switched my irritated glare from them to him.

"What?"

"Oh my god did you hear his voice!?" Squealed strawberry blondie. Jugs now had placed her hands on his bicep and pectoral. She was practically groping the man. My fingers increased in pain and I hissed in a breath. *Jesus!*

I opened my eyes not realizing they'd close from the pain. I stared at Don, waiting for his response.

"Just go on and shop, It's not like they're company will be the death of me."

My jaw dropped. "You're kidding me right?" I glanced at the chicks in disbelief that this is the sort of company he wanted to keep. I shook my head in disgust and grabbed my clothes to purchase.

Idiot men, ugh! I'll never understand what guys see in girls like that. I was beyond irritated, especially since Don had been acting as if he actually liked me. I had to remember I was just a job to him, that he was just my guardian until this whole thing blew over.

"I wish I had a man like that." I looked up to see the woman ringing me up daydreaming, her gaze just to the right off my shoulder. I snorted in response.

"A man like what? A man who ignores, lies and deceives you? Have at it lady." I snarled the last at her and grabbed my bags heading towards the door. I didn't need this, I'd call my mom for a ride home. Don could go to hell for I cared, the ass.

I wasn't paying attention, so lost was I in cursing out the angel of death that I walked into the glass door. What threw me off was the glass door grabbing hold of me before my ass landed on the floor.

"What the . . . ?" I shook myself out of my daze and looked up. Great, just wonderful.

"Hey, 'Azel. Nice hair." Than smiled down at me and I melted at his touch and delicious smile. He liked my hair? Had it only been two or three days since I'd seen him? That day he'd shown up at my house and took me away seemed like months ago. Did I miss him? I seriously ran into him too hard.

"W-what are you doing here Than?" I know he was still holding onto me but between Don's seeming betrayal and Than's warmth I didn't pull away.

He pulled his glance away from me to look in Don's direction. "I need you to wait outside." His tone brooked no argument, something was wrong. I just nodded dumbly at him.

"O-okay." He looked back at me with a grim look and gently pushed me towards the entrance. I didn't look back at whatever it was Than had been looking at behind me, but ran, I ran out to the entrance me and Don had entered only a couple hours ago.

Breathing a little harder than usual, I noticed as soon as I'd left the vicinity of that store, the burning in my fingers had left me. I held my hands out to examine but nothing was different about them. *How odd.*

"Did you know that there's a high percentage rate of pedestrian deaths in random mall parking lots?" I squeaked in fright at the teenage boy standing next to me, holding my hand to my chest. I took a couple of breaths before looking at him again.

Freezing on the spot I finally recognized the boy for what he was. A spirit. It'd been awhile since the little girl in the bathroom that I didn't recognize the abnormal chill. Shit, I so didn't need this right now! Slow breath in, slow breath out. Okay, I didn't want to die, I was only comforted a little that Than was in the mall right behind me if anything happened.

A car drove by us a little too fast and I took a step back seeing as his side mirror had a possibility of clipping us as it moved on.

"Hey move back from the curb!" The boy took a step back just as another truck sped by recklessly. I was holding a breath I realized and let it out.

"Do you know the speed limit in a parking lot?" The boy asked me without looking at me.

Starting to wonder where this was going and how this boy had died I moved back towards him. "5 mph?"

He turned his head to look at me, a sad smile curving his lips. "That's right." I saw it a millisecond before it happened and something pushed me to grab the boy. I saw the truck out of the corner of my eye and the screech of the brakes as I pushed instead of grabbed.

"JANE!"

It was too late. My momentum to get the boy out of the way had me falling to my hands and knees. The last thing I remembered was blinding pain in my shoulder, ribs and hip as I was hit across the pavement by the GMC.

—~—

Than couldn't process what his brain was feeding to him. He had just opened the doors to leave the mall, Don right behind him when he heard the telltale screech of someone breaking. Hard. He flicked his gaze up to see Jane throw herself off the curb directly in front of the oncoming truck. Terror ripped through him.

"JANE!"

He shifted to her too late as a horrifying crunching sound tore through the air, signaling the breaking of multiple bones. He crouched down beside her unwilling to touch her just yet.

"Shit! Jane?! Jane!" Her shoulder looked dislocated. As for the rest of her body, he'd say she resembled a rag doll, thrown carelessly to the ground and stepped on a few hundred times. Blood trickled down her forehead and from the corner of her mouth.

He could hear the human in the truck get out as Don tried to calm him down from overreacting. His focus never left Jane as he brushed the hair from her face. He placed his other fingers to her neck to check her pulse. "Fuck!" Barely there, they needed to move. Now.

"Don!" He called out to him still not breaking his focus on her. How could he have let this happen? He had finally allowed her to remain home, trusting that Don would be around so that he didn't have to deal with the onslaught of emotions she made him feel. Like a fool and a coward he'd taken the time off freely, boozing with other demons and trying to enjoy the enticements provided at their parties.

All for not, no one made him burn like his Jane. His little mortal. Now look what it'd cost him. She lay dying on the floor, for what? Trying to do what was thrust upon her. Damnit! He was supposed to be helping her! Hadn't that been the deal? He'd never forgive himself. So lost in his thoughts, he growled when someone gripped his shoulder, crouching in front of Jane to protect her.

Don held his hands up. "Than, Jesus, calm down before someone sees you!" Don positioned himself in front of him to shield his appearance from mortal eyes. He could just imagine his eyes burning like coals, fangs protruding from his gums and pass his lips. He closed his eyes, focusing on receding to his human form. "Good, damn, Than I have to take her."

He growled out a negative. "Touch her and I'll rip you're damned arms from their sockets!" He was losing control again but he wouldn't let him take her away from his sight again. His nails started to turn to razor sharp claws as his wings strained to release from his back.

"Thanatos!" Don was shouting for him to calm the hell down. That they'd take her back to his own place if he'd remove the shields. "You can't do this on your own. You weren't meant to heal a mortal." Finally, Don got through to him. Breathing heavily Than nodded in agreement, turning to lift Jane ever so carefully into his arms.

"I'll see you there." He didn't wait but shifted to his room. He placed Jane on the bed, laying her limbs out so that Don could work on her. A growl slipped past his lips. *Heal* her, he amended for his demon's piece of mind.

Don appeared across from him with another angel in tow. Than release another growl in warning but Don held out a hand. "This is Mumiah, Angel of Longevity; she will do what she can."

Mumiah looked at Than with calmness. "She was hit on which side?"

"Her right." Don responded.

"Alright, please leave. I can't have any interruptions, this will take awhile."

"Like hell! I'm not leaving." Than refused to leave her alone again. Don was at his side instantly.

"C'mon Than, she doesn't have a lot of time left. Can't you feel her?"

He let out a frustrated breath before pushing past Don to remove himself from the room. Don was right. Because of the unnatural and violent situation, he could practically feel her soul calling to him. She was close to her death. In any other situation, with any other mortal, this is what he lived for. But not with Jane, this was *killing* him.

Don shut the door behind him just as a scream rent the air. Jane's scream.

CHAPTER 14

I've never felt pain like this. Like all the bones on my right side were rearranging, popping back into place or even regrowing if that were possible. I screamed and begged for it to stop but it never did. I finally blacked out after what seemed to be hours of torturous agony.

I waited for the nightmares to come. The ones of me running through the casino only to end up crying and saying goodbye to my father once again. Those never came, instead I dreamed.

I dreamed of my hopes and fantasies. Dreams of my father, but happier. Ones that also included my mom and Jordan. Then like a blur, my dreams shifted to Than and some of Don. Those were vivid, as if it were real; I could even smell that familiar smell Than emitted. The comfortable smell that I finally recognized as the same scent of my father. No wonder I loved it so much! I wondered if I would remember that when I woke up.

The pain visited me again. Not as intense but still agonizing to go through. This went on in the same pattern of pain and dreams until I became numb to it. I was in the middle of another pain session when someone called my name. Deep, masculine tones which reminded me of the best hot chocolate I had ever had one time in France.

"Jane?" I awoke but didn't open my eyes. Did I really want to wake up? What would I miss really? But then I recalled my dad telling me to be strong, to not leave mom and Jordan alone. I finally cracked my eyes open. Not that it made a difference, it was pitch black.

"Wh—" My voice cracked and my throat was so dry, it must have been awhile since I've had anything to drink. I tried to clear it but that only burned and a whimper came out instead.

A hand found my own on the bed and squeezed. "Here, drink this." Than? Why was I here? I had to assume I was at his place, in his room yet again. I lifted my right hand with effort and found what felt to be his thigh. Gulping, I raised it to finally land upon his arm and followed the path down to the glass of water he held.

"I'm going to help you sit up alright? Take it slow."

I didn't know why he was being so cautious, my body was sore but it didn't feel that bad. He placed his left hand at my right hip and his right arm slid around my head to lift me. I clenched my abs to help sit up and immediately let out a ravaged scream.

"Jane!" He placed me back down gently but I'd dropped the glass of water as soon as the pain shot up my spine and traveled down my right shoulder into my arm. I squeezed my eyes shut, tears escaping down my face. Okay, so I was wrong, the pain was excruciating.

Than removed the now soaked sheet covering me and threw it in the corner of the room. I immediately shivered at the cool air touching my damp skin. I could now see, my eyes having adjusted to the darkness. Than returned his focus on me, he looked frustrated, like he didn't know what he should do. I just wanted to curl into a ball but after that first attempt at moving I settled in to staying on my back.

"Jane, I'm sorry. Damnit, where does it hurt?"

I moved only my eyes to give him a painful glare. Seriously?

"Alright, alright I get it. Everywhere, I'm going to go get a bottle you can drink from." He left the room and I lay there staring at the ceiling. What the hell had happened? I tried to think back to the last thing I remember doing before this.

I remember the mall, Don being a jerk in the store when he'd been surrounded by those babbling idiots. Then I remembered Than and how weird he'd been acting when he'd arrived. I moved past that memory to me standing outside of the mall and encountering that spirit boy. My eyes widened, had I really done that?

Than returned then with a bottle of water. He pulled up the top, unlocking it for water to flow freely from it and placed it to my lips. I drank like a parched woman and closed my eyes in relief. After a couple more breaths and sips, my throat finally felt normal. He placed the bottle on the table and placed his warm hand on my own. How odd, since when did Than show that he was worried or cared? I would have moved my hand but didn't dare after what I just felt.

I tried for talking. "What happened . . . . afterwards?" I refused to name what I'd done, was I stupid or just had a death wish?

He looked away, closing his eyes in what looked to be pain. "After you were . . . hit, I brought you here. Don had Mumiah—"

"Who's Mumiah?" I cut in.

"Angel of Health. Bitch in my eyes." I nodded and he continued on. "She healed you, well most of you."

Most of me? "What do you mean?"

"Well, after the first night—"

"Wait a minute." I struggled and winced in pain when I raised my arm and a finger to halt him. Looking at him and hoping I was seriously wrong I asked him, "How long have I been like this? Here?" He looked away again. "Than?" The hand he covered, I upturned and gripped him, willing him to tell me.

An exhausted sigh left him. "It's been a week. It's Sunday afternoon."

It was worse than I thought. I closed my eyes in disbelief, opening them again when I realized my family didn't know where I was. "Did you tell my mom?"

At this he got up and started pacing. I didn't want to look too closely at what I felt after he let go of my hand. I made a fist to ignore the bereft feeling. I refocused on Than and he looked beside himself, was that a blush on his face?

"Than?" I asked worriedly, Than did NOT blush. Hell, men as manly as he was did NOT turn pink period. Something was really up. "What is it? You did tell her where I was right?"

"Of course I told her where you were." He said as if I were an idiot.

"Well then what has got you blushing?" I asked him.

A shaky scoff left him. "Blushing? Are you insane woman?"

"Than. You can scoff all you want until you're out of breath, I know what I'm looking at and that's a man blushing!" I winced at the force I used to shout at him. Than noticed though and moved back to sit next to me.

"Will you stop straining your body? You're nowhere near ready for big movements or shouting matches." He leaned over me, still blushing by the way, and fluffed my pillows behind my head. Seriously, he did fluffed my pillows.

"Okay, I'm freaking out. What did you tell her that you're blushing about?"

"I told you—"

"Yeah, yeah you're not blushing. Whatever, spill it."

"The only thing I could tell her was that we have been dating, that you never told her, I didn't know why and that's why you've been staying over so long and so much." He peeked at me for my reaction.

I was speechless, nay shocked to my core. "Excuse me?" I said in a low, monotone voice.

He arched a brow, a little of his arrogance showing. "What's so unappealing about it? You'd rather I tell her you were hit by a truck trying to save a spirit and every bone in your body was pretty much broken, shattered or dislocated?"

I winced with every new description. I looked away when I answered. "No."

"Okay, so that's what it is."

Sunday, why was that making me worry my bottom lip? Shit! "Oh my god, I start my new job tomorrow! I'm so screwed!" It was almost enough to make me cry. "Oh, I hate this! If it weren't for this stupid spirit fiasco, I'd be happily settling into my new job tomorrow, a normal life!" Than's hand covered mine again, this time in comfort. Okay, I had to know. What was with this?

I looked back at him. "Who are you? Why are you so nice all of a sudden?"

He looked away. "No reason. What happened at the store?"

Wow, total one eighty on me. I let the subject drop and recounted what a jerk Don was.

"You didn't notice anything about the 'bimbos'?" He used my term for the gaggle of girls with a devilish grin. It almost made me smile it was so sexy.

"Besides them all looking artificial? No, why?" I waited curiously.

"They were all shadow impersonators of Jealousy." I looked back blankly. Was I supposed to know what that was?

He rolled his eyes. "The shadow demon Jealousy was using her powers to create those women to distract Don from protecting you and in turn making you jealous of them, unfocusing you. I'm actually surprised you couldn't tell. Usually by now a *descendion* can sense demons that are close."

My eyes widened, remembering the burning in my fingers. "I did. My fingers were burning, but with more intensity as I left the dressing rooms." Than simply nodded.

"That's your powers telling you to destroy the demon. I don't know what you can do yet but it's already starting to appear."

"Okay fine, but Than, what were YOU doing there?" I asked him archly. That's one part of the puzzle piece I couldn't figure out. I wouldn't have believed it but another blush appeared on his hard cheeks.

He mumbled out a response I didn't catch. "What was that?"

"I'm never far." He mumbled a little louder.

"You follow me?" How was that possible, wouldn't I have noticed somehow? "Everywhere?"

He finally looked at me and gave a sharp nod. I studied this man before me. My own personal protector, fierce and everything a girl fantasized about. How did a girl end up so lucky?

I blew out a long breath. Okay, there were a lot of questions in the air. I just wasn't sure if now was the time to deal with it all. What was I going to do about my job? I was starting to deflate at ever finding a normal way to live this life of mine.

"So Don was subdued and couldn't help me?" I asked, backtracking my thoughts to the conversation.

"No, normally he would have been fine. This demon came straight from Erebus though, more powerful than most angels can handle. Only one of the first origins would have been able to surpass four or five of Jealousy's shadows."

I only understood half of what he'd said and nodded, agreeing with the rest I didn't. I closed my eyes at how exhausting all this knowledge was. I left them closed, they were so heavy. I fell into a heavy sleep within seconds.

—∾—

Than watched over Jane while she slept and healed. He'd left out certain details to keep her calm. Yes, he'd called her mom and never had he been more fearful for his life. That woman asked more questions than a kid with a magic eight ball. She'd questioned him until Than decided he'd keep communication with her minimal after that. Yes, Ms. Rivers had fallen for his explanation, but barely.

What Jane didn't know was that he was serious about keeping her. At least half of him was. The other half was still wary of messing around with a mortal, no matter that she was a *descendion*. That just made her more unattainable. Of course then there was that little problem of him sending her father to an early grave out of impatience. He winced at what she would do if she ever found out.

Don was also still here, but Than wouldn't let him near her. He only allowed him to check in on her every so often. Mumiah never came back, had said that all she could do had been done. He was grateful but he still detested her throwing him out of the room.

It was Monday morning but he didn't wake her. Instead he called her new job from her cell and left a message saying she'd been in an accident and that if they wanted to contact her, to call his number which he'd left. It was only two in the morning so it'd be awhile until they got it.

He honestly didn't know what he was now feeling for her. They'd started off at such a rocky start at the mall all those weeks ago. Sitting down in the window seat, he made sure he was able to see both her and the grounds outside, just in case Erebos decided to send more demons after her or if she had any more nightmares. Frowning, he noticed she had a lot of those.

He thought back on what they'd been through. Laughing quietly to himself when the memory of her pulling him into the fountain to get back at him pushing her in because she wouldn't be quiet. He shook at himself at the asshole move on his part.

His skin heated when he thought of the stolen kisses he'd gotten from her. Her hot response in return, how she'd made him lose control so easily as if he'd never had sex before. He was practically putty in her soft capable hands. Had she freaked out when she saw his true form? Maybe a little but she'd quickly moved to curiosity, his little mortal.

He brushed his hair back in frustration, standing up to pace. This wasn't how it was supposed to be! He was supposed to seduce her to pick his side but she was reeling him in instead, however unintentional she was being. He knew she responded to his touch but did he want more? Did she? He didn't dare act on his feelings, that's how people got dead. No, he'd have to put some distance between them, it was the only way he could protect her and still have her persuaded to his side. He felt torn at the decision but was distracted by the light knock at the door.

Moving to open it, Don stood on the other side. "What?" He growled impatiently.

Don glared right back at him, barely civil about it. "How is she?" His gaze tried to flick over Than's shoulder to get a glimpse of Jane.

Than looked back to check if she was still asleep. He turned back to him and removed himself from the room making Don take a step back into the hall.

"She's in pain when she moves but I got some water down her throat when she woke up. She knows what happened, everything's been explained."

Don snorted. "Yeah how did that turn out?"

He rolled his eyes and crossed his arms over his chest nonchalantly. "She's okay, only had a few questions."

"You're a terrible liar. Either that or she doesn't know *everything.*" He raised a brow in question.

He only shrugged off the obvious question. "She knows all she needs to know."

Don shook his head. "You're an idiot if you think she'll choose you over me after she finds out." He whispered harshly.

Than's aggression and frustration broke loose and he went for Don, pinning him to the opposite wall. "You say anything and I'll personally make sure your wings never work again," he growled low so that Jane never heard them.

Don sneered back at him. “If I could, I would still tell her you arrogant ass!” Throwing a right, he took Don’s hit like a champ and only clamped his vice grip around his throat tighter and slammed him against the wall.

“Can’t you see how badly she hurts?” Don spit out after chucking up some blood. Bringing his right knee up into Than’s groin, Than finally released his throat.

Trying to catch his breath, he lost his upper hand as Don tackled him to the floor and threw in a few more punches. Since Than had willingly let him past his barriers, their interference pact was pretty much for shit now.

Than grabbed his next punch with his right and twisted, cracking the bone immediately. Wincing, Don used his other hand to finish what his other fist had started, effectively splitting open Than’s lip. Than rolled but Don countered him and they rolled around throwing knees and fists whenever they could get one in. They finally kicked apart from each other, both crouching into stances that put them at the ready for attack if provoked.

Don released an irritated breath and stood up ending his side of the fight. “Look, I know how she looks at you. My job isn’t to win her over anymore as a priority but to protect her. This situation has taken a new priority on our side of the spectrum. But just know that if you hurt her I’ll be after you faster than you can shift demon.” At that Don turned around and made his way down the stairs.

Than shifted to a spot he liked to go sometimes to think, a forest not far from his estate in a clearing surrounded by trees. Frustrated he fell to his knees and roared to the heavens that were against him.

—ꟽ—

My eyes opened at the vivid dream of Than, his roar so painfully sad with frustration that I swore it woke me up. I shifted my eyes to the window to my right, light was shining through. What time was it now? What about my job? Somehow at this moment I couldn't care less. I was so tired of being responsible and attempting to make my life work when fate was so obviously against me!

I wanted to get up but remembering the pain I went through with even Than's assistance I had to rethink that. Taking a deep breath I wiggled my toes and fingers with no pain. Hmm, that was better than whenever that night was that I tried to get up. I moved on to my arms and calves to encounter pain that reminded me of muscle cramps. Okay, I could deal with that. Next I did my entire legs, arms and lifted my head. I got a little dizzy so I lay back down to take more deep breaths.

Once I thought I was ready I rolled over onto my stomach, bringing my hands up next to my head with a grunt. This was actually more comfortable I thought to myself. Taking another deep breath, I pushed myself up onto my knees. Damn my stomach cramped worse than my worse days going through PMS! Sucking in a painful breath, I went to put one foot on the ground and then the other so that I had my entire upper body on the bed. Already I was feeling a fine sheen of sweat on my body from the exertion. I seriously need more water, I felt so dizzy I was bound to fall on the floor as soon as I lifted up from the bed. *Damnit!* I would not give up, I wanted a shower and the door to the bathroom was just a few steps away so that I could use the doorframe for support if I made it that far.

Turning my head, I measured my steps in my head and squeezed my eyes shut to mentally support myself. Okay, I got this. Opening my eyes, I took a breath for strength and pushed off the bed. One, two, three. I was starting to stumble and winced at the pain to my right part of my ribcage. I flung a hand out and grabbed onto the frame of the door for dear life. Panting now, I rested my left hand on my left knee. So out of breath, I came down to my knees as slowly as possible with a faint thump of contact. That would surely bruise. Ignoring the pain, I crawled the rest of the way and left the door open. At this point I really could care less about who saw me in the buff.

After much struggling and breaks for breaths, I finally found myself in the tub with warm soapy water filling up around me. "Ahh." A satisfied smile broke out across my lips at the luxury of finally getting a soak. I folded a hand towel and placed it under my neck for comfort. I wouldn't be able to wash my hair but maybe later in the day I'd have more strength for that. As for right now I rubbed the wash cloth of lavender across my aching limbs enjoying the soothing scent.

Unwilling to remove myself, I rested my eyes and leaned back in the tub. This of course brought me to thoughts that have been racing through my dreams and conscious mind alike. I seriously couldn't see myself living a normal life anymore, but I knew I'd have too. How else was I going to live if I didn't have a real job? But the job I had studied all my life for didn't seem like it would last more than a week if I had a spirit encounter at work. I'd have to look elsewhere for a simple job I wouldn't care about losing. Of course if I ended up dying in one of these processes, there was no point anyways. But still, I couldn't live with my mom forever If I was going to keep this up.

Sighing out loud I sunk lower in the tub. This was a serious disaster. I still had tons of questions for Than though, I had let it pass before but he was definitely acting different around me. Don wasn't even in the picture anymore. Sure he was comfortable to be with and made me feel something but not like Than. Not that I wanted to start anything serious with Than, I told myself sternly. I felt so safe and protected with him but only when he opened himself up. I didn't even think he did it knowingly; he was too worked up for that, playing the arrogant asshole. But I knew there was more to him than he let on.

My eyes were closed when I thought I heard the door from the bedroom open and close silently with a click. *Oh, no.*

"'Azel?" Thumping footsteps made their way to the bed and I heard rustling like he was trying to find me in the sheets. I covered my mouth as a giggle slipped out. Really Than? In the sheets? I'm not that skinny.

"'Azel!?" Now he sounded worried, I didn't want him to see me naked though! Ugh, what a predicament I put myself in.

At that moment the bathroom door flew open, banging against the wall. The lights flicked on and I covered myself immediately with a small screech. "Close your eyes damnit!"

He of course ignored me. "What the fuck Jane!? How did you get in here? Are you insane? What if you'd fallen and cracked your thick head on the damned floor!" The last was shouted. Okay I guess I never thought of that scenario, but still. Was he seriously that worried? I sank a little lower in the water to get away from his anger.

He sighed out loud and ran a hand through his hair. Blowing out another breath as if to calm himself, he moved to sit on the edge of the tub. If possible I sunk lower and stared at the broad expanse of his back.

"Why didn't you answer when I called?" He said in a quiet voice seemingly trying to calm himself.

I lifted myself out of the water only enough to answer. "I was trying to think of a way to keep you out of here but still know I was alright."

He turned his head to look at me, his gaze never leaving my eyes before turning back to look straight ahead. "Are you ready to come out?"

"Yeah . . . but . . ."

He only got up to grab a towel and held it out in front of me. I tried to stand up while he closed his eyes but I seriously overestimated my own strength. Embarrassed I stayed in a sitting position with my arms wrapped around my legs to cover everything. I cleared my throat to get his attention. He dropped the towel, revealing his questioning gaze.

I looked away. "I can't get up." A small laugh left him before he walked out of the bathroom.

"Hey! You can't just leave me here!" I barely got the last word out before he was back with a huge smile on his face. I leaned back away from him, a bit wary of his intentions with that look on his face.

"What are you smiling about?"

"Oh nothing." With that he leaned down and picked me up, out of the water as if I weighed little to nothing. I almost uncrossed my arms to hold onto his neck but checked myself just in time to avoid giving him a full frontal show of my girls. God, how embarrassing! I was sure to be as red as a cherry when he placed me on the bed and wrapped me up with the towel he'd placed there.

I mumbled a thank you and grabbed the comforter he offered me to cover the rest of my body. Looking up at him I only saw the man in the middle of a forest, screaming to the heavens in anguished sorrow.

"What?" I didn't know what to say, so I shook my head and said nothing.

"Is Don still here?" I asked to fill up the awkward silence that'd taken place.

Looking annoyed he answered, "Probably."

"Can I see him?" Suspicion flashed in his eyes and my own eyes narrowed at what the reason would be to cause that look in his eyes.

"Why?"

"Do I need a reason?" I shot back.

He only growled and got up from the bed. He opened the door and Don was standing there as if knowing I had wanted to see him, weird.

A tense look was exchanged between the two imposing men in front of me. Almost as if they were warning each other about something. I gulped not sure I wanted to know the cause of those looks or the outcome if either one of them went against the others warning.

Than walked out and Don took the spot he'd just vacated. He placed a warm had on my stomach and gave me a comforting smile. "How are you legs?"

Shifting I really needed to dry off and I trusted Don way more than Than. "I'm doing better but can I ask a favor?"

He tilted his head with curiosity. "Sure, what's up?"

Feeling a small blush form I rushed out my request. "Can you help me dry off and change?" I removed the comforter to show him I was only in a seriously wet towel.

His smile turned into a frown. "Does he seriously have no brain? Why didn't he help you?"

"Honestly, I don't want to get into it." I felt awkward sharing my feelings with one man about another man.

He held up his hands. "Alright, far be it from me to pry. Let's get you out of that wet mess."

Not once did Don look below my neck as he helped me stand, dry off and help me into my clothes. I'd say that's rather miraculous if you ask me. I felt safe and I trusted him, knowing that he would never push me into an awkward position. Finally finished I asked if he would sit with me on the window seat and open the window to catch some fresh air.

I inhaled as he opened the windows and glorified in the smell of the nearby garden. Don picked me up and placed me in between his legs, allowing me to lean against his chest and he against the wall. Why couldn't I relax like this with Than, my heartbeat was always a mile a minute with him.

"What are you thinking?"

I snorted. "About impossibilities."

A soft chuckle sounded behind me and I snuggled deeper into his embrace as we watched the outside world go by. Closing my eyes I tried to bring up a list of the questions I'd been meaning to ask him as soon as I got the chance. That chance was now, whether it ruined this perfect moment or not.

"Don? How come I can't see your other form like Than?" I asked with my eyes still closed, tuning into his rhythmic heartbeat.

"Probably because he lost control of it." That was a test question; she'd wanted to know if he'd tell the truth since she'd already known the answer to that. More comfortable, she moved on to the tough questions.

"This God, Erebos . . . he's already sent one deadly demon after me to try and get me away from both of you. I think if it hadn't been for Than's stalker ways, I'd have been 'collected' as you'd told me before." I paused before asking the inevitable question. "Is it possible for me to have a normal life?"

It took a while before Don answered making me dread the answer even more. "If there is a way to stop Erebos, to discover whatever it is that he's using to collect spirits. There is a possibility you'd have a chance of normalcy." A chance, how much of a chance? One percent? I shook my head in defeat.

"I know it'll never happen, deep down I feel it. It's why everything has been going so wrong. Something is missing from this puzzle Don. I'm obviously not supposed to do this alone. Are there others I'm supposed to be working with? Some kind of society that takes my kind in and we work together and live together?" Don pulled me closer but somehow I still felt the cold seep down into my chilled bones.

"No, there is no society." I knew the answer but I was reaching for any ideas. I knew I was right, that something was missing. I wondered if they knew but couldn't or wouldn't tell me for both of their advantages. She wouldn't put it past them; they'd lied and deceived her from the start.

"Then how am I supposed to live a mortal life with immortal powers and talents? How did the ones before me do it?"

"They chose a side."

"Right, it's easier once you choose a side. That's right, I forgot that part. But how will it be easier? Will I be supported monetarily? I just don't see myself working at a law firm and battling spirits in the lobby Don." I glanced up at him sarcastically and watched a small smile form on his face. He truly was a magnificent creation, why was I attracted to the wrong man!? It was so frustrating.

"You just worry about getting better and continuing on your regular routine until you're ready to choose a side legs. Leave the shadow demons to me and Than and you handle the spirits." I sighed in defeat and closed my eyes. Listening to Don's heartbeat had me falling asleep again. I didn't fight it but instead did what he'd suggested. I'd sleep, get better and do my job. I knew that if I didn't, I might as well cut the thread that would end my life myself.

I left my eyes closed then asked one more question. "Hey Don?"

"Mhmm?"

"Why are both of your faces bruised up?"

CHAPTER 15

I was huffing and puffing trying to catch up to him. I knew he could outrun me in a heartbeat, hell he could shift and I wouldn't even know where he'd be. Behind me? Back in the house? Asia? Hell if I knew.

I was currently running through the forest that expanded after the garden. I know he'd come this way, or was it the right fork in the path he'd taken? Damnit, he had me all twisted! I stopped in the middle of nowhere and bent over to catch my breath.

Another week had passed by and I was back to my regular health as a 'pathetic mortal'. Than was back to being distant and an ass. He could never take back those nights where he'd taken care of me though. He'd given himself away and I'd use it against him one day to get what I wanted. Answers, the ones I knew would solve the missing pieces of this f'd up situation I'd found myself in.

A twig snapped to my right and I took off after the sound. I was so out of shape that my breathing was a sure dead give away to where I was. No wonder I couldn't catch up to him.

Now, you may be wondering why I was out here running around like a chicken without a head, chasing after this snooping piece of crap you'd call a man. Well, since I practically started living with the likes of him, I of course had to bring certain items with me to the house. One item in particular that is the cause of my adventure today.

Yes, that item. The one thing almost every girl on the planet has. Guessed it? Yup, he had my diary. The sonofabitch had found it this morning while I was eating breakfast. How he'd found it? I really have no idea. I'd hidden it in my jumbo box of Pearl tampons. What man goes into a box of tampons?! Well I definitely knew my sacred hiding place was no longer so secret. If he ever got to the end, I'd kill myself and end my misery myself.

"'I don't know how I feel about him, only that if I keep going on like this I'll drive myself mad.'" His silky voice mimicked a female voice to copy me as he read an entry out of my diary. I turned towards his voice, fuming that he was reading it as I chased him through this stupid maze of a forest. I took off in that direction before I heard him behind me reading a different entry entirely.

"'I just couldn't be with him anymore; I don't have the same feelings I used to when we were just friends and first starting out our relationship.'" He was getting to the end of my entries. That's it I'd kill him, then myself so that my secrets were never released ever again. I'd burn that stupid diary before anyone else found it first.

Silently I followed the ending of his voice. That was a pretty long entry he'd read and I finally saw him as I hid behind a large tree trunk. His stance was strong, back to me as he flipped through some of the pages to find another entry to taunt me with no doubt. I slapped myself mentally as I caught myself staring at his perfectly formed, muscled ass. I bit my lip almost giving myself away with a sigh. His deep laughter dragged me from my daze as he started reading a damning entry. I sprinted and lunged as he read.

"'Don seems nice enough, but it's Than- . . . . OOMPH!" I slammed into his back, effectively taking him down with my fury of force.

I ripped the book from his hands and jumped off of him. I started to run and rip at the same time, crumpling the entry he'd been reading and shoving it into my mouth to destroy with my spit. Disgusting? Yeah, well you'd do it too if your diary were about to be read by someone you had the hots for. I formed as much spit as possible but something slammed into me from behind causing me to spit the paper out of my mouth onto the ground just out of reach.

Male laughter greeted me from my back. "Give me that 'Azel!"

"NEVER! Over my DEAD body you fiend!" I struggled from beneath him, dragging him and myself to the paper inches from my fingers. It was amazing, the strength you received from sheer will. Just as I was going to grab it and rip it to tiny, itty bitty pieces, he snatched it and I deflated with defeat. My only hope now was that my spit had destroyed what was left of that entry. I dropped my face into the patch of grass I'd face planted into and waited for my demise.

"Aw 'Azel that's disgusting." Making a sound of disgust he must have thrown the paper wad because it landed back in front of me. I couldn't help my reaction after that. I laughed so hard and forcefully he must've been bouncing on top of me.

"What is so funny?" I laughed even harder. I'd done it! I beat Than, it felt so good! I had to rub it in his face.

Lifting my face from the floor I shouted out, "I WON! YOU OVERBEARING, PERVERT JOURNAL READER!" I continued to laugh like a maniac in his arrogant face. I'd saved face today; he'd never know what I thought of him or where my feelings led me. Hah! Take that!

I finally realized I couldn't stop laughing. Now I knew why, because he was death tickling me! It hurt so much; I had to make him stop!

I squealed out a peal of laughter and snorted a couple times, it was too much. "THAN, STOP!" I struggled and giggled, I even tried to drag myself away but it was no use.

"Give in! Surrender and I'll stop!" Damn him! He continued to tickle me relentlessly and without mercy.

"NE—" more giggling ensued before I took a breath, "NEVER!"

He intensified the tickling if that were even possible and I was completely out of breath. "Okay! Okay, I give, I give!"

He paused. "Say it!"

I growled but when he made for my sides again I flinched and immediately surrendered. "I surrender! You win!" He laughed in my face. But it wasn't over yet, he thought he'd won. Ha, we'd see who would have the last laugh. I steeled myself against his charms as I grabbed hold of his neck, forcing his mouth to my own.

I forced my way in, taking what I knew my body had been craving for the entire week Than had been ignoring me. At first he tensed and stilled, slowly pulling back out of my grip but I wasn't having any of it. I wrapped my legs around his waist, refusing to release him from my play in this game of ours. I'm sure he could've easily broken my hold but instead he only stroked his tongue against mines eagerly, finally giving in. A smile crossed my lips but I quickly smothered it against his lips.

He gripped my ass and lifted me up from the ground causing me to gasp in delight at how I seemingly weighed nothing to him. It was nothing like when Don picked me up. This was hard, this was aggressive even animalistic.

A hard surface pressed against my back and I realized he brought me up against a tree. A moan escaped me unbiddingly but he was so rough and so hot. I'd never been taken this roughly thinking it wasn't something I'd find sexy at all. Boy was I ever wrong.

I took a gulp to refortify myself on winning this match. He was not going to win! I undulated my hips against him throwing out a moan for extra measure. Or was that real?

I held onto his shoulders while he gave all his attention to my neck. Oh, God not my weak spot! I squeezed my eyes shut and threw my head back against the tree a couple times to have myself focus on the pain instead of the warmth spreading through my core. This man/demon or whatever was going to be the death of me!

He stilled, panting against my neck, his fingers slowly gripping my hips firmly. I winced slightly but forced myself to bring my head down to his neck and bit his ear. A low growl filled the air. "'Azel . . ."

"Hmm?" I continued to nibble on his ear and watched goose bumps run down his neck happily. That's when I also noticed his wings in full standing attention to his sides. My mouth formed an "O' in appreciation.

He ran his lips lightly against the spot he'd been kissing and slowly brought them to my own, forcing me away from his neck. My eyes locked with his and I was almost lost in the heat reflected back at me. I bit my lip and tried to hide in the crook of his neck but he removed one hand from my backside and forced me to look at him. *Shit, no I can't look at him and focus at the same time!*

Gazing into my eyes, he never broke contact as he stared for a good full minute breaking down my defenses. God but his hot stare was stripping me bare to look into my soul for answers.

Taking a deep breath of my scent he finally spoke. "What was the ending to that entry Jane?"

I could do nothing but stare back into his eyes with a hopeless expression on my face. I gulped down the truth as I would've done with that piece of paper to save my sanity and my heart. I slowly shook my head in his light grip on my chin. This game was over and I was done playing with my own feelings. Done with him playing my heart strings, even if he didn't know what he was doing.

I would never understand what I'd wanted in that moment I decided to kiss him, thinking I would be able to beat him at his own game. I tossed my head out of his grip and unwrapped my legs from his waist, forcing him to drop me to the ground. "I don't know what you're talking about." I turned and started walking away, giving him my back as he would've done to me not a month ago.

Had I completely lost my mind? A human and a demon? What was I saying? I didn't even KNOW what Than was. The more I thought about how much I didn't know, the more pissed off I became. That's when a strong hand gripped my arm.

"'Azel . . ."

"STOP calling me that!" I flung out as I whipped around fuming in his face. I brought my palms up and pushed him in the chest, completely ignoring his impeccable, bulging muscles. He didn't budge which only pissed me off further. I slammed my hands against him again with complete anger at my lack of knowledge about what the hell was going on in my own life.

"Stop Jane." So calmly he spoke, so unemotional. Ha! The only time he showed emotion was when I was dying. And why? Probably because if I didn't choose his side, he'd probably be punished or something totally selfish on his part.

"No! I won't stop! You tell me what I want to know right now, or so help me God I will kill myself first before I choose anyone's side!"

He seemed to take in my words and discard them. "You're lying."

"You don't know me! How dare you presume to tell me what I will or will not do to save myself? Better the devil you know . . . ." I was panting with my exertion of energy put towards my emotions. But really, this was ridiculous, it's been a little over a month and I still didn't know what the hell was going on.

He only crossed his arms over his chest and looked as if he were irritated. "Jane, enough. You're not going to kill yourself anymore than I would dress up as the Easter bunny on Halloween."

I ignored him, he was only trying to distract me. Funny how I was starting to pick up on all his little tells. "What are you Than?"

"You know the answer to that." He answered in a monotone voice, his poker voice. That voice I hated. It was the one he used when he was calling me an idiot but in reality he knew I knew something was wrong, that he was lying to me.

I shook my head and asked again, louder. "What are you Than?"

"I told you—"

"STOP lying to me! I know what you aren't and I don't know what you are. You are a demon but I want to know your title. Don is the Angel of Death. What ARE you?" He tried to get near me but I backed away swiftly, if he touched me it would only be to distract me from my purpose and no other reason.

I stood with my feet apart, hands folded across my chest with stubbornness. "Tell me what you are, or I choose Don's side." This was my ultimatum, this would decide everything from here on out. If he couldn't answer me this simple question, then I knew I was choosing the right side.

Than's arms dropped to his sides, fists clenching and unclenching in frustration no doubt. He seemed to be grinding his molars and cursing in every language he knew under his breath. Dragging a hand through his already mussed hair, he stared me down in finality. "You want to know what I am Jane? Who I am?"

His tone was so cold, so deadly I almost shook my head. I had to know though, otherwise this was all a lie. All the feelings he ever made me feel were used to manipulate me to do what he wanted me to do. Which ways he wanted me to swerve, duck and hop. I was not his puppet, I would not be his plaything. I nodded in affirmative to finally have my answer.

He looked into my eyes and stalked me until my back once again met the trunk of a tree. His breath was hot as he leaned down and whispered in my ear. "I'm Death's son." He leaned back and waited for my reaction.

I scrunched my eyebrows in confusion. "Death's son? Is that possible?" He only arched a brow as if I was dumb enough to ask since he was standing right there.

"Does that even mean you're a demon?"

The look of slight surprise on his face let me know that he wasn't expecting Ms. Inquisitive after that load off. "That's your biggest worry?"

I looked at him with confusion. "Just answer the question."

He sighed in frustration and glanced around. "This is not the place to do this." Reaching over before I could react, he grabbed my arm and shifted us to a beach boardwalk that contained a small carnival. Never releasing my arm, he dragged me to a bench close to the end of the walk, staring out into the endless horizon.

I dropped down next to him and felt the chill with the sea breeze and night air. I ignored that for now and got back to the question. "Well?' He flicked a look at me and refocused on the water ahead.

"Since there is no other term for Death, I believe a demon is the best word I can use to describe us."

That was as confusing as ever. "So, yes?"

"Sure why not." Irritating man.

"Why didn't you tell me?"

He looked at me as if I were nuts. "When should I have told you Jane? When we first met? Hi, I'm Death's son, can I tag along with you for awhile? Or no, I know, how about when we were making out? Hmm? Oh, just so you know, I'm Death's son and condoms don't work against me, so be prepared to make a demon baby. Yeah, I don't see any of those times coming up as a good intervention moment 'Azel."

I stood up in anger. "Okay don't be such a smart ass! There are plenty of ways you could have mentioned it. Like when I was first interrogating you? Or after the encounter with Don at the mall when I realized I could sense demons?"

"I couldn't tell you because of the no interference rule that is of course no longer in effect and the second case I didn't think it important."

I pointed at him in accusation. "Ah! See! Right there, you could have told me but thought it in YOUR best interests to keep it from me."

He stood up now, his head heating up as much as mine was. "No! I kept it from you to protect you!"

I scoffed in his face. "Protect me from what!? Knowing who I was trusting?"

He grabbed my shoulders and shook me once. "No you idiot! I was protecting you from ME!" After his confession he practically deflated, seeming to realize what he'd said.

Now I was really confused. He was hanging his head but kept contact with my shoulders. I placed my hands against his cheeks to bring him up to look at me. "Protect me from you?" He nodded once.

Taking a deep breath he was about to speak but I didn't get to hear him. My own pulse started to pound erratically when I noticed the burning in my fingers. Than must have notice something had changed because he'd started shaking me and I finally refocused on him.

"Jane? What's wrong, your face is as pale as death." He started glancing around but that was the thing, no one was by us. The only people nearby were at least yards away from us. How was I picking up such a strong demon vibe now?

"I'm sensing a demon Than. How can that be?" I'd inadvertently moved closer to him, using his body as a shield. That's when I notice the couple, the ones I had said were yards away. They had moved closer but didn't seem to be paying us any mind. I brushed it off and turned to Than. He wrapped his arms around me and moved me behind him. I peeked out from one side to see what he was hiding me from.

I was now staring into burning green emeralds for eyes on a very familiar face and a black tar colored set on the man next to her. The couple I had thought to be just that, wasn't that at all. I felt Than tense in front of me. Why didn't he just shift us out of here?

"Ah, Thanatosss, ssso nice to ssee you again." The woman spoke with an exaggeration on her S's as if she were a snake.

"I can't say the same for you bitch."

The man spoke next and I cringed away from his voice. "Tsk tsk, Thanatos, I thought we were friends." It was the voice of a child molester, a rapist. It was the sound of a calm psycho, 'I'm going to kill you slowly but if you beg me I might go a little faster' voice. It was a sound that put fear in my heart.

"Consider yourself unfriended." Than responded in a snarky tone.

My fingers were burning like crazy! I really just wanted them to stop; I clenched them to quell the feeling. It didn't do much but it'd have to do for now. Who were these nut jobs anyways? Well at least the man. I had an idea of who the woman was.

"Charming Thanatos, but ah, where are your manners, hmm?" He directed his gaze to me. "Mademoiselle, I am Fear and this striking woman beside me is Jealousy, although I do believe you were informally introduced a week ago no?"

They were the one's Erebos had sent after her? I tugged on Than's shirt, trying to tell him to shift.

He didn't spare me a glance but answered all the same. "I can't."

What he'd said earlier about their powers not being at maximum registered in my head. Shit, now what?

"Give the girl to usss, and we'll leave you be." Jealousy stated simply.

"Touch her, and I'll rip your head off you slimy insect of a demon." Than's growl was so low it was almost impossible to understand him.

"I think not mon ami. We will be taking her and leaving you in pieces." With that Fear lunged to one side, Jealousy to the other dissecting Than's attention.

"Jane, down!" I didn't hesitate but crouched into a ball. A whoosh of air knocked me on my side and a screech sounded to my left. I'm guessing the bitch got hit. Brushing my hair out of my face, I looked up to see what was going on. At first I didn't see anything. But then I realized they were so fast I couldn't really follow their movements at all. A fist thrown here and a tackle down to the ground there. I didn't know what to do but stay frozen on the ground, afraid if I ran for it, it would either distract Than or I'd just get in the way and end up dead from one of their deadly blows.

Just then a shadow came from my right making me flinch into movement. I raised one leg and kicked with all the strength I could muster, I succeeded in knocking her in the face, stunning her long enough to run in the opposite direction. I stumbled but thankfully caught myself before I could fall, putting me in the exact same position as before.

About ten steps into my run I heard the rendering of skin. Flinching at the sound, I slowed down and turned around. On his knees, one hand supporting the rest of his body while the other held onto his stomach, Than was in full demon form. He was beautiful, I couldn't think of him being anything other than magnificent. Weird? Maybe, but all the same I couldn't take my eyes away from him. Or the fact that he was bleeding profusely all over the boardwalk. His wings were drooped on either side of his body and he looked up as the demon Fear made a final attempt at ending his life.

Before I even knew what had happened, I had moved from where I was standing to being in-between Fear and

Than. As if watching myself in an out of body experience, I watched as I blocked Fear's blow, knocking it out of the way as if he were nothing more than a pestering fly. Using my other hand I gripped his throat, picked him up and threw him to the ground. Gripping harder, I leaned in close and saw his own Fear in his eyes. His fear was of me. As if I knew what to do all along, I brought my other hand and placed my fingertips over his pulsing demon heart, where the soul was kept. *How did I know that?* Closing my eyes I concentrated and found my grip on his soul, when I opened my eyes a scream pierced the night and there was nothing under me anymore. The only remnant of Fear was my black, glowing left palm that no longer burned with the need to collect a demon soul.

I moved my gaze to Jealousy, not standing too far away. Scowling, she turned to an inky shadow and disappeared through the cracks of the walkway. Turning around to kneel next to Than I scanned his injuries. They were terrible if not completely deadly. His entire torso had been ripped apart as if a giant clawed hand had slashed at him. I could see his insides for crying out loud!

"Than?" I pushed him lightly onto his back, hoping to keep the blood in him for a while more before help came. I couldn't call anyone for help, they'd freak out the moment they saw him. His demon skin was matte black that extended to his wings. He had claws extending from his fingertips and fangs. Other than that he was pretty normal, nothing to be that alarmed about. Oh, well and he was at least three times bigger than normal. That'd be hard to explain to cops or the ambulance.

I wiped my face, feeling something running down my cheeks. My hand came away wet. I was crying? No, I wouldn't think like that, Than couldn't die. I placed my hands on both sides of his cheeks, praying that he'd open his eyes. The blood was just everywhere, overpowering my senses. I scrunched my nose at the smell but only continued to try and wake him up. "Than, please wake up, please?!" I shook him a little but no change came over his features. Damnit! I couldn't move him on my own. That's when I thought, duh, Don! Sobbing now, I reached for my phone and couldn't find the damned thing. Ugh! It was at the house!

I frantically searched the ripped pieces of Than's pants searching for his phone. Why would he have Don's number though? They were enemies, it didn't seem likely that he'd have it but I had to try.

Eureka! I pulled it out and searched the phone book for his number. Unsurprisingly there weren't many numbers and she didn't see a Don anywhere. Then she came across a most interesting name that sounded just like something Than would do. She selected the name 'Jerkoff' and waited for someone to answer.

After three rings she got a growled reply, "What do you want dickwad?"

Ignoring him she quickly answered, "Don? Oh God, Don it's me. Something's happened. I need help and I don't know where Than brought me . . . I-I . . . Oh, Jesus Don quick he's dying!"

"Jane, don't move a muscle I'll be right there. Don't move an inch!" The line went dead.

She tossed the phone aside and crawled to Than, placing his head in her lap. Brushing his hair back she leaned in and kissed his forehead. He couldn't die, not because of her. Not another person she loved. She cried harder at the realization of what she just thought. She loved the idiot! After everything they'd fought about, everything he kept from her, lied to her about she still couldn't help the fact that she still loved him for all his faults.

"Don't you fucking die on me Than!" She screamed out in frustration at having realized too late that she could have lost everything at the cost of her questions. What did it matter if he was protecting her? Why did it matter what or who he was? She didn't even know who she was! Who was she to judge anyone else?

Footsteps sounded behind her. Coming too fast for her piece of mind. It had been at least ten minutes from when she'd spoken with Don. She'd lost half her mind rocking Than back and forth with no response from him at all. Her nerves were fried. The person grabbed her arms none too gently to remove her from Than. She finally lost it. She kicked, clawed, even threw some punches at those who would try to take her from him. She screamed death threats in a voice she'd never guess as her own until someone finally knocked her out.

CHAPTER 16

I dreamed of blood. On the walls, dripping from my fingertips, falling from my hair. It wasn't my blood but someone else's. Who's though? I looked around and saw nothing but darkness . . . and the blood.

Come to me.

I jerked around at the voice that called to me. Chills ran down my back at the sound. Deep, deceivingly calm, calling me to him. I didn't recognize the voice, only that it wasn't one I would follow, ever.

"Who are you? What do you want?"

The voice laughed a slow, deceptive laugh. I waited but the voice said no more. I felt as if I should know it somehow. I moved from the pool of blood, causing red, inky footsteps to trail behind me. "Come out! Who are you?!" Only silence met my ears as I walked aimlessly in no direction at all.

The sound of grunts and fists connecting with flesh brought me around to my left. Out of nowhere, there stood three demons and Than in a heated battle. More blood flew, including bodies when Than sent them flying away from him in different directions.

I tried to call out to him but my voice was useless. So I started to run towards him, only to find that my feet were stuck!

What the hell? I pulled and pulled but it was no use. I was forced to watch as one then two of the three demons got hold of Than's wings to hold him down before taking very thick blades from harness's on their bodies and plunging both daggers into his wings, pinning him to the ground.

I screamed a silent scream and tried to release myself from this invisible hold on my body while Than roared from the pain. I couldn't take my eyes away from him. I watched hopelessly as the third demon drew a sword from his back harness, flashing it's deadly sharp blade before Than's eyes.

I struggled futilely once again and tore the flesh in my throat when the final scream released from my lips as the demon swung the blade down on Than's neck.

—ɱ—

I screamed myself awake and thick arms were there to catch me. Only remembering being on the boardwalk, I fought and pushed away from my attacker. I had to get to Than, he was dying! Where the hell was Don?

"'Azel! Shh, shh. Calm down, I got you its okay!"

Than? I stopped my struggles and turned to face him, not believing my ears. Sure enough I met his endless black eyes that I'd lost myself in more than once. I couldn't believe it, that dream had felt so real! And on the walk? What had happened? I'd been sure that he was dead before . . . who had taken her away from him? All my heart knew was that I was so happy he was not a corpse right now because of me. Because he had been protecting ME. I finally broke down and started sobbing in his arms.

He tightened his hold around me becoming the Than that'd taken care of me while I was lying in bed almost dead myself. He rubbed small circles on my back and massaged my neck with his other hand trying to soothe me. My crying faded into small hiccups and I'd realized I'd just cried almost the hardest in my life in the chest of a man I now knew I loved. The man I had killed for to protect, the man I'd kissed while dying in my arms. How had this happened? I attempted to think back to when it came to be.

Was it when he'd pushed me into the fountain? Or when he'd first shown that he'd cared? I didn't know when but I knew it wasn't a faulty decision on my part. I felt in my soul. It had only taken his dying form to knock some sense into me. But would I tell him? Not until I knew what he felt about me. He had pulled back after I'd become better after the accident. On purpose? Probably, but why? Again, she was looking at empty spaces that could only be filled by Than.

I'd finally calmed down enough to lay silently wrapped in his arms, simply inhaling that scent I loved so much. There were still things I needed to ask but I was so tired. Also, where had all the spirits been lately? It's now been two weeks since the boy and now my hands were full of demons instead.

My hands . . . that reminded me of what I'd done to Fear. Actually, what HAD I done? I sniffed and lifted my face away from Than's chest to see if he knew anything about what I'd done to him. I hadn't even been ME when it'd happened.

"Than?" My voice was so small, made hoarse by all the screaming I'd been doing lately.

"Mm?" He wrapped me up tighter as if I'd disappear. Hiding a smile I continued.

"When you were on the walk and I came to interfere? Something happened."

He finally looked down at me. Just by looking at him I knew he knew. He knew and had seen what I'd done. "What did I do?"

He shifted to lying on his back, pulling me flush to his side. I didn't care anymore; I wrapped my left arm around his waist and placed my head on his shoulder. "You collected Fears demon soul." He rubbed my arm in comfort while I absorbed the news of my newfound powers. I guess seeing Than dying had finally triggered those strong emotions Don had been talking about.

"Where does it go? The souls I mean." I didn't like the sound of this.

He sighed heavily. "In theory, the soul becomes a part of you. This means you'll have to learn how to control them eventually. The more souls you take in, the more difficult it will become, especially demon souls. They may even overpower you and control you instead. Damnit, everything's going to hell in a hand basket." By the end, he was already talking to himself as if trying to figure out a way to get Fear out of my body.

I pushed off his chest and turned to face him, sitting cross legged. "Well it's simple; I'll just not do that anymore." I waved my hand in the air, dismissing it as if I could just cease to use my powers and go on happily with my life.

Than closed his eyes and remained quiet for awhile. I perused his handsome face, strong jaw and sharp cheek bones. Silky hair I could run my hands through all day and night. I closed my own eyes and hung my head in my hands, massaging my temples in concentration.

Don had said my powers were to help me empower and protect myself. I would have to use them, that's what Than wasn't saying in his silence. Okay, then another burden had been placed upon me, to control this power and make it work for me and not against me. Great.

Erebus

"What do you mean, she got away?" Erebos sneered in Jealousy's face.

She took a step back and with good reason. This time, there was no getting away, he had a hold on her powers and waited impatiently for a recap on what had happened to his other demon.

"It's just as I said sir. The girl has come into her powers and destroyed Fear with her bare hands. It was nothing I have ever seen before."

He stared back into her eyes with hate and anger, but most of all violence. But by all that was unholy he would restrain himself until he received every detail from her. "Continue, what exactly did she do?"

Gulping, she explained how the mortal had changed before her eyes, interfering in the fight between Fear and Thanatos. Swatting his hand out of the air as if an annoying bug and throwing him down to the floor. Then as she proceeded to suck the soul from his very body.

He came to stand before her, so close she tried to take another step back but he grabbed her by the throat squeezing ever so gently in warning. "She 'collected' a soul? A *demon* soul?" Having her air supply cut she could only nod.

How was this possible? Not even he, Erebos, a primordial God of shadows and all that went bump in the night could collect a demon soul. Who was this mortal? She was more important for his collection than just any *descendion*. Turning back to his demon minion he flung her from his grasp.

"Do whatever you have to; I don't care how you do it. Bring that mortal to me or die a painful death." Rubbing her neck she disappeared and he moved to Charon's Orb. Two of his most trusted demons left, he thought as he stared at the souls gently moving in the orb. He didn't want to have to fetch the mortal himself. Technically, primordial God's weren't able to travel between dimensions. However, there was a certain God in debt to him if the need should ever arise where he needed to do this himself.

Scowling at this snag in his plans, he moved to sit on his throne of souls and spirits to plan ahead of the impending failure of Jealousy and Sorrow.

—∞—

"Are you ever coming home or are you living with this person now?" My mom was impatient and irritated at my absence of late at home.

"I can come home if you want me to Mom." I looked over at Than who'd begun to shake his head. I turned around ignoring him.

"Well then get your butt home tonight. Also, what's going on with your job?"

Crap. "They understand my absence and small setback, I'm still a go there mom, don't worry. I've let them know that I'm coming in next Monday." What a lie that was. Here I was in Than's living room, lying to my mother yet again. I never called them since Than had left a message for them after the accident. The one my mother still had no idea about. I bit my lip and flopped down onto the couch in exhaustion.

Earlier we had ended the conversation on me controlling my powers and came down at my rumbling stomach's request. I'd decided to talk to my mom since I hadn't in a long while.

"Alright well get your butt in gear Jane. Remember you have bills to pay that I'm not forking the money over for anymore."

"Alright, I got it. Also, mom what's for dinner?"

She sighed as if this was not important at the moment. "Steak, why?"

"Would you mind if I brought Than over for you to meet at dinner?" I asked hesitantly. Than immediately appeared next to me looking horrified. He started shaking his head comically. A small smile broke over my face as I remembered how he'd described my mother as a detective harpy. His face was priceless, probably the most human I've seen it since meeting him.

"Whatever, just get home."

"Thanks mom, be home soon. I love you." I said the last as an afterthought. There were too many close calls these days. I wanted her to know that I loved her and always would.

A pause held on her side before she answered me in kind. "Love you too. See you later."

"Okay, bye."

"Bye." *Click.*

"Are you insane? I am NOT sitting at a dinner table with your harpy of a mother." I tossed the phone onto the coffee table and closed my eyes. I sighed at his claim.

"Yes you are because I'm not going to lie to my mother more than I have too. You got us into this dating mess so you help be a part of it." Why should I have to carry all the weight of HIS lie?

"Fine, I'll go on one condition." I snorted, I don't think so.

"No, you don't get conditions."

"Fine, enjoy your miserable dinner, answering all her questions with lies." I heard a shrug in his voice.

I growled in frustration. "Argh! You're so selfish!" I glanced at my watch; it was already four in the afternoon. If I were going to make it there for dinner I had to leave soon. I knew what he was going to ask and I was so not dying to answer him. It would mean opening up my heart to him, basically holding it out for him to safe keep. I trusted him to protect me, my body, even if for his own purposes. I didn't know him enough to keep my heart safe too.

All of a sudden I was being lifted into the air and placed in his lap. "What the he-?"

He held up a finger. "Shh." His face went sober with seriousness. I could almost see into his soul as if he was trying to be open with me.

I shifted my weight and leaned my head against his shoulder, keeping my hands in my lap. I waited for him to continue.

"Jane, why would you put yourself between me and a final blow that way? You could've died again! I wouldn't have been able to save you by how injured I was. Why'd you do it?"

There it was, that big elephant in the room. What we had both refused to acknowledge as soon as I'd woken up. I started drawing random patterns on his shirt, feeling his ribbed abs underneath his shirt. I shrugged in response and he continued.

"Don told me they had to knock you out because of how out of control you were." He paused making me nervous. "You were speaking in a demonic language Jane." I pulled back surprisingly and looked at him in shock.

"I was?" I don't remember speaking at all, just screaming at anyone who had tried to take me away from him at the time. He nodded in answer.

"Apparently you were cursing them for taking you away from me, that I was dying and to save me. To take you back to me." He had been looking at the far wall lost in memory but finally looked back at me, coming back from whatever he was seeing in his mind.

My mouth opened a couple of times like a fish gasping for air. My heart pounded in my chest at the emotions churning around in there like butterflies trying their damnedest to get out. That's when I started to hyperventilate and felt a phrase vomit coming up. *Oh, no.*

"Jane? Jane! Are you okay? Look at me." I had been flicking my gaze around the room looking for an out. He shook me and I found myself straddling his hips in his attempt to get me to look at him. I couldn't breathe; I couldn't keep it in anymore!

Staring straight into his eyes it came out as a shout. "I love you!" I widened my eyes as I stared in shock for his reaction. I slapped both of my hands over my mouth. *Oh, God, kill me now!*

His grasp on my biceps loosened somewhat. The look of shock on his face would have been comical if it weren't for my own embarrassing situation being a part of this.

"What?" Barely a whisper but I heard him.

I shook my head helplessly and dropped my hands into my lap. There it was, his to destroy or do with as he would. God, how could I have been so stupid?! Why couldn't I keep my mouth shut?

He tilted my head up but I pulled my head away and looked somewhere off to my right. "Go ahead; laugh at the weak little human who fell in love with Death's son."

I sneered out pathetically. There was no reason why he shouldn't. Who was she to think that someone like Than would ever love her in return?

"Jane look at me." Softly spoken but I refused to be fooled. As soon as I looked at him he'd throw it back in my face, I just knew it. I continued to stare off to the side of the living room. A sigh sounded in front of me.

"You silly mortal." Before I knew what'd happened we were shifting to a whole new room I'd never been in before. This room was a neutral color and a great deal larger than his own room. Two windows graced the far wall with window seats on both. The windows faced the garden and the forest beyond whereas Than's room faced the front of the house.

I held onto Than's neck, my legs still wrapped around his waist and looked to my right where a door led to a bathroom no doubt. From here I could see the marble and bright lights that seemed to go on forever. A double set of doors to the left of the bathroom looked as if a closet lay beyond. I finally looked at Than for his reasoning on bringing me here.

"This is your room now." Wait what? My confusion must have shown on my face but he only chuckled and brought me to the bed to set me down.

Gripping the comforter, I looked back up at him. "I don't understand." I eyed him suspiciously, noticing something had changed in his demeanor. I wasn't sure if he was going to laugh out loud or was waiting for me to ask him why he had a foolish grin playing on his lips.

He finally decided on a exhausted sigh. "Of course you don't Jane." He placed his hands on his hips and stared at me in . . . fondness? Ookay, I was officially freaked out. Pulling my feet up, I attempted to scramble back from him. I wasn't quick enough and he grabbed onto an ankle before placing another hand next to me putting his body over me, effectively caging me in.

"Ah ah, where exactly do you think your going?" His smile was wickedly gorgeous, sending a warm shiver down my spine and setting off sparks in my core. I was so nervous before this Than, I wet my lips, immediately drawing his attention there.

Releasing my ankle he placed his other hand next to me and leaned in slowly, giving me the chance to pull away. I only stared back at him in disbelief at his reaction to my declaration of love, waiting for him to make his move. Or as I had expected, for him to pull back. He didn't though, finally taking my lips on a soft caress.

It was so affectionate I moaned instantly. He gripped my thigh, pulling it up to wrap around his waist. I didn't hesitate and wrapped my other around his other hip, putting him flush against me. I bit back another moan as he lifted me and carried us to the middle of the bed before sinking into me and the bed.

Was this real? Or was he just playing me and going to pull away any minute? He stopped kissing me, staring at me in annoyance. "Can you stop?"

I was confused again. "Stop what?" Bending his head he nibbled a path from my collar bone to my ear. I squirmed and wiggled a little away from him.

"Stop thinking." I smiled as he took my mouth again, he bit my lower lip demanding entrance but I denied him.

"Make me." I looked at him with a challenge in my eyes. His glinted with mischief causing another fire to burn in my stomach.

Rising up, he grabbed the hem of my shirt and tore it up in half before I could say anything. I gasped in mock outrage. "You are so buying me a new shirt!"

His cocky smile made me blush. "Why? They're all just going to end up like that one." He nodded to the shredded piece of shirt now on the side of the bed.

I laughed as I lifted myself up and pulled at his shirt. "Why am I the only one who has to be naked?" I pouted for effect but he only dusted my hands away.

"First of all, your not even half naked. Secondly, because I'm only focusing on you right now." Replacing his weight off to the side of me, he lightly brushed his fingertips across my chest, causing my skin to break out in goosebumps. I never broke my eye contact, making things even hotter.

He smirked and I noticed his fang poking out before he leaned in to my chest and bit through the middle part of my bra. I watched them fall apart in heated amusement. As he licked a path from the middle of my chest to pay greedy attention to my nipple.

Gasping, I arched into his mouth. I ran my fingers through his hair, holding on as he sucked, licked and moved on to the other side. I made small moans of pleasure when he used his right hand to pinch, pull and play with the nipple not occupying his mouth. I ground myself into his pelvis asking for more. I wanted *more*.

Seeming to know what I wanted, Than removed himself and undid my shorts pulling them down my legs, following the path with kisses. With a bite on the inside of my ankle he dropped my shorts off the side of the bed. He stared down at me with all the hunger a wolf possessed when staring at his prey.

Lowering himself back down to me he grabbed my thighs, placing light kisses and some bite marks all the way up until he met my core. I held my breath as he met my eyes and dove in without preamble.

"Oh my . . . Than . . ." I sighed his name as if it were a prayer. Thanking the lord for creating such a fine example of the male species. I watched the muscles bunch and played with his shoulders while he used his tongue to plunge and lick, making me feel unspeakable things. He sucked on my nub until I screamed his name. I was so close to release, I didn't know I could ever come this fast. Ususally I had to work a little harder just to make sure I beat out the guys. Figured Than would be the one to surpass all of them.

A thick finger found it's way into my core and he added that friction with his tongue causing my hips to lift off the bed making him delve deeper. "Than! I'm going to . . . to . . ." I screamed, gripping the sheets as an orgasm like never before broke over my body, causing me to shudder and my walls to spasm around his finger. He was an animal! Oh my God, he'd ruined me for anyone else now if he ever left me.

Still in between my legs, Than licked up any remaining juices and finally pulled up to lay on me. He wasn't heavy, his weight was comfortable and I was so relaxed that I couldn't care less. I watched him rub his chin off on his shoulder before leaning down to place a kiss on my lips.

I smiled thinking about what had happened and what the subject was before this. I pulled his head down onto my chest and ran my fingers playfully through his hair, causing him to relax and lay a bit more heavily on me. I can't believe this happened. I was seriously in awe but I pushed it aside thinking his clever way of trying to distract me.

"Than?" I murmured with my eyes closed.

"Hmm?" His breathing was even and his whole body was relaxed. I smirked, thinking about how I was about to ruin his peave.

"You're still coming with me to dinner."

Groaning he lifted his head to look at me. "I am NOT spending an hour or more with that tyrant you call mother."

I tried to sit up, leaning over to look at the clock. Giving a groan of my own we were going to be late if I didn't move now. I shoved him off me, already missing the heat his huge body provided. "C'mon, it'll be fine. Besides, I'll protect you." I gave him a cheeky smile and danced out of his grasp before he could grab me. Laughing, I made my way to the closet where the sneaky devil had all the clothes I'd brought over hung on the bars.

I was wiggling into skinny jeans when I felt him behind me. Still trying to pull up my pants I gave him an arched stare. "Yes? Can I help you?"

He stalked towards me with hunger in his eyes and I held up my hands trying to ward him off, waddling back away from him. My back came up against a dresser in the closet causing me to stop and look up at him towering over me. I've never seen a more intense stare before, as if he was drinking in every feature of my face. Leaning in close, he brushed his lips past my lips, onto my cheek and to my ear. Goosebumps broke out all over my body and my hands landed on his chest, clenching his shirt in my grip.

He grabbed my pants, playing his fingers lightly on the flesh of my hips. I shivered and bit my lip, closing my eyes at the sensations he made me feel. He grabbed the top of my pants and yanked them up the rest of the way. He pulled away with a smile and kissed me. "Let's go."

CHAPTER 17

"So what do you do Than?" My mother's demeanor had relaxed somewhat now that I was finally home. She was feeding our dog who was currently bouncing up and down against her thigh, begging mercilessly for food. I scowled at him in disapproval, continuing to chew my food.

"I'm sort of a broker between companies." Chewing, he paused seeming to think of a lie. At least, I knew it was a lie. "I work for a company called Scythe Industries. My father owns it."

Looking down at my dog my mom commanded him to sit before looking back to Than. "Is that your last name? Scythe?" Than nodded in response. I looked at him curiously, was it a lie? If it wasn't I'd laugh, really? They couldn't think of a more ironic last name for death?

"Where did you two meet? If I recall, Jane said she'd met you not even a month ago." She cut another piece of her steak while I gripped my fork and looked up to answer her but Than beat me to it.

"Well I'd happened to be at the in-store Starbucks while Jane had been standing in line." He looked at me with mischief before turning to look at my mom. "She'd dropped her keys and didn't even hear them, so I returned them to her but only if she would have coffee with me." It was too bad our dinner table was glass, otherwise I'd have kicked him in the shins for putting me in another lie.

My mother shook her head. "Well that's her, always forgetting one thing or another. You really should be more careful." I glared at him. She looked at me and asked if I were staying home tonight. I strove not to look at Than when I answered her. "Yeah, sure."

Although I was dying to stay with Than, I needed to take a step back and take a normal life break. Now that I've told him how I felt and was effectively left hanging since he hadn't said it back, I needed time to think. I mean of course he wasn't going to say it back, maybe not at all. I was crushed at the thought of another oncoming heartbreak. I always saw things that weren't there! I got up, already frustrated with the situation I'd put myself in.

I cleaned up and washed the dishes while Than stood next to me and dried them. "You don't need to do that you know. That's what the rack is for." I didn't look at him but just continued to wash. All he did was grunt in acknowledgment to my words.

Finally done I decided to say goodbye. "Mom, I'm going to walk him out, I'll be back."

"Alright. Than it was truly nice meeting you!" My mom called from the couch.

We walked out down the pathway to my gate and when we got there I didn't know what to say. I kicked a rock out of the way, drawing out the silence. "Thanks for coming," I started awkwardly.

He snorted. "You better be thankful." I couldn't help the smile forming on my lips. Always an ass no matter what. The difference now was that I knew a different part of him. Maybe not all of him, but the cracks were sure starting to show.

"Will you be alright?" He asked with worry in his voice. You see? Crack.

I finally looked up at him. "I really can't say Than. Things just seem to be popping up to destroy me where ever I go." I said it as a joke but the seriousness was there under my light tone. Than only scowled at me.

"Not exactly what I wanted to hear if you expect me to let you stay here alone." I'd had the thought also. What if they showed up at the house? What if they came after my family? Maybe this wasn't such a brilliant idea.

"What are you thinking about?" He moved in front of me. I could feel his intense heat, making my toes curl. I wanted nothing more than to go back to his place and dive back into my new bed. Preferably with his warm embrace around me. I shook myself out of my daydream.

I looked up at him, worrying my bottom lip and looked away thinking.

"Do you need Don here?" He growled out Don's name. I looked at him in confusion. Why would I want him here? What was he going to do, stand outside all night? I knew he probably would for my safety. But what if it wasn't enough? What if they appeared inside somehow without Don knowing? I shook my head.

Sighing I crossed my arms over my chest. "No, really it'll be fine. I'll be fine." I said it more to myself than anyone else to convince myself I didn't need these guys around all the time.

Nodding he stepped closer bringing my gaze up to his towering form. He leaned down and tipped my chin up. "Be careful." It was more of a warning than anything else. He kissed me, hard. I leaned into him, kissing him back and enjoying the warmth I was sure to miss while I was on my own. Pulling back, he locked eyes with me for a second before turning away. I don't know what he'd been trying to tell me but it was too late as he got into his sleek Lamborghini and peeled off down the street.

Touching my lips, I turned away and went back inside.

Next Afternoon . . .

"Hey sis! What's up? Long time no talk, I'm in serious need of girl time." I hadn't had a smile like the one I was flaunting now since forever. My best girlfriend in the world Mysti, had called me up for some friendly chitchat and catch up. She wasn't really my sister, that's just how close we were.

"Well I was thinking we should do a photo shoot. C'mon you know you want to. It's the perfect time for us to catch up." I laughed at her rushed out and hopeful words. Mysti was an amazing photographer. Her phases doing it came and went but anytime she picked up a camera, it was magic.

"You know what, yeah let's go get some sister downtime. Then I can tell you all about the new hunk I've been hanging around with." I waited for it and sure enough she responded in her sly way.

"Ooh realeh? Alright well I'll grab my stuff and be at your house in ten, be ready sweetness."

"Yeah, yeah I will be." I laughed out in response.

I hung up the phone before my mom came in from outside, our dog rushing ahead of her to rub himself all over the couch. Ew.

"Who was that?" She asked, out of breath from her exertions from working on her garden in the backyard.

Still smiling I turned to answer her. "That was Mysti, we're going out to do a photo shoot. She's picking me up in ten."

A genuine smile appeared on her lips. “That’s nice, you haven’t been out with your friends in a while.”

I shrugged, heading to my room to change. “You know that I couldn’t really, since I’m tight on money mom. But for her, I’ll sacrifice.”

She laughed. “Alright, well be careful and what about lunch?”

I paused, damn I didn’t have anything. “I guess I’ll pick something up on our way to where ever she’s kidnapping me to.”

“Okay.”

I rolled my eyes as I had forgotten to ask Mysti what the heck she had wanted me to be wearing. Grabbing my phone, I sent her a quick text. My phone beeped seconds after.

Doesn’t matter, I’m going to make you change anyways. ;)

Shaking my head, I sent my response. **You’re always trying to get me naked. ;)**

lol grr baby

I laughed out loud and moved to my closet to throw on a loose white cropped top and then to my drawers for some shorts. It was nice and sunny out with some clouds. No wonder she was in a tizzy.

Five minutes later I was out the door planting a kiss on my mom’s cheek in the garden, finally making my way up front to my gate. I swung it closed just as a car honking behind me made me turn around.

Mysti leaned her head out the window with her signature sunglasses on and trucker hat. “Hello gorgeous. Wanna go for a ride?”

I rolled my eyes at her mocking male voice and bent down to rub my leg all the way up to my hip. “I don’t think you can afford this.”

We laughed as I dropped the act and flopped into her passenger seat, hugged her tightly and strapped in.

She drove out onto my street. "Well?! Who is he? Wait, he's not abusive right?"

I actually paused about that last bit. Was he?

Jane!" She said it as if I were crazy to even contemplate an abusive guy again.

"No! No, I swear he isn't abusive! Don't worry."

She looked at me suspiciously, squinting. "Are you lying because you want my approval?"

I rolled my eyes at her. "Scouts honor, to my knowledge he's not abusive."

"How long have you known him?" This would definitely piss her off.

I fidgeted with my shirt and nails and finally mumbled, "A month . . . or so."

Sitting up straighter she whipped her head in my direction. "What?! You never told me! What the hell bitch?!"

Wincing I put on my best apology face. "I know, really but I mean we only got together last night and really I don't even know if he's into me!" It all came out on a rush. All my insecurities that I'd needed to talk to someone about. Not that Mysti was an encouragement since I had warned her time again about her now ex-boyfriend Liam. Now we were just two girls with broken hearts, trying to get by on giving each other advice and being cushions for one another. I pointed to a Taco Bell drive thru, she turned into the driveway.

"This is not getting better Jane, only worse. Where'd you meet him?"

"Barnes and Nobles."

"How old is he?"

"Er . . ."

"You don't know how old he is?!" Mysti shook her head in complete disbelief.

Can I take your order?

"I guess it never came up. Hmm . . ." How odd, I guess knowing he was an immortal I never cared to know, wouldn't make a difference anyway. I yelled my order out the window and confirmed her repeat of it. Mys drove forward to pay her as I handed her the money.

"He's not some old looking geezer is he?" She looked at me after the worker took the money.

"Really? You really think that's the kind of guy I'd go for?" I asked sarcastically.

She just looked at me. "You haven't exactly had a great track record Jr." Mysti had come up with the nickname since my initials were technically J.R. The first time I called her senior, it didn't go so well. So I have yet to come up with anything that stuck yet. She was only a month older than me so it would've worked perfectly. Maybe I should give it one more try.

She grabbed my food and placed it in my lap. I dug in, famished since I hadn't had breakfast.

But alas, she was right. I HAD gone out with some of the worse stereotypes ever. "Okay yeah, I have almost the worst. BUT . . . !" I held up a finger. "You will lose your ever loving mind if you see him." I slumped in defeat. "I just don't think now would be a good time since we are just finding out footing.

"Uh huh." She probably thought something was definitely up, but how could I tell her all that was going on in my life? She would flip, knowing her she would probably WANT to tag along to encounter these things. Daring, my darling sister. I loved her so.

Mysti finally pulled up too a small part of forest area that wasn't far from home. As a matter of fact, I'd say this same forest linked up to the forest behind Than's house. *Great . . .*

"Forest theme this time?"

She smiled in delight, I could practically see the ideas floating through her head. "You're incorrigible Mys."

She shrugged as I followed her through the trees. "What can I say, I'm awesome."

We started bouncing ideas off of eachother, her providing the setting and me throwing out ideas to add to her thoughts. She finally stopped in a spot that had enough light but not too much and twirled around to face me. "You see? That's why I love bringing you! We come up with such awesome ideas together!"

I snorted at her claim, we didn't really have a choice. When Mysti needed models, we were hard pressed not to say yes. "Just remember to make me look good, my ass is growing as we speak." We laughed together and she started to throw a different bunch of combinations of clothes at me to try on. We both decided on the plaid long sleeve shirt and beige khaki shorts, going for a woodsy look.

We went through a series of looks and poses, using fallen tree trunks, high grass patches and nicely lighted ground to lay on looking up into the light shining down on us.

"That's good, just like that. Don't move." I heard her shutter a bunch of times before she finally got up from kneeling.

I sat up holding onto one knee. "Alright, give it here. It's your turn to show me the love."

We moved away from where I'd been and started the whole routine again. I got around to taking at least thirty pictures of her in different lighting, poses and looks when it started to get chilly. I rubbed a calf against my other trying to warm them up as I finished another shot of my friend. I checked my watch to see what time it was. Two hours in and it was this cold already?

"Hey are you cold?" She walked up to me and hefted her camera over my head to peer at the pictures I'd taken, deleting some on the way as she made faces of approval or sheer horror.

"No, not really." Ignoring me, she continued to look through the pictures.

I looked around but no one was around. I didn't hear anything but I couldn't shake the feeling that now, someone was watching us. Without looking at her I warned Mysti, "We should go Mys . . ."

Popping her head up in attention she pouted my way. "What? C'mon my trigger finger isn't even tired yet. Let's do one more with a change of clothes." I looked back at her to tell her that we should really leave when I noticed the look on her face. It definitely did not match her excited tone just a second ago. I've never seen her look scared before, only concerned when she knew we had to get out of a situation.

Turning back around, I swore as I took a couple of steps in front of my friend. I stared back into one familiar pair of eyes and a set of the most sorrowful gaze of a stranger. I hadn't had time to realize the feelings in my fingers. They'd been smart, they must have followed us and then shifted here like how Than was able to. I cursed mentally once more and tried to think of what I should do next.

"Can we help you?" Mysti said from behind me in a warning tone. God this was a nightmare, how would I get us out of this?

Their eyes became lethal sneers. Jealousy stepped forward first threateningly. "You'll pay for what you did to my brother bitch."

Her brother? Crap, I'd destroyed or rather collected Fear, her brother's soul. Wonderful.

I never took my eyes from them but whispered to Mys, "Run to the car and drive as fast as you can Mysti. Now."

"You're kidding right? Who are these losers? What'd you do to her brother?" Never one to run and leave her friends behind, I knew it'd been a long shot for her to actually leave. I refocused fully on the demons before me when they made small movements to trap us between them.

Without taking my eyes off both of them I began to explain to Mysti for her own survival. "I need you to listen and understand Mys . . ." The man, the one I didn't know started to murmur gibberish I didn't understand, I spoke faster. "I'm different than I thought I was, I have the power to send lingering spirits on from this earth . . ." I turned to look at Jealousy who was closer, I shifted with her, blocking her from a frontal attack at my friend.

"What?" She asked, confused and a little dumbfounded.

I sighed, "I know, it's weird but that's why I've been hanging with Than and stuff. Just take it and believe it because it's real and these people are demons. Not human, got it?"

"Um, Jane . . . ?" At her worried tone I looked at the man. Well at least that's where he used to be. In his place was someone I'd only seen in nightmares and then in my fondest dreams.

My jaw dropped. "Dad?" I took an untold step forward. That's all the distraction she needed for enough space between me and Mys.

I was knocked to the side, about five feet and landed hard in the dirt. I placed my hands on the ground to lift myself up when I heard struggling behind me. I spat out leaves and twigs from my mouth, bringing myself up to run to my friend. How could I have been so stupid!? My father was gone, never coming back, why had I fallen for it? Before I could get to her though I was back handed back onto the ground. The image of my father leaned down to sneer in my face. "You'll pay dearly *descendion* bitch." Spittle sprayed onto my face from his rage. I didn't get a chance to respond because he grabbed what little hair I had left from cutting it and yanked me up. My fingers were literally on fire at this point. I felt the change and so did he because he cut me off from completely nuking his ass.

Giving a firm tug on my hair, he tugged my back to his front, caging me in with one huge forearm. "Change, and your friend dies." His hot disgusting breath fanned across my cheek and I leaned away. He only tugged me back harder. "Are we going to have a problem?"

I refused to let the tears fall from my eyes. I shook my head, no. I stared in horror as Jealousy held Mys in an almost similar position as me. The only difference was that she was fighting for all she was worth. Oh, I could kiss her, she was so brave! Her efforts however, only received a vicious knee to the back, causing her to land sprawling on the ground in front of me. She wasn't moving.

"Mys!" I started to struggle, failing at escaping his tight hold.

"Grab the girl and let's go. He's waiting." My holder growled to Jealousy.

Picking Mys up as if she were nothing more than a sack of potatoes, she threw my friend over her shoulder. Before I knew it I was staring into hell.

CHAPTER 18

At this moment Than didn't think anyone would ever feel as confused as he did. He was currently nursing a bottle of Jack's, staring into the fireplace. It'd been a full day and all he could think about was Jane.

Jane' eyes he'd nicknamed her over, her body, her voice, hell, her bloody hair follicles. He felt like shit over what'd he'd done to her. Guilt consumed him, hence his current condition now.

Hearing the shuffling of footsteps behind him, he didn't bother acknowledging the ass of an angel.

"Drowning our guilt are we?" Don took his chairs companion next to him. The bloody angel had been here frequently ever since they broke the pact seperating the interference rule that had been set before Jane had almost died.

He snorted in denial. "Hardly." His voice was completely slurred. Damn, how much had he drunk? Bringing up the bottle he dangled from his fingertips, he stared in disbelief at the now empty bottle. He dropped his spinning head back against the chair, dropping the bottle to the floor to join it's friend on the ground.

"You're a terrible liar."

"No one asked for your opinion." Than kept his eyes closed as he tried to focus on remaining upright in his chair.

"No one has to, but don't you think you should lay off the bottle if something should happen to her?"

"Isn't that yooour job?" He responded sarcastically, if not a bit childishly. The alcohol was making him petty. "She likes you better anyways."

If he'd been looking at Don he would have seen his wide eyed look of disbelief. "You must be blind. Or just stupid, but then I knew that already." He heard Don relax into his chair.

Ignoring his claim since he didn't want to feel more than he already did for his . . . . THE mortal, he corrected, he asked him, "What the hell are you doing here anyway? Aren't you supposed to be watching over her now?" Though she'd claimed she didn't need one of them with her, he'd still told Don about her plans. She had an uncanny ability of knowing when he was near apparently. He, at the time, hadn't wanted her getting mad at him for going against her wishes. The angel had shook his head in disbelief at his stupidity and flashed instantly to go to her. Angels were snobby, they called it flashing instead of shifting, trying to make it seem more than it was.

"She was with her friend taking pictures when I left them. Nothing of interest there."

Something niggled in the back of his mind. Call it a warning, but something didn't feel right about this. He shook his head to clear it, blaming the alcohol. He was being ridiculous of course, she was simply with her friend taking pictures. Where was the harm in that? He scoffed at his own paranoia and got up in search of another bottle. He was still thinking and he didn't want to be. He wanted her pink lips and hazel eyes out of his head.

"Do you really think that's wise?" Don said snobbily, eyeing him from his spot in front of the fireplace.

"Oh, put a sock in it. You said it yourself, the mortal is fine." He found another Jack bottle hidden in the back of the bar cupboard and uncapped it, immediately taking a swig. "'Nothing of interest there,'" he mocked him.

He watched unfocused, as Don got up in irritation. "Whatever, do what the fuck you want." With that he 'flashed' out of the room, leaving Than to his drunken state.

He dropped himself back into his seat and drank. Staring into the fire he contemplated his growing attachment to the girl and how the hell he was supposed to tell her he's the reason her father was no longer here. *Fuck.*

—∞—

Lachesis watched as the mortal was taken. She watched as the angel and son of death talk of senseless things.

Shaking her head, she moved the scene back to the girl. She'd be there for a couple of days. This was the hurt and pain that she'd foretold in the thread of the mortal's life. In order for harmony to reside between the two, there must be pain from truth and lessons learned. It would be painful, but if things played out right between the two, there would be the brightest light of love and harmony that anyone's seen in a long time.

"Why do you waste your time with this mortal?"

Atropos approached from behind, gazing over her shoulder to watch as the demoness of Jealousy and demon of Sorrow carried the mortals to the cells Erebos had in his domain. She normally would not show feelings for such an event, always watched indifferently. But she shuddered now to think of the things they would do to her if they did not get what they wanted.

"How do I waste time sister, by doing my job?" She turned to look at her, waiting for her response.

She only stared at the vision before them, sneering at it. "I still say he should die."

"Sister, your job has nothing to do with mine until I give the say so."

Atropos sniffed disdainfully. "Would it were I, they'd both be dead by now." She turned to walk away as Lachesis remained focused on the scene.

"That is why you are not in my position," she murmured. The scene went dark as Lachesis turned away herself to go back to the mortal's thread. She must do this carefully as she still had rules to follow.

With that in mind, she sat down at her table that held the delicate thread of white for the mortal, and the black for the demon. It was time to complete her work.

—⁓—

I screamed until I didn't have a voice, until I couldn't cry anymore. As Sorrow raised the whip again, I still flinched even though I knew exactly what it felt like everytime he did it. I didn't know where Mys was anymore. They had seperated us down two different chambers where the cells were.

He'd moved me to a room that was damp and dark. All the better for him to whip me without me seeing it coming. *Bastard.*

Where the hell were those two bastards now? She couldn't help but feel betrayed and forgotten. When she needed them most, where were they? A tear tried to escape, but no. If she could hold in the tears from this whipping, she could definitely save them from those men.

I realized it'd gotten quiet and that the whipping finally stopped. His footsteps left the chamber only to be replaced by a sinister presence. This I definitely did not recognize from the time I'd been here. I shivered uneasily at the sickly smell that permeated the air. If Than was the son of death, this only reminded her of decaying bodies.

"So, you are the *descendion* I've been seeking." I almost whimpered at his voice, it was almost as bad as his body odor. Sickly sweet and deceivingly soft as if he'd lash out any moment. I said nothing and waited for the abuse to happen.

"Do you know who I am?" I remained silent still, hoping against what I knew to be true. Those tears may just appear anytime now.

"WHO AM I, DISGUSTING MORTAL?!" I whimpered and cringed, trying to move away but the chains holding me down didn't give me any length to work with.

That's when he kicked me in the ribs, one or two definitely cracked as I fell to the floor crying out in a silent cry. The tears finally came.

He yelled the same question a couple more times, each one punctuated with either a kick or a backhand to my face. I couldn't open my eyes anymore, they'd been forced close by the swelling. I finally got his name out, fearing this being before me as I lay in a fetal position on the ground. I could only hope Mysti was being treated more kindly than I was since I was the one he wanted.

His breath fanned over my face, if I were even half as lucid, I'd have gagged. "Where are your faithful protectors now?" He moved away and left me there, slamming the door behind him and locking it.

Indeed, where were my protectors now? That was my final thought as I blacked out blessedly.

—ᴡ—

I think it'd been a day or so now. I was starving and dying for a glass of water. They never allowed for me to be unchained so my clothes were disgustingly ruined, or whatever was left of them after all the whipping I'd endured.

Still, there was no sign of me ever leaving this place. I didn't even know where we were and no one but Sorrow, Jealousy and Erebos visited me. Jealousy was the worst of them all. She was vicious, not needing weapons to make me suffer. She used nails, hands, feet, and teeth to break me down.

I stopped asking about Mys as that only earned me more abuse that I didn't think my body would handle anymore. I wondered instead about what they were waiting for. Wasn't the whole point of my capture to collect my *descendion* soul to make Erebos more powerful? Did his hate reach so far for my kind that he was just playing with me until I was mindless and broken? Whatever the reason I wish he would just do it. I was obviously forgotten by those two useless idiots. I'd given up on them finding me already after a day or however long I'd been in here. Who knows with all the blackouts I'd been through, but judging by my stomach I'd take a guess at two or three days and nights now. Who knew a human could survive the torture these demons have been making me succumb to for even that long?

The door to my cell scraped open as Sorrow shuffled inside. I still couldn't see because of the swelling so I was forced to use my other senses. Sorrow always shuffled,

Jealousy sauntered with soft steps and Erebos just reeked of malevolence.

I felt the chains move away from my wrists in surprise. Were they moving me to another room for a different kind of torture? But why would they do that? Wasn't this room as good as any?

I couldn't say anything and was a useless rag doll, having no energy from lack of food and water to put up a fight. Sorrow picked me up and the pain pierced me viciously. I wasn't able to cry out but only whimpered in pain.

I was moved for what seemed to me like a few minutes until I was again placed on the cold stone floor. Only silence met my ears and I strained for any sign of noise or movement from my surroundings. It seemed to be a bit lighter and cooler in this area, judging from the lightness I saw through my eyelids.

Finally, that hated voice filled the room. "Bind her to the pole. I'm done waiting, she should be ready now."

I panicked and tried to move but it was useless. I couldn't see and had no muscle mass left, what was the point? Might as well end this misery while I could. I was seriously lucky there were no spirits I had to guide down here, but then Erebos probably had control of that. He definitely wouldn't like it if his current power source was taken from him by a simple spirit.

Sorrow and Jealousy took either my feet or hands, one holding me up to the pole while the other shackled me to hang. The strain on my broken body was so outrageous that had there been anything left to me I'd have made some kind of noise in protest.

It was silent once more as I waited for whatever lay in wait for me. I could feel Erebos move forward, sensing his malicious cloud waver just before me. I tried to open my eyes and succeeded just a little to recognize his blurry shape and something he held in his hands. Something round which glowed the brightest white I'd ever seen. My eyes watered at the bright globe, ending my small accomplishment of sight.

At first nothing happened as if time stood still. Then it was sudden and harsh, something inside of me suddenly moved, being pulled towards the being in front of me. This time I did scream, though it may have sounded more like scraping metal since my voice was basically useless. But the pain could not go with silence.

". . . Why isn't it working?" I barely heard Sorrow ask hesitantly in concern.

I heard him curse foully and the pulling sensation stopped thankfully. What the hell had he tried to do to me? All the torture I'd endured had nothing on the rendering of something trying to leave my body at that moment.

"She is still holding on. This was unforeseen, she is stronger than I imagined."

That's when I finally realized what he'd been trying to do. To collect me, but why hadn't it worked? I didn't know there was more to it. A spark of hope flashed within me. Maybe I stood a chance after all. All that torture had been to break me, to make me weak as if he couldn't collect my soul with my strength and will intact. I was finally beginning to understand.

"Leave her there, she'll break eventually. They always do. Continue as usual until I deem her ready." I felt him move on and the other two follow him.

So, I had a small reprieve. Did I still have a shot at escaping this hell? If so I would harden myself as much as possible so that I would never break for this evil. I would not be responsible for making him more powerful. But how long could I hold on?

—~—

Erebos didn't understand it. It was always the same with every single *descendion* he'd collected over the decades. Usually it only took a day or less to break them and bring Charon's Orb to release their soul from their weak and broken bodies.

As he sat on his throne, he contemplated the reasons this could be but couldn't come up with anything significant. For once, the screams of his tortured souls and spirits did not calm him. The mortal was more important than ever before, he could practically taste the power she'd provide for him. Maybe even enough for him to leave this realm forever and move on to the human realm.

A smile formed upon his lips in fondness of the havoc he would wreak on their unsuspecting plane. But first he had to figure out why he couldn't collect her after everything they'd done to her. His smile disappeared from his face.

Hmm, he thought. Maybe a new tactic would break her spirit. Getting up he moved to summon Sorrow and Jealousy to his side. They appeared instantly and he smiled cruelly at them. "Find Secrecy, it's time to break this mortal."

CHAPTER 19

Once again saltwater was thrown onto me, waking me from my hanging position. My body burned as the water slid down into the gashes and any small abrasions left on my body.

I had lost track of time, having stopped when it seemed pointless. Since the last time I was awoken a new demon had been introduced to me. They called him Secrecy and his talent was above all the worst of the three.

Standing before me now, they'd finally let my eyes heal so that I could see his deceivingly beautiful form. It was impossible to look away. Not because I had some kind of infatuation or anything like that. It was literally impossible to look away from him once he had you in his sights. It's how his powers worked after all.

He inched closer, gracefully moving like a prowling panther. He seemed more graceful than Jealousy if that were possible. So far he'd gone through my earlier memories, the worst ones. The ones he could use against me, making me go insane with a thousand different feelings. They'd left my body alone, moving on to my mind to break me.

He finally stood directly in front of me, not three inches or less from my face. He was tall, even as I hung from this six foot pole, his eyes were directly in front of mine. He brought his hand up to brush some of my hair out of my face and I flinched away, glaring at him.

He smirked, then backhanded me once causing my face to whip to the side. I hung my head, not able to hold it up after that. I'm pretty sure my tooth came loose at that hit.

He grabbed my face and stared into my eyes using his demon to find my inner secrets, things that I held in a box. Things I detested to remember.

He'd had to start from my birth and work his way through all my years. That was almost a blessing and a curse at the same time. He'd found memories I'd suppressed that I'd honestly forgotten about in my adulthood. But the worst one was the one he was pulling from the darkness now. The nightmares I'd been having recently. *Oh God, no.*

I attempted to pull from his grasp but it was useless. He pulled forth the memory as clear as if it were yesterday.

We finally finished our meal, stuffed out of our minds. "I don't think I can move." I laughed and pushed up from my chair, moving to make sure my mom had room to push my dad through a cleared path out of the restaurant.

"Well that was dinner so I hope you last because we aren't buying anymore. You'll have to do with leftovers at the hotel if you want more to eat." My mom said as she hung my dad's backpack on the back of his wheelchair and started to move him forward. I moved ahead of them making sure people saw that we were coming and made a path for us.

Turning around the border fence separating the sitting diners from the shoppers, I moved on ahead turning my head once to see if my parents were following safely behind me. They were and I refocused ahead of me staring at the H & M clothing store ahead of us. I'd been stealing looks at the store throughout the whole meal hoping to persuade my parents to let me shop a little.

I could hear them talking behind me as I asked without looking, "Hey, can we go inside H & M?" There was no response to my question but I heard my mom behind me talking in a worried tone. I turned around to see what was going on.

"John? Johnny? What's wrong? John?!" I looked on worriedly as blood started to fall from my father's mouth. Beginning to become scared but not wanting to cause a scene, I walked (WALKED?!) quickly to the bathroom that was just down the hall passed H & M. By the time I was halfway there I ran the rest of the way and pulled paper towels until everyone was looking at me as if I were crazy.

Not caring, I ran from the bathroom and made it back to my parents. I stared in horror at how much worse it was in just a minute. Blood coated his shoulder and ran down his wheelchair to create a puddle on the floor as he hung over unable to speak to my mom but able to move his hands trying to tell us something.

My mom stood in front of him trying to understand what it was he was telling us. "I can't understand you John! Oh my God, Jane get help!" I gave her the paper towels and she put them to use immediately. As I moved quickly to the restaurant to ask for help I could hear some of the people around us gasping and crying out.

"Did someone call 911?!?" Someone called out.

"I'm calling them now!" Another woman replied. I felt like an idiot. Why didn't we do that!?

I made it to the counter before saying in a rush to the worker there. "Do you guys have cleaners or anything to help us?!" The man looked confused and I didn't have time for his reply. He was saying no and that he was sorry but I was already turning back away to run to my parents.

From the point on I remembered the rest vividly. Secrecy had pulled from my mind leaving me to drown in my guilt at our unresponsive nature to my dad's need for medical help.

I remembered the EMT's coming just as I did. Walking . . . as if they had all the time in the world to reach my father. I recalled how the mall security tried to move my dad to the floor, laying in his own pool of blood. How his head had cracked onto the marble floor because he was too heavy for one man to carry his dead weight. The tears started falling rapidly from my eyes.

I moved on to when the EMT's had finally made it to him, trying to pump life into him with a machine I didn't recognize. My mom standing next to me as they tried to push us back. Me snapping and throwing his hand off me saying not to touch me in a voice I didn't recognize.

I remembered their forlorn faces and I the thought that I still hadn't let a single tear fall, refusing to believe what was so obvious. I held that hope when they took him to the ambulance, when we finally made it to the car to go to the hospital and even when we were sitting in the waiting room for about forty-five minutes.

All of that hope was destroyed and crushed with a heavy fist when the doctor came up to us and told us. Told us that he was gone. That it was a stroke, quick.

I was the first to cry, sobbing at first and then finally creating a flood of tears. No amount of tissue could have helped. My mom finally followed suit as we were led to where he layed on a gurney in the room they'd placed him.

Back to reality I realized where I was, how real it had felt to remember that memory again. My face was covered in salted tears, my nose running madly. My body shuddered at the guilt I've always held in my heart, never letting myself forgive my soul for the inactivity of calling the stupid ambulance at the first sign of the unnatural blood coursing out of my father.

A voice called me back to attention. "Sweet Jane, do you know why you've never understood the suddenness of his death?"

My sobbing subsided as I felt my heart being stabbed with a sharp knife. I had always thought about that, always wondered how it could be that we were just having a good time sharing a meal and laughs about the trip and then he was ripped cruelly from my life.

I only stared at the ground from my position in hate and anger for this demon that brought up pain of my loss.

"Hmm? Can you take a guess? Anything at all ringing a bell?" I saw his legs moving him to pace in front of me. Why was he doing this, dragging out the inevitable?

"I'll give you one hint." I could hear the glee and excitement in his voice at something he'd discovered from my memories. "This allll has to do with the person you love."

I felt absolutely naked in front of him. Now not only did I have to suffer the pain from the worst event in my life, but now he would throw this in my face too. Then I went over his hint again, refocusing on what he was trying to tell me.

He laughed at my sudden stillness. "Oh, she's figuring something out." He said in a sing song voice.

How? What did Than have anything to do with my father's death . . . ? Unless . . .

"Ding, ding, ding! We have a winner ladies and gentlemen!" He called out to no one in particular.

I refused to believe it. I wouldn't, how could I believe such an obvious lie? But of course there was something about his tone that held no deceit.

"No . . ." I finally whispered in a ragged tone. I tried to shake my head in denial at his claim.

"Oh yes! That's right my dearest! The demon you've fallen in love with is a lying, deceiving, unforgiving and selfish killer! Who would've thought? The son of Death, taking a life?! It's ridiculous, no?" I was literally going into shock. My body started to convulse and fresh tears poured down my cheeks.

Rough hands lifted my head up as I met Secrecy's truthful eyes. "Ask me how, little Jane. How in the world did Thanatos take your father's life?"

". . . How." It wasn't a question but a whispered statement, simply doing what he wanted me to do. I didn't want to know but I did.

"I'm so glad you asked. Well if you must know, Thanatos is actually quite new to his job of meeting people at the time of their deaths. Being the selfish youth that he is, let's just say that he tried to speed things up a bit to get your father's death out of the way to free up some time."

I sobbed pathetically after every word that left his truthful lips. Oh, how I wish it were a lie. I wish he were making it all up so that I still could hold out on that hope that I'd met someone who'd actually made me feel alive again. Someone I thought hopelessly, who would help me through the years and make me a strong person again.

But no, of course not. Fate was a cold hard bitch who wanted me to suffer. Fine then, suffer I would. I couldn't stand the betrayal, Than had been my only hope and just like the hope I'd carried for my father in his last moment, it was crushed brutally.

Secrecy laughed madly and left me there to wallow in the guilt he'd surfaced within me. They'd finally succeeded, now all I had to do was wait for the inevitable.

—∞—

Something was wrong. He felt it in the very pit of his stomach. Than was pacing madly in his living room trying to figure out why he was having this sick feeling in his stomach.

Against his better judgment he'd stayed away from her. Unable to grab hold of his emotions and feelings, he thought it'd be best to just let her be. Don would handle it, though it made him crazy thinking she was spending time with that horse's ass.

It'd been three days and this was the outcome. He also hadn't heard from said horse's ass since his drunken night alone in sitting room. Something was definitely up. It could be her stubbornness, but he'd sent a quick text to her seeing if she was alright. She never answered but there were a million and one reasons why she wouldn't have considering the way he treated her.

Than jerked out of his focused gaze on the carpet when he heard his front door slam open. Sensing that it was Don he only paused and waited for him. What he expected to see wasn't at all what was now in front of him.

Don was a wreck physically. His eyes were crazed and he didn't even have control of his form, his massive white feathered wings arched in tension as if he were ready to take flight once again.

Than swallowed his insults, worry over Jane taking over instantly. "What happened? Where is she?" His voice grew in volume as he moved toward Abaddon aggressively.

Breathing heavily and trying to calm down, he finally broke down. "They took her. God DAMNIT! They took her and I wasn't there!" His house rattled at the angel's fury and Than clenched his own fists, trying to understand what the fuck was happening.

"Who the FUCK took her and when did this happen?!" He growled out menacingly.

Guilt crossed his features and that's how he knew without the answer. "Erebos." That's when he lost it, shifting and breaking forms, he'd left Don standing in his home and found himself walking down the corridor to his father's domain in the nether realm. He didn't care what it took he had to find her and get into Erebus somehow without the primordial God knowing of his presence.

"Ah, is that my son come to tell me of how he cheated more lives?" His father was doing much the same as he had been only a few nights ago. Just instead of human liquor, he had a tumbler of some demon wine.

"I need to get into Erebus." He ignored his father's jibe and watched as his menacing form stood from the chair.

"Why's that?" He asked calmly as if discussing the weather.

"I need to save her, she could be dead already for all I know." His words were rushed trying to hurry this along.

"Who son?"

"Don't play with me father, you know just as well! Take me to Erebus!" His father's power was ever powerful as he slammed Than's body up against the far wall without so much as lifting a finger.

"Watch your tongue boy. If it weren't for you, the mortal would never have been in this situation in the first place."

Than refused to be cowed when the one he now knew he loved could be dying this very moment. "You think I don't know that!?" He yelled in frustration. "You think I haven't learned my lesson? I love her father! LOVE. HER."

Taking a breath he calmed himself to speak rationally to his father who'd finally turned around at his unnatural claim.

"Love?" He scoffed. "Don't be ridiculous boy, you wouldn't know love if it slapped you in the face then spit twice on your feet." He laughed at his son's ridiculous claim. But Than knew he'd grabbed his attention with his claim. Knowing his father wouldn't be able to turn down a deal, he did the most unselfish thing he'd ever done in his life.

"Fine, I'll prove it to you." He licked his dry lips knowing this could end badly on his part if it back fired and he was wrong about how Jane felt about him. His father arched his eyebrow in question.

"I'm listening." He released Than from his hold on the wall and turned back around to pace slowly before the hearth, sipping his spirits.

"If I save 'Azel, and return her home, AND tell her the truth about her father . . ." he paused knowing there was no going back. He honestly did love her now that he'd admitted it and would do anything to keep her. Even win her over all over again if she hated him eternally after. He glanced back to his father, standing up straighter and holding onto his resolve. "I'll do anything you want of me. Anything, against my will and all."

"That's a grand proposal son, but I honestly don't see the benefit for me." Than was about to protest but his father continued.

"However, should you do all the things you claim and indeed love this mortal . . ." He turned around from his thoughts and looked at Than. "You will marry the girl and she will be eternally in my service." At this, Than began to protest but his father cut him off once more.

"I also want the Orb. Charon's Orb to be exact."

This stumped Than as he didn't know what his father was talking about. "What does an Orb have to do with this?"

Sighing his father turned back around once more and Than was seriously losing patience as every second wasted here was a moment wasted in saving Jane. "The Orb is what Erebos is using to hold his power over the collected spirits and souls. It's what he will use to collect your mortal's soul as well if you don't hurry. Do you accept my terms?"

"Wait, what happens if I fail?"

His father smirked. "Well then you stand to lose everything don't you?" With that Death opened a portal with a wave of his hand. "Do not fail Thanatos, I can't save your soul if you do."

Without a backward glance or farewell, he ran through the portal to find 'Azel before it was too late."

CHAPTER 20

Once again I found myself facing evil incarnate. All four of my torturer's stood before me ready to collect my soul and I could do nothing but let them. My will was gone and my heart was shattered to pieces. I was such a fool! Had I not told myself in the beginning not to get caught up with him? Then after knowing he was a demon I still continued to love him more and more. I wish I could slap myself. Maybe I deserved all the torture they've been dishing out, I though cynically.

I observed my surroundings, depressed that this was the end of my life. That this is what I'd lived my life for. To have my soul sucked out of me to be used for an evil primordial God and have my heart rendered and snipped to tiny little pieces blowing away with the wind without a care.

I was a bit angry when I thought of the powers I could have used against them if I hadn't brought my best friend into the picture. But wouldn't have they gone after my friends and family eventually? There was no way out I concluded. It was inevitable, this was my fate. Death, it always had been since I was born.

It's funny because I'd always thought after every failed relationship that I just wasn't meant to be with anyone.

That I was meant to be an independent woman who lived with her cat until she grew old.

I was distracted from my morbid thoughts when Erebos brought the same Orb before me. Charon's Orb, they called it. This was what me and Than had been wondering about. The device he used to collect souls. Not exactly the way I wanted to discover the thing, but I guess beggars couldn't be choosers. Maybe I could warn the next *descendion* of its existence once I was a spirit. Could a spirit do anything other than relive its gruesome demise? Hell, would I even become a spirit? What happened after being 'collected'?

I didn't know but I guess I'd find out soon enough. Erebos stepped forward and this time I heard the small demonic chanting they all used together and my throat had healed enough for me to start screaming at the painful tug of my soul attempting to connect once again to the bright Orb.

My eyes watered and I threw my head back against the wooden pole staring at the cave like ceiling. I widened them at the sight I saw above me. *Impossible!* What I'd seen disappeared with the blink of my eyes and that only made me cry in frustration. At first I thought I'd been saved, that he'd finally found me at last. But no, it was just the vision of my desperate mind. But what was I saying? He'd betrayed me, had lied to my face knowing what he'd done to me all this time and acting as if he . . . as if he . . . I shook my head. *NO, STOP!* I would not make excuses for that bastard of a man. Holding onto my anger, I couldn't stop the flailing of my body as it struggled to hold onto what rightfully belonged within me.

That's when all hell broke loose. A roar like I'd never in my life heard before in movies or in reality pierced the cave, ringing in my ears. That didn't stop the tugging though, I continued to whimper and scream, my body thrashing against my bonds and my voice box tearing once more. I used what strength I had left to lift my head to see what had caused such an angry, animalistic sound.

What I saw in between thrases made my heart stop completely. A demon the size of an elephant was ripping into all three of the minor demons who'd tortured me all this time. I strove to watch as he tore them limb from limb, tossing their body parts into every which direction. His razor sharp canines tore into their throats as his claws dug fiercely into his victims ribcages, puncturing lungs, organs and heart all at once. His wing span was incredible as they swatted oncoming attacks without a care, protecting his back from all of them.

All this and Erebos didn't flinch once. Sure, why should he? No simple demon could defeat him. I was fading in and out of consciousness as the fight continued, my heart beginning to slow rapidly. I finally dropped my head, not able to hold up the weight any longer. Another roar pierced the air but I couldn't acknowledge it as I finally blacked out.

—∞—

*NO!*Than roared at the slumping figure of the mortal he loved. He fought harder and finally slashed his claws across the last of the demons he'd been fighting, severing the head clean off of his neck. The body dropped and by the time it hit the floor, Than had shifted to slam into the God. He barely moved but was in enough of a trance in severing the soul's ties with Jane's body that he'd been distracted. Good.

Than punched the bastard with all the fury and strength he possessed. Only his head whipped to the side and turned slowly to glare at him. "Not so smart demon." He shifted back to his throne where he replaced the Orb and shifted so quickly before Than could figure out where he'd turn up next, that he was flying across the room, his lip split from Erebos' own punch.

Before Than could even drop to the floor, Erebos had him in a chokehold, slamming him into the stone wall behind him. "Are you stupid or just have a death wish?" He punctuated his last word with a tight squeeze of his fist around his throat. Than's gaze refused to flick behind the God, not wanting to give anything away.

Erebos' powerful body was suddenly thrown across the cave, clear to the other side. Don dusted his hands off, striding in full angel form towards the God. "I'm told he's both, but then who am I to judge?"

Than quickly recovered, using the distraction Don provided to shift to Jane. Reaching up to unshackle her from the pole, he caught her frail form and was almost unmanned with tears at the sight of her abused body. He growled as he held her to him for a moment before kissing her forehead and placing her down on the ground. He had to help Don, leaving here would mean not being able to come back.

Checking once more to see if she were breathing, he shifted to where Don was currently punching Erebos' face to a pulp. Before he could land one in himself though, a powerful blast sent both of them flying. "ENOUGH!" The God roared throughout the hall. He started to move towards where they hand landed but used his powers to hold both of them up in the air and slammed them against each other as if they were his personal dolls to smack around.

Thanatos, you have to grab the Orb and get Jane out of here.

Get the fuck out of my head.

Suck it up you faggot and get her out!

I kind of would but I'm in as much of a suck ass situation as you, please enlighten me.

There was no response from Don on that count. The Orb was closest to him but he didn't look at it, not wanting to give away his intentions if he was given the opportunity. An invisible vice grip started to constrict his throat and he started gasping for air.

Be . . . ready . . .

What the hell was the delusional talking about?

With a great flash of light, Than closed his eyes, still struggling for breath. Reopening them, the cave was full of angels with flaming swords. With Erebos' focus diverted to too many entities, both him and Don dropped to the floor without warning.

Now Than!

He didn't need to be told again. He shifted to grab the Orb and then to Jane, picking her up lightly. Right before he was about to shift, Jane whispered something.

"Friend . . . . Mys . . ." They'd taken her friend too? Fuck! He didn't have time for this.

Don, I've got her. Her friend is somewhere down here too.

Go, we'll find the girl.

He didn't respond but was in his father's realm instantly. He placed her in his room where he used to stay before he was of age to apprentice as his father's heir. Laying her down gently, he called out for his father.

Walking in slowly as if he had all the time in the world he stood next to Than, staring thoughtfully at Jane. "Bravo son, and the Orb?" Without preamble, Than offered the Orb to him.

"Her pulse is thready at best. He obviously didn't succeed in collecting her soul in time, but something's wrong." He brushed his fingertips across her face, her chilled lips and closed eyes.

"Move aside." Than wanted to growl but knew his father wouldn't hurt her. It was in his best interests not to touch a hair on her head if he had any say about it. He watched as his father placed the Orb on top of Jane's chest, gently taking her hands and placing them over the Orb to hold it in place. Then he moved next to her head and looked as if he were whispering something to her.

About to question his father, he stopped as whatever he'd whispered to her seemed to be taking effect. The Orb glowed a fierce blue as a whisper of some kind of mist was drawn from it and moved to Jane's mouth, seeping through her lips. Her eyes flew open as a gasp for air was drawn into her mouth. Her hands dropped from the Orb and his father swiftly caught it before it hit the floor.

"Jane!" He moved past his father, grabbing hold of her much too skeletal frame between his arms, placing light kisses all over her face.

"Than?" Her voice was full of confusion. Then he watched as her eyes filled with tears but quickly heated with hate and venom. "Get away from me!" She tried to push him away but he simply held onto her, her efforts much too weak to gain much movement away from him.

"'Azel? What's wrong? Talk to me, please. Stop struggling, you'll only lose more strength."

"You lying SCUM! Let me go! You . . . you KILLER! OH, I HATE YOU!" She started to sob as he placed her down onto the soft bed before she hurt herself.

That's when the worst came to mind. She knew, he didn't know how but she knew the truth. He was in so much shit right now. His face drained of color as his father stepped next to him. "Why don't you give her some time?

I'll watch her." Than scowled at him, he didn't want to leave her with him. He wanted to take care of her himself.

His father saw the resistance in his eyes and showed him the door without breaking a sweat. Than sat outside the door like a petulant child waiting for the outcome of his father's efforts with her.

A week later . . .

"Would you stop with the pacing already? You're seriously going to make a hole in the floor."

"Shut up! It's my house and I'll make as many dents, holes, and fucking wear and tear that I want!" Than picked up the dining room table, hefting and throwing it across the room to crash into the wall. It splintered and a leg flew towards Don, but he caught it without blinking and placed it down on the floor where he was leaning against the wall.

All of the furniture in his mansion was now destroyed from his frustration. There were even great, gaping holes in some walls so that you could see right outside. The only things he refused to destroy were his cars. That was untouchable three days ago. Now? Even those were looking tempting.

After the first day of waiting outside for Jane, his father effectively shifted him outside of his realm, barring his return for the time being. It was the worst for him in the beginning of the week. Don had turned up to find him destroying everything in his household as a demon. They had a go at each other because the stupid angel was trying to calm him down. Had said he was going to cause neighbors to call the local police and that was the last thing they needed.

As soon as he calmed down, Don had gone on to explain that Erebos was stripped of his Primordial God rights because of all the rules he'd broken and scheming he'd been about to accomplish to overthrow both the Greek pantheon and mortal Earth. He was now rotting in Tartarus as a weak mortal, being sentenced to be tortured as he'd tortured 'Azel and countless other victims that had been wronged by his selfishness.

Than would personally like a go at him, but left it to the ex-God's pantheon to deal with. Clashing pantheons was something no one needed or wanted to deal with.

The week continued on as such with no word from his father and the company of an annoying angel. Said angel currently stood up and dusted off his pants that was covered with debris from the oncoming flying objects whenever Than had thrown something.

"Look, this is not going to solve the problem of you not seeing her. Would you just relax?"

He glared at the angel. "I swear if you tell me patience is a virtue, I'll rethink this pact we have going on at the moment."

"Honestly, I'd like to have a go at your annoying ranting but I'm just as worried as you are alright?"

Than scoffed. Sure they'd cleared the air about the kind of love Don held for HIS mortal but he still had possessive issues that couldn't be cured. "You don't have to be worried about her hating you and never loving you again if she doesn't forgive you for killing her father."

Don shrugged. "That was your selfish decision. Lesson learned and hopefully forgiveness is coming your way. I however do have to worry about her hating me for knowing and not telling her all this time."

Hmm, the snob had a point. It kind of made his mood lighter but his situation was by far worse off. He dragged his fingers through his already thinned out hair from that exact movement and sighed a frustrated sigh. He stared up at the ceiling hoping his father would hear his plea. "Any word would be nice right about now father!"

—∞—

The first two days were spent healing the mortal woman. His son always referred to her as a girl but Death saw little innocence in this woman's eyes. Only hate, death, sorrow and life. For her age, he was surprised at the life she'd lead so far. At the loss she'd endured with strength. She'd make a fine wife indeed. A fine wife for a man who deserved her. Whether or not that man was his son, was up to her and for him to decide.

By the third and fourth day, she had enough strength and meat back on her bones to sit up and eat on her own. She also found her voice though it was scratchy from the repair her throat was going through.

She was sitting up, propped against her pillows and sipping some chicken noodle soup when she placed the bowl in between her legs to look up at him. She'd been wary and she should be. He was Death after all. Until now she'd never spoken.

"Do you have another name I can call you?" It was barely a whisper but of course he heard it. He smirked at the request. No one had ever asked him what his real name was before he'd become Death.

"John."

She nodded after the smallest widening of the eyes. He was curious at the reason why.

"Why are you surprised?" She was startled by his answer, unaware of how observant one became over a millennia of existing.

"It's just that it's so simple."

He tilted his head at her confusion when he realized she didn't know of whence he came. "I was born just a little before . . . his death and rebirth." He pointed up to indicate that which he could not speak literally about. "All names were simple and reused back then."

Her eyes glazed over for a second and he'd wondered if he'd have to save her from falling over onto the floor. But she snapped out of it and gave a small shake of her head. "Right. Of course, how silly of me."

Clearing his throat he moved on to more important questions. "You know why you are here?"

She shook her head but he could detect a lie before anyone ever made the move to do it. It was all about body language.

Sighing he realized she would not speak of it. Not yet anyways, he could hear his son throwing out curses and doing who knew what to his possessions while he ranted like a child. He wouldn't force her though, she needed time.

"Very well, you need more rest." He stood and took the bowl from her and made his way to leave. Not before she cleared her throat to speak.

"Thank you John." She gifted him with a small smile that he would never forget. The more he stayed with the mortal, the more he figured how his son had come to love her. Without responding he left and shut the door behind him.

CHAPTER 21

Friday

"Do you like your job?" I asked around a mouth full of sliced pieces of steak.

"Not particularly but it pays the bills." I looked up in shock only to find a smile upon those lips that looked so much . . . My face fell and I returned to eating. I had to gain my strength back if I ever planned on leaving this place.

It'd been a week now and I was getting more and more attached to John as a person. He was funny when he wanted to be and didn't push me into the one thing I didn't want to talk about. Since Wednesday, when I'd first spoken to him, we've done nothing but talk of mundane things. I asked him questions about his life before this and he asked me about my likes and dislikes since being Death, he'd know how I'd spent my life, being able to flash through my memories. At first I'd found it disturbing but I shrugged it off knowing he wasn't able to help it, that it came with the job.

I placed the plate on the side table and dragged my legs to the edge of the bed. "Ready for my walk?" I looked at him expectantly. We'd been doing some motor control routines to get my body back in motion so that I'd be able to function on my own without my family having any sign of what had been done to me.

John only looked at me in worry this time though. It was the look where I knew he was about to try and push. I sighed, as we'd come to be very observant of each other. He'd been surprised at how empathetic I was once I was finally strong enough to be awake for more than a few hours at a time.

He also sighed and crossed his arms in front of him, sitting up straight and staring at me with a no nonsense look. "Jane, we have to talk about it."

"No, we really don't."

"Girl, it's eating you up inside and if you let the parasite nibble away, I can't help you." He glared at me. It was the first time he'd shown anything but growing affection for me, so suffice it to say I was a bit shocked at his tone.

"No one can help me and I never asked you." I regretted saying it as soon as I said the last word. He knew though as he again sighed patiently as if dealing with a child.

"I've never seen you as a child until now little mortal. Please don't prove me wrong."

I crossed my arms and pouted, lifting my chin in defiance. "I don't ever, EVER, want to talk about your deceitful bastard of a son!"

I watched as he seemed to mull this over and rethink his strategy. Shrugging he got up. "I guess you leave me no choice but to bring him here to talk to you then." I sputtered in indignation at the thought.

"Don't you dare!" I yelled at his back before he could leave.

"Then talk to me about it. Or I swear he'll be here so fast, it'll make you go straight back into a coma."

I glared at him, my mouth now uncontrollable in my anger. "That might just be a great idea. Send him on in! That way I won't have to deal with either of you. Like father like son, I never knew why I couldn't see it before!" I snapped my fingers in mock shock. "That's right, because you are both liars and deceivers!"

Before I knew it he was before me, sneering in my face. His form was also changing but he controlled it a lot quicker than Than had, his power apparent. "Listen here *girl*, the ONLY reason you are alive is because myself, my son and Abaddon risked our necks to get your ungrateful ass out of a situation that yes, my son had caused. However, he did it out of love for you. Even though he knew you would hate him upon knowing, he risked everything to bring you home safely. But what does he get? Thanks? No, he gets the mortal girl who can't see that she's swimming in her own pool of guilt. Too bothered to see the new life that's been thrown to her."

"OH, and I suppose I should just forgive him then? Just like that hmm?" I yelled back at him. "He took my father prematurely at the worst possible time all for his amusement for free time! Well forgive me if I don't become so forgiving. Also! It's not like he ever declared his love for me or even bothered to show it!"

"Are you deaf or just stupid?! I just said he'd planned your rescue, on his own I might add. He had no idea that Abaddon would be there or that they'd have more help. Or when he saved you after your first spirit encounter?"

"That was a coincidence! He didn't know that he would save me with his abnormal body heat!" I raged back at him. But he ignored me and moved on.

"OR the time he took care of you back to health after you got hit by that truck?"

"Don could have done the same." I said, not so convincingly anymore and he knew it.

His sigh was only aggravated now. "Jane, my son has made terrible mistakes in the past. It was why he'd been sent instead of another to bring you to our side himself. It was my order that he do so as his punishment. He had to learn what his rash decision would cost others. I'd say he'd learned his lesson very well." He said the last part as an aside to himself. I snorted in disbelief.

"So let me get this straight. Not only was I a pawn for whichever side I chose, but now I'm also just a lesson learned?!" I was so angry but there was nothing to throw unless these pillows turned to something vicious on impact.

"Will you stop seeing the face value of things and look beyond that?"

"Just get out! That's enough; I've had enough for today. Leave me alone!" I turned over in my bed weakly and pulled the covers over my head ignoring John.

He got up to leave but before he shut the door, he said, "Just think about it Jane. Try to see past the misdeeds and betrayal. I'll see you tomorrow." With that the door snicked closed. I didn't think about it but fell straight to sleep from exhaustion and dreamed about it instead.

Saturday

"I think I've got it." John was holding onto my forearms as I stood on my almost there legs again. We were going through the drills of trying to walk and muscle memory.

He looked doubtfully at me. "Are you sure?"

I nodded and he slowly released me. I held my hands out to balance myself and smiled as I could stand on my own.

Walking though, that was another story. Without warning I took a step and my knee buckled, but John caught my upper body swiftly before I could fall.

I swore in irritation. "Damnit!" He sat me on the bed once again.

"Alright I think it's time for you to eat Ms. Stubborn."

"No! I want to keep going." I tried to get up from the bed but he only pushed me back down.

Ignoring me, he moved to the table which held a tuna sandwich with a small caeser salad. My diet was slowly getting better and I was glad I was able to consume the hardy stuff. It was definitely helping with my strength, just not my body movements.

"Eat first and we'll try again after some rest." He placed the plate in my lap and I didn't want to admit it but I was hungry. I shoved the sandwich into my mouth and picked up a chip, biting into it.

John looked at me uneasily. I stared back at him warily as I chewed; wondering what was on his mind. "What?"

He sighed and leaned back in his chair. "I need to get you out of this room. I fear though as soon as I do, Than will sense that you are on that plane." He looked thoughtful trying to solve this issue. Shrugging he stood and grabbed onto my arm before shifting us to Earth's realm.

I looked around, already used to the sudden movement and found myself in a field of grass that went on for miles around me. The only other object with us was a great willow tree, its vines brushing the grass peacefully with the light breeze. "Where are we?"

He shrugged and sat down under the willow, patting a spot next to him. "Somewhere up North, Than wouldn't remember but I used to bring him here when he was a child." I stopped chewing, the subject of Than having been on my mind all night. I dreamed of nothing else as if John had planted the dreams there himself. I furrowed my brows in suspicion and looked at him askance.

Nah, he wasn't the demon of dreams and nightmares after all. Sighing I continued to eat and dropped down next to him. We sat there in silence simply enjoying each other's company and the fresh air around us. After I finished my meal, I dropped down and folded my hands behind my head, listening to the wind blow through the willows branches, rustling the leaves against each other. It was very peaceful here; if I could have a house here I would definitely build one.

I closed my eyes and started the long averted conversation. "I don't think I can do it." He only patted my hand, being the listener.

I took the time to think about my options. I could hate him forever and never see him again, leaving me to my own devices with my *descendion* job. Or, I could forgive the bastard and try to love him again, having someone by my side to help if anything ever went wrong again.

I gulped at the realization that I didn't have to try and love him. As soon as I saw him in that cave before he went nuclear on those demons, I'd already forgiven him. I sat up in surprise and looked at John. He only stared ahead, gazing on into the never ending field.

"You knew didn't you?"

He turned to look at me in mock surprise. "Knew what?"

I rolled my eyes and stared ahead too. "You knew I'd forgiven him as soon as he came to rescue me." I was simply too full of hate and too stubborn to see it. To see and feel the lightness in my heart that had taken place once my pained and hopeless gaze landed on him. Hanging my head I groaned knowing I'd have to see him soon to confess and apologize. With the worry came a spark of excitement though. I guess I did miss the big oaf. A smile crept across my lips.

"Can we start again?"

John stood and pulled me up. "Sure." I couldn't ignore the relieved smile that formed on his lips. "Anything you want little mortal."

—ꟺ—

That's it, he thought. I'm done, she hates me forever and I'm never going to have the chance to see or love her right.

Don grabbed his wrist before he could drink from the bottle he'd just opened. A fresh one to drown his sorrows and pity in.

"Damnit Thanatos! Give me that!" He ripped the bottle from his grip and poured it down the drain, dropping the bottle in after it.

"Hey! Prick, that was a perfectly good bottle of Henessey!" Half drunk already, he turned and threw a weak punch in Don's general area. Missing, he sloppily fell forward but Don caught the back of his shirt pulling him back to steady him.

"It's only been a week! Pull yourself together before she shows up out of nowhere and sees you like this!"

He dragged his drunken ass over to the sofa and pushed him into it. What did he mean, she would show up? "What are you talking about?"

"I'm just saying that if she were to show up by chance that you would be in a shitty position to talk to her don't you think?" He shook his head and went to sit in another chair. "You know this baby sitting is getting really old. I could be doing more important things."

Than snorted in disbelief. "I seriously doubt that." He dropped his body horizontally on the sofa to stare at the ceiling. "This waiting is killing me."

A shuffling noise came from the other side of the sofa and Than flicked his gaze to Don in question. He had someone in his house the entire time? Sitting up he came face to face with a mortal who looked to have some of the same features as his own. She had long sandy blonde hair, a round face with serious eyes and an athlete's body. Again he glanced over to Don but he only stared at the girl with a look Than knew all too well. Recognition came to him. This was Jane's friend, the one who had been captured with her.

She hadn't suffered the brunt of the demon's torture, not being the goal. Of course if things had been any different, they could have used her to get to Jane if they'd wanted to.

"Uh, it's been a week Don, where is Jane." Don turned to me accusingly and then her friend did the same.

"What?"

She put her fists on her hips with her feet apart, ready for an argument. He didn't even know her and she was going to argue with him? Definitely Jane's friend then. "What did you do to her!?"

He sneered at her accusing tone. "I didn't do anything! I'm simply waiting for my father to grace us with her presence." With that he dropped back to the sofa, nursing the oncoming headache.

She continued on though, not taking the hint that the conversation was over. "Well that's just great! Wonderful, Don where is she?" Her tone had softened noticeably when she spoke to him but was still accusatory. Hmm, there was something going on there.

Don fell back into his chair and blew out a breath from exhaustion. "Leave it alone Mys."

"She's my best friend, is she at least okay?"

"Obviously, or this idiot would've offed himself already."

Than growled in response.

"You two are impossible." With that she moved to squeeze herself in between Don and the end of the chair he was in, grabbing the remote to turn the TV on.

They all remained silent as Mys flicked through channels while Than's mind was constantly on Jane. If she was better, if his father were treating her right, if she'd ever forgive him. Not able to take it anymore he got up.

"Where are you going?" Don asked suspiciously.

"Easy 'dad', I'm hitting the gym to work off some frustration." He didn't stop but kept moving. It was going to be a long work out.

CHAPTER 22

I started breathing a bit heavier than usual as I stood fidgeting before the massive mansion.

"Stop that, you'll be fine." John pulled my hands apart. I hadn't realized how hard I'd been gripping them together, watching as the white turned back to pink.

I frantically looked up to his steadying gaze. "Let's just go, he'll never know we were here." I grabbed his hands and started to move back to the car in the driveway but he held me firmly and turned me back around.

I don't know why I was nervous to see him again. What if he had lost hope on us because of what I'd said? What if he never loved me? Once again I started to back up into John's strong frame.

"Jane, breathe your starting to make ME nervous and that makes no sense." He gently gave me a small push towards the front door and I panicked. Turning around I took one step but froze at his voice.

"Jane?" It was barely a whisper and I just stood there not wanting to turn around and face him.

"I leave the rest to you Thanatos, don't fuck it up." I heard the glare in John's voice as he brushed some stray strands of my hair behind me ear and the small breeze as he left us.

"Jane?" His voice was closer, as in right behind me closer. I hunched over and took a deep breath before turning around. I looked up and up, finally meeting his eyes. God, it was like seeing him again for the first time. As a matter of fact, I felt exactly how I did the first time I locked eyes with him. Floored and out of breath.

I flinched out of my trance when he raised a hand as if to touch me. Taking a step back, I looked at his hand warily then back to him. The hurt in his eyes made my heart clench. This was not the Than I remembered before I was captured. This man before me looked tortured himself, as if he'd been abusing himself every day since I turned him away.

I swallowed nervously. "Walk with me?" My heart felt a bit lighter as his grim expression turned up a little at my invitation.

We walked towards the back of the house where I'd found the expansive garden the last time. In silence, I led us to the bench past the centerpiece tree and sat down. He sat down next to me and I could practically feel his anxiousness radiating from his body. I wasn't sure where to start or if I should just wait for him. Soon though he saved me the trouble.

"Jane?" I looked at him, stared into those obsidian eyes I hadn't seen in a week. Had missed when I'd been sure I'd be dead in a matter of days. I urged him to continue with my eyes.

"I know that no apology would ever be accepted for what I've done. What I've put you through because of my selfish actions." He turned his body to face me lifting his hands but dropping them knowing instinctively that I wouldn't allow his touch just yet. So instead he ran it through his hair, making me miss how I used to do that and enjoy it.

"Look I'm no good at this. All I know is that I almost imploded when I found out that you'd been taken." He looked away and I watched his eyes harden as he got lost in a memory I wasn't a part of. "I know that as soon as I knew where you were and who had taken you, that I would destroy all who stood in my way and that I would have gone to the ends of the Earth and every other realm trying to get to you." He turned again to face me, a haunted look in his eyes. I yearned to brush the creases away from his forehead and the worry from his eyes with a kiss, but I needed to hear more. I needed to hear the right words my heart has been longing for.

"I don't think I deserve your forgiveness now that I know how it's affected you all this time. Now that I know that the one precious thing in my world had been betrayed by the one she loves." He closed his eyes and placed his forehead in one hand, frustrated. When he looked back to me, I had to duck my head to hide the small smile on my lips. I was enjoying his groveling too much.

"Please 'Azel, please say we can be friends at least?" He looked at me longingly, a puppy dog stare that I'd never seen before on his hard, masculine face.

I hid my smile and looked up into his eyes, shaking my head slowly. "No . . ." Jane watched as he began to crumble before her eyes but before he could plead his case or his life or do something rash, I continued. "That's not what I want Thanatos." I used his full name to make sure I had his complete attention and would take my next words very seriously.

I stood, playing with the hem of my dress that fell to my mid thigh. I twirled around to finally lay out my rules.

"I want you to be mine forever." I smiled as his head flew up and his surprised eyes widened even more. "I want you to make me laugh, make me happy. I want you to make up for what you've taken away from me for as long as I live. I will settle for nothing less, and if you ever, EVER betray or lie or any such vile action again, I'll personally have your father castrate you, repair you and then I'll castrate you again and have you thrown into the deepest pits of hell to be tortured as no one has." I glared as a huge smile began to form on his beautiful mouth. "Do you accept my terms Thanatos?" I almost lost it and began to laugh as his face lit up with happiness.

"Is that all my little mortal?" He stood up slowly and took the two steps it took for him to stand before me, gazing down into my eyes. I finally allowed his fingers to brush my face, pushing stray strands of my hair from my face. I shivered at his warmth and closed my eyes to savor his touch, leaning into him.

"Terms are subject to change." I whispered, and he laughed out loud.

"Anything, I'll do anything you wish Jane." With that he bent his head and claimed my lips in the most passionate kiss I'd ever encountered. This was better than the lustful kisses we'd shared before. These were filled with love, care and tenderness. Entwining his hands in my hair, I felt the Earth move as he shifted us to my new room.

"Anything?" I said, breaking the kiss.

He smiled devilishly, picking me up and laying me on the bed. "I am yours to command my love."

I smiled and arched my brow. He laughed once again; I'd never get tired of hearing it. He rolled his eyes and kissed me again. "I LOVE you, Jane. Are you happy now?"

I made as though I were thinking about it and he tickled me before repeating his declaration of love. "I love you, adore you. I will never forsake you or break the trust you've so graciously given me. Your heart is safe in my hands 'Azel." I brought him down to me to claim his lips hotly.

"I love you, Than." I fisted his collar and locked eyes with him. "But if you don't make love to me I may just rescind this offer. His eyes darkened and he smiled, beginning to strip my clothes off.

"Yes my love."

He then began to show me that he was truly mine to command.

EPILOGUE

Lachesis moved away from the scene, not wanting to intrude on a moment that was fated to happen. A smile crossed her lips and she looked at her two sisters. "All is in order sisters; disaster has once again been diverted."

Atropos gagged and shook her head in disgust. Clothos simply nodded and moved back to the spindle and thread room. Easing her way to her own room once more, she couldn't stop smiling. They truly were made for each other, just as she'd intended and predicted.

Had Jane's father not been taken in such a way, she would not have had the strength of mind to deal with Thanatos' world. Had that not happened, Erebos would continue to grow in strength eventually taking over both realms with nobody strong enough to stop him. Without the unity all three had shown, this would have been impossible.

They would move on to have two kids, after they married of course. Just as John had wanted. As for his claim of ownership over Jane, he'd simply meant in his twisted way that she would be his daughter in-law, his to protect against all including his own son if necessary. Jane of course would punish Thanatos for keeping that tidbit from her and move on to lecturing his father for doing the same. The love they shared kept things light though and would keep them strong in the future.

Her 'decision' to become immortal however was something Lachesis couldn't have helped. Once entwining an immortal's thread to a mortal's, the mortal took on the dominant life thread of the immortal. She wouldn't know this of course until she noticed that she didn't age or grow. A small snag for her when she had to tell her family.

They would thank her later when she attended their wedding in the summer. She had a few more 'gifts' to bestow on the happy couple who unknowingly saved Atropos from a lot of snipping. Not that she ever complained of course.

Lachesis moved to sit on her chaise and looked over thoughtfully at the two threads lying on her backlit board once more. One brown mortal thread and another as white as snow, which glowed as bright as the heavens.

Laying back to rest she smiled to herself as she thought of what she had in store for the angel.

GLOSSARY

Abaddon—Angel of Death (Ritaya)

Atropos—Third sister of the three fates. Her job was to choose the cause of death and eventually cut the life thread of mortals.

Chaos—Formless or the void state preceding the creation of the universe.

Clothos—First sister of the three fates. Her job was to spin the thread of human life.

Descendion—A mortal descendant from the daughter of Zeus and Aphrodite, charged with the responsibility of guiding spirits to either Heaven or Hell.

Erebos—Primordial deity of deep darkness and shadow. One of the first five beings to come into existence from Chaos.

Erebus—Region of the Underworld where the dead have to pass immediately after dying.

Lachesis—Second sister of the three fates. Her job was measure how long a thread of life would be.

Lefate—A Descendion swayer, the left hand man or hell's side.

Moirai—The three fates.

Ritaya—A Descendion swayer, the right hand man or heaven's side.

Thanatos—Son of Death (Lefate)